MW01697483

TIMELESS *Regency* COLLECTION

Road TO GRETNA GREEN

TIMELESS *Regency* COLLECTION

Road TO GRETNA GREEN

Lucinda Brant

Julie Daines

Heather B. Moore

Mirror Press

Interior Design by Cora Johnson
Edited by Haley Swan and Lisa Shepherd
Cover design by Rachael Anderson
Cover Photo Credit: Archangel Images: Jill Battaglia

Published by Mirror Press, LLC

ISBN: 978-1-947152-77-9

TABLE OF CONTENTS

Other Timeless Regency Collections

Autumn Masquerade
A Midwinter Ball
Spring in Hyde Park
Summer House Party
A Country Christmas
A Season in London
A Holiday in Bath
A Night in Grosvenor Square
Road to Gretna Green
Wedding Wagers
An Evening at Almack's
A Week in Brighton
To Love a Governess

Saving Grace

-Lucinda Brant-

One

Carlisle, Cumbria, England, 1788 (a leap year)

"MY DEAR, WAS it necessary to extend an invitation to the entire population of Carlisle?" Lord Salkeld complained from his wing chair by the fireplace.

"Very necessary, Papa," Edith Meredith replied politely. "But not everyone is here. Just our closest friends and acquaintances."

His Lordship looked out across the crowded drawing room from under hooded lids and then up at his eldest daughter with mild surprise. He could count his good friends on one hand; as for acquaintances . . . He had no need for superfluous connections.

"Indeed? I was unaware I had so many—friends."

Edith pretended ignorance of his meaning, mindful that while her irascible father had the respect of the community as was his due as a peer of the realm, he was tolerated rather than liked.

"Had I not invited everyone who mattered, they would have felt justly aggrieved to be forgotten. After all, it is not every day the daughter of a viscount marries. So to receive a gilt-edged invitation to His Lordship's tea party is an honor indeed. Did you not see how low Mrs. Paley curtsied? She is the wife of an archdeacon to be sure, but her grandpapa was the Bishop of York, so she is very mindful of rank and consequence."

Lord Salkeld was slightly mollified by this recognition of his superior social standing amongst Carlisle society. His chin went up as he regarded the press of persons who constituted this society: lawyers, merchants, a magistrate or two, vicars, retired military types, and a handful of country squires, and all here with their wives. When his wife and two eldest sons were alive, most of these persons would have gained entry to his house only via the trade entrance. And yet, here they all were, in his drawing room, drinking his Bohea tea from fine porcelain cups.

Somewhere deep in the room someone burst out laughing.

Lord Salkeld grimaced at such boorish behavior.

It was a further reminder that this border town was as far removed from the environs of London's superior society as it was possible to get without crossing into Scotland. Just ten miles north, Scotland was the outer reaches of civilization as far as His Lordship was concerned. London was where he belonged but did not venture these days due to his infirmity and reduced circumstances. And Scotland was where his daughter was to be married and where she would then reside. His irritability returned.

"But why a tea party? A tea party! *Tea.* This lot would've been well satisfied with small beer and punch."

"But as your daughter, a tea party is what *I* deserve, Papa," Edith explained with a slight flush to her cheeks, aware their guests could not help but overhear her father's complaints. "Besides, Royston approved, saying cake tastes much better with tea and would be what the wives would want."

Mention of his heir had Lord Salkeld grinding his teeth. While he might hold the title, it was his only surviving son who held the purse strings. Royston had conspired with the family lawyer to curtail his spending, his travel, and the lifestyle to which he had been accustomed for most of his sixty years. He'd been lectured to like a five-year-old, been told that what he considered the necessities of life were indulgences he could live without, all for the good of the estate. And yet his heir had seen fit to dip into the purse for coin to waste on tea and cakes to feed what amounted to a bunch of savages. His resentment of his son increased tenfold. And what was in fact a gesture of brotherly love in allowing Edith a tea party regardless of the family's financial constraints, His Lordship construed it as another example of his son's high-handedness. His voice dripped with sarcasm.

"It is as well then that you are marrying a man who can supply you with as much tea and cake as you want, Edith. Sir James Murray may be a Scot and his grandfather hung for treason for supporting the Young Pretender—"

"Papa!"

"—invading my country and laying siege to my town, but I am prepared to overlook his traitorous ancestor for your sake. And because he is a wealthy young man with a fine estate who is distantly related to the Kinross dukedom, a Scottish duke but a duke nonetheless. And—"

"—because he loves me," Edith interrupted. "I am marrying James because I love him and he loves me, and that is the only reason."

"Balderdash! Do you think I'd have permitted a daughter of mine to marry just any man? Egad! If that were the case, your sister would've been married three times over by now."

"But I did not fall in love with just any man, Papa. And Grace is too young to know her own mind. I do not doubt she will fall in love a half a dozen more times before she finally settles on *the one*."

"*The one*—ha! I wish your brother would settle on *the one*. *Any*one would do at this late stage. I'm only getting older and more ill, and he is not getting any younger. He's one and thirty. I—*he*—needs an heir. By his age I had sired four children, *three* of them sons. And what has he sired? Eh? Who knows!"

Edith was appalled. "I'm sure I couldn't say, Papa. It is not something I have ever thought about—"

"Nor should you," he demanded darkly, and to mask his slip of the tongue alluding to his heir's nefarious activities, of which he knew nothing and had therefore no right to comment, said, "You can serve up tepid brown liquid and crumbs to this lot, but I want something stronger to toast my eldest daughter's impending marriage. Have Hale fetch up a bottle of Bordeaux."

"Yes, Papa," Edith replied placidly, but did not signal for the butler.

She fixed her smile, hoping Royston would return home soon. Better still, that Cousin Helen joined them. Her father had a soft spot for Cousin Helen. And Edith knew that if anyone could placate the old nobleman, it was she. In the interim she did her best to do so.

"You must not upset your humors, Papa. Remember that tomorrow morning we travel to Comlongon Castle, and you need to save your strength for the journey and the wedding ceremony."

"I won't be squeezed into my own carriage to sit shoulder to shoulder with others for hours on end. That would indeed upset my humors."

"Why would you? Have you forgotten the arrangements? We are going on ahead, and Cousin Helen has her own carriage. And you know very well Royston always rides and is never without his medical satchel."

Lord Salkeld sat up. He grimaced. "Medical satchel! Pshaw. Carrying it about like a tradesman with his tools. A viscount's heir a—a common blood spiller and bonesetter. It's a disgrace."

"Royston wasn't your heir when he chose to study medicine."

"He was not. And I do not need reminding that in losing Thomas and Matthew I am left with a country physician to follow on after me. Matthew at least had the decency to obtain a posting in the Foreign Office. Royston would have served us all better had he gone into the law or—or politics, both suitable vocations for a gentleman. But there is nothing elevating about getting one's hands dirty with the blood and filth of persons riddled with disease. He should've given it away on Matthew's passing."

"You cannot mean that, Papa. Royston is an exceptional physician, and the community cannot do without him or his expertise, not now that Dr. Rawlings has retired and—"

"I can and do mean it! If he continues to spend his time around the sick and dying, it stands to reason he will get sick himself. But he doesn't care for his birthright, or for me, or for the fact that should he die before me, I will have no one to succeed to the title. It will become extinct. Is that what you want, Edith? For the title to die with your dear papa?"

"Papa, you are upsetting yourself for no reason. Royston is as healthy as your best stallion, and as strong. You do him a disservice if you believe he does not think, and think daily, that one day he will be Viscount Salkeld. But he—we all—hope that day is far into the future. So until it arrives he must occupy himself. So why not put to good use his medical training? But I agree with you. He must think of the future and marry, which is why, Papa—" Edith paused for effect and waited for her father to look up at her. She opened wide her eyes. "We both know, do we not, what needs to occur for that to happen, and what you must do to ensure it does."

His Lordship waved a languid hand. "I do. But I am not convinced this scheme will work. But as I do not have an alternate strategy, I am prepared to be swept along with your matchmaking, and yes, I will be on my best behavior, as promised."

"Thank you. And . . . ?"

"And what, my dear?"

"Papa! You know very well!"

Lord Salkeld pulled a face and resettled himself before glancing up at Edith, who was staring at him fixedly. He repeated what she had said to him at breakfast.

"I have two eyes and one mouth, and I am to use them in that proportion."

Edith relaxed and smiled. She swiftly kissed his cheek. "Thank you, Papa."

He caught at her hand and in a rare show of sentimentality gave it a pat. "I shall miss you, my dear."

"And I you, Papa. But I will not be so very far away . . . And . . . This is what we both want, is it not?"

"It is."

Edith nodded. Feeling the tears well up, she made a show of brushing down her silk gown while blinking her eyes dry before looking toward the double doors, which were opening wide.

"Shall I see if it is Cousin Helen who has joined us?"

Her father's lined face softened. "Cousin Helen is here?"

"She arrived from London yesterday. It was late, and we did not wish to disturb you. She took breakfast in her room. The journey fatigued her."

Lord Salkeld looked toward the door expectantly, but it was not Helen, Lady Dysart, who came through the crush of guests but His Lordship's third and now only living son. The smile fell away, and his features hardened. Before his heir had taken more than four steps toward him, Lord Salkeld had lifted his walking stick. This he waved about before pointing it at his son's top boots.

"Where are your manners, sir? Where are your shoes? This is a drawing room, not a stable! And a tea party, not the hunt!"

Two

Royston Meredith ignored his father and crossed to the sideboard over which hung a full-length portrait of his mother, the late Viscountess Salkeld, in her prime, a most regal and beautiful woman, with dark hair and dark eyes, and whom he, perhaps most of her five children, resembled greatly. He had not only inherited her beauty but her love of animals and the outdoors. He also had her forbearance. Finding the whiskey decanter and glasses, he poured himself out a drop, raised it to her, then downed it in one. He then joined his father and sister, who were looking concerned.

"Forgive my lateness, Edie. I had the muck removed and polish applied to my boots, but there was no time to shave or to change for your party."

Edith glanced him over, from polished boots to knitted riding breeches, to the slightly crumpled dark wool riding frock coat with silver buttons, and on up to his windswept black curls that were inexpertly scraped back and tied at the nape with a ribbon. Her frown lifted. He was most handsome when slightly disheveled, the shadow of stubble on his square chin and cheeks adding to his manliness. Far from being offended by his appearance as was her father, she was pleased he had not shaved or changed, all because she wanted Cousin Helen to see him at his best.

This tea party might be an occasion for Carlisle society to

celebrate her upcoming wedding to the wealthiest Scotsman this side of Edinburgh, but it also proved the perfect excuse to have her brother and Cousin Helen in the same room for the first time in years. And with both attending her wedding, they could not help but be in each other's company. She only hoped there was enough time to achieve the desired outcome. She would not have been so confident about her matchmaking machinations had she not the help of her father, her sister, and her darling Sir James, with the couple none the wiser.

"You're here. That's all that matters," she said brightly, and quickly schooled her features lest he wonder at her unusual buoyancy. Discussing medicine never failed to divert his thoughts to what truly mattered most. "And the Waugh boy . . . Was it a break?"

"A dislocated shoulder, nothing more gruesome."

"That is a relief. For everyone. I dare say he won't be astride for a while?"

"Not for several weeks."

"If you ask me, the sooner the boy gets back in the saddle, the better!" Lord Salkeld said.

Royston Meredith rolled his eyes at his sister before saying levelly to his father, "We did not ask you, sir. It is as well for Colin I am the physician in the family."

Lord Salkeld gave a dismissive snort.

"This family does not require a physician, sir. What it requires is an heir thinking about marriage, not gallivanting about the countryside attending on fools and miscreants as if he were their servant. It is your wedding we should be attending—"

"Papa! Remember: two eyes, one mouth."

Lord Salkeld instantly shut his mouth, but he did not allow his daughter's chastisement to stop him from grumbling under his breath. Royston was surprised and intrigued to see his cantankerous parent suddenly docile and was about to ask Edith what she meant by *two eyes, one mouth*, when she made a pronouncement that had him not only forget the question, but that he had a mouth at all.

"Ah, here is Cousin Helen come at last!"

A woman of above-average height with slender limbs and a swanlike grace glided across the carpet, and every head turned to watch her pass by. She wore a pale-blue silk gown *à la anglaise* with a fringed paisley shawl draped off her shoulders and over her arms. But it was at the messy abundance of bright red curls, piled up and pinned and looking as if at any moment the weight would topple and the long tresses tumble to the small of her back, that Royston's eyes fixed. His throat dried. He swallowed. The dryness remained. He managed to pull his gaze away from her coiffure to look into her eyes. They were the same light blue as her gown. They stared back at him, bright and unblinking. His cheeks flushed with heat. He dropped his gaze, but not away from her. It fixed on her mouth. If her hair had dried his throat and her eyes made him blush, her slightly parted lips sent him deaf. There was a sudden buzzing in his ears he could not explain.

Finally, he tore his gaze away when she bobbed a respectful curtsy to his father, then leaned in to kiss the old nobleman's forehead. Royston had no idea what she said to make his father chuckle because the buzzing was still in his ears. She then spoke to Edith before surprising him by turning and addressing him directly.

He did not hear her words, so he could not give a reply. He hoped a curt nod would suffice. He was still in a mental fog. And that fog had him hurtling back to the last time he had seen Cousin Helen. It was a little over a year ago, when his greatest wish had finally come true. She had been made a widow and was free again, free to re-marry, and thus free to be his again. But the truth of the matter was she had never really been his, ever. She might now be a widow and able to marry whomever she pleased, but he was very sure that he would never be that *whomever*.

On that sudden depressing realization, his ears went pop, and his hearing returned.

"Oh, do not concern yourself, my lord," Cousin Helen was saying. "I am reconciled to it. Cousin Royston was just as talkative the last time we were in each other's company, and just as polite. To be fair to us both, that was a somber occasion, whereas this"—she smiled brightly at Edith and affectionately touched the young woman's arm—"this is something different entirely. It is a joyous occasion and one I am exceedingly happy to celebrate with . . . with—" She glanced at Royston, who still stood as a plank beside his sister. "With you all!" She then looked about her as if she had lost something or someone. "But where is Grace?"

Three

THE SOMBER OCCASION to which Cousin Helen alluded had occurred thirteen months earlier. It was a commemorative service held to celebrate the long life and distinguished career of the Member of Parliament for Carlisle, Sir William Dysart. Sir William had died peacefully in his sleep at the relatively young age of fifty-two, leaving behind five adult children, fourteen grandchildren, and a much younger second wife, Royston's cousin, Helen. A kind and generous man and a pillar of society, everyone who knew him mourned his passing. Everyone, that is, except Royston Meredith.

Royston had been in London for several weeks attending a series of medical lectures given by the celebrated anatomist Dr. John Hunter, when he heard the news of Sir William's passing, and in the most surprising of ways. He had accepted an invitation to an inaugural meeting of like-minded gentlemen who wished to form a society for the prevention of cruelty to animals. The meeting took place at Old Slaughter's Coffee House in St. Martins Lane, and he had been keen to discuss with these men, many of whom he had corresponded with over the years, their enlightened views on the rights of animals, in particular beasts of burden. The meeting had opened with a prayer for one of their founders, Sir William Dysart, who had been instrumental in drawing up a bill for the ethical treatment of horses that he was set to put before the

House at the next sitting of Parliament, but who had recently passed away.

There was to be a service for Sir William the very next day at St. George's, Hanover Square.

Royston attended with two of these like-minded gentlemen and sat as far back in the church as was possible. He could have taken the pew behind the grieving widow as a representative of her family. After all, Helen was his cousin and a Meredith, and she had no immediate family other than his. So it would have been entirely appropriate for him to join her. But he did not. He slid onto a bench behind the assembled congregation of family members, dignitaries, and people connected to Sir William who had come to pay their respects.

He felt a charlatan because he had not come to offer his cousin sympathy for her loss. While he did indeed commiserate with Sir William's family for losing their father and grandfather, with Sir William's friends and acquaintances, those who had benefited from knowing the parliamentarian, and with his fellow animal rights advocates who had lost a valuable patron, he had little sympathy for the widow. This was because his overriding emotion was a selfish one.

He hoped by attending this service he could finally eradicate the bitterness he harbored toward Sir William. In marrying Helen, the parliamentarian had robbed him of the only woman he loved. Sir William and his cousin Helen had married two months after her eighteenth birthday. He had learnt about it in a letter from his sister whilst studying in France; it was the most miserable day of his life.

After the service, the congregation had spilled out into the watery sunshine of an inner courtyard to pay their respects to grieving family members, assembled to receive their condolences and sympathies. Royston had gone forward, features schooled in solemn reflection and with heart beating hard. Six years had elapsed since he had seen her, when she had been living in his family home as his father's ward. As children they had spent every summer together exploring the

Cumbrian countryside. She a thin wisp of a girl with a tangle of bright red braids and a dusting of freckles across her nose and cheeks. He an awkwardly loose-limbed boy who dreamed of attending medical school and who confided his hopes and dreams in her and most probably bored her silly. Though the little crease between her dark-red brows was evidence of a studiousness far beyond her years.

Remembrance of that tiny detail made him smile, but such nostalgia considerably sobered his mood as he waited in line. His attention was caught by a gentleman at the grieving widow's left shoulder, whispering in her ear as persons approached. He presumed he was offering up the identities of these people so Helen would not make a social gaffe at not knowing them. And when this gentleman dug deep in a pocket for a handkerchief and gave it to the widow to dab at her eyes, Royston scowled. The scowl was still there when he stepped up to Sir William's young widow and made her his bow.

How sophisticated she appeared in her black silks, and much older with such dark circles under her eyes, evidence of her sorrow. But then, as now, she had the same effect on him. He swallowed hard. His throat was unaccountably dry, and there was a buzzing in his ears that set him slightly off-balance. And then, as now, he lost the ability to speak, or at least to form a coherent sentence. He mumbled several platitudes and did not give her the chance to respond, instead moving on quickly to speak with Sir William's heir, who stood on her other side. Whatever happiness he had felt at Sir William's passing, whatever his selfish reasons for attending this commemorative service, evaporated. One look into Cousin Helen's pale-blue eyes and he saw the pain and suffering of her loss, and he knew himself for an unfeeling and selfish oaf.

He had been under the delusion that his cousin had married Sir William for any number of reasons but that love was not one of them. But seeing her as a grieving widow, he realized that she had indeed loved her husband. It was a rude awakening. How naive had he been in thinking the love they had for each other as children would mature into something more than cousinly affection. All confidence in the possibility of Helen, Lady Dysart, accepting a proposal of marriage from him now she was a widow vanished. He was so melancholy it left him with a pain in the chest.

Thirteen months should have healed the wound of his disappointment and delusion. But it had not. This was starkly evident when Helen only had to glide into his father's drawing room for the scab to be torn off the wound, a wound that still festered. Nothing had changed for him since his seventeenth birthday when as a thirteen-year-old orphan Cousin Helen had come to live at Salkeld House. Her arrival was the best birthday present he had ever received. It was love at first sight for him, and he was still in love with her.

Four

HELEN, LADY DYSART, had entered the drawing room and immediately searched the unfamiliar faces for her cousin Royston. It was not that she was eager to see him, not yet. In fact, she hoped he might still be out and about on his rounds tending to his patients. She needed time to compose herself, to have ready a witty rejoinder to what would surely be a monosyllabic and unemotional response from him to her presence. She'd had endless hours in the carriage ride up from London, even a night at an inn staring at the low ceiling, to practice her insouciance, to hide her true feelings, and to show him she remained indifferent despite an end to her mourning and having cast off her drab widow's clothing.

Yet, seeing Royston standing by Edith, broodingly handsome and austere as ever, she gave a start, and her knees wobbled. She told herself she was being ridiculous. She was no longer a doe-eyed girl who had pinned all her hopes on marrying him. She was a confident widow, calm and in control, a woman of the world who did not need the support or approval of any man. So she squared her shoulders and stepped up to her family members with all the self-assurance of an experienced dancer making her appearance before an appreciative audience.

And what did she do or say when finally before her cousin? She forgot the rehearsed offhand remark carefully constructed on her journey. Instead she had teased him about the last time they had seen each other, at her husband's commemorative service. Not the most auspicious of starts to her visit, to throw her marriage in his face yet again. As if marriage to Sir William was a trophy she had won, a triumph of her own making. When in fact she blamed Royston as the catalyst for her accepting Sir William's marriage proposal. Not that either man had forced her into marriage. But it was Royston who had broken her heart.

Foolishly, as a girl she had believed him when he said he loved her and that he meant to marry her once he'd completed his medical studies and returned to Carlisle and set up practice. Would she mind being the wife of a country physician? She had given him an emphatic yes to the idea of being his wife, and she did not mind in the least he was to be a physician. In fact she was very proud of his strength of purpose. But she did have one worry, and that was his father's determination to marry her to his brother Thomas. And then when Thomas had died, to marry her to Royston's other brother, Matthew.

Royston had assured her he would not let that happen. If his father tried to force her into marriage with either of his elder brothers, he made her a solemn promise to run away with her across the border into Scotland and to Gretna Green, which was only ten miles away. He assured her that while the law in England forbade her marrying without parental consent before her twenty-first birthday, the law in Scotland was different. They could marry in Scotland, and no one could stop them. She had to trust in him, and she did.

But he had not asked her to marry him. Not even after the tragic deaths of his elder brothers left him the heir to his father's title and estate did he seek her out and reassure her they would be married. There was no further talk of running away to Gretna Green. Then one day she discovered he was off to France to further his studies. He had returned to Carlisle from Edinburgh only to collect his trunks and say his farewells to the family. And it seemed he was never going to marry her, here in Carlisle, or across the border in Scotland. This she discovered for herself one afternoon when she was witness to a heated exchange between father and son.

She remembered that day as if it were yesterday. And she remembered it now as she glanced about the drawing room, determined to avoid looking at Royston again—though she knew his gaze never left her for a moment—wondering at the whereabouts of her youngest cousin Grace.

Five

THE INCIDENT IN Lord Salkeld's book room occurred a handful of days before Helen's eighteenth birthday. Her uncle had summoned her. He had important news about her future. When the butler told her that Royston was with his father, her heart skipped a beat, hoping upon hope that the important news was the announcement of their engagement. Finally! The happiest day of her life had arrived.

To the Meredith household it was a forgone conclusion that she and Royston would marry, now that His Lordship had lost his two eldest sons in quick succession. Thomas had tragically died in a hunting accident. Twelve months later Matthew succumbed to pneumonia. That left Lord Salkeld's third and now only surviving son, Royston, to marry Helen, daughter of His Lordship's brother who had made a fortune in trade. Helen's dowry was a staggering £25,000. So it was unsurprising that her uncle would want to keep such a fortune within the family. And the only way to do that was to marry her to one of his sons.

She had arrived at the book room all smiles of expectation of the announcement of her engagement to Royston. What she walked in on was a blistering argument between father and son that left her in no doubts as to her cousin's feelings on the matter of marriage and about his feelings for her . . .

Lord Salkeld slammed his fist down hard on the polished wooden surface of his desk, rattling the pounce pot.

"You will marry, sir!"

Royston stared at his father, hands clenched at his sides. His voice was low and resolute.

"And I repeat—*sir*—I will not."

"I know what's best for this family and its future, and it is time you faced up to your responsibilities—"

"I won't be lectured to by a man who never faced up to his!"

"How dare—"

"All those years spending months away at a time in London, living with your mistress, lavishing trinkets and baubles and God knows what on a pack of whores. Gambling away our future in gaming hells and at the racetrack—"

"Why you—you sanctimonious whelp!"

"—while your wife and children practically starved, living in a house without coal or adequate firewood, its roof in need of repair, with servants who were stealing the plate to feed themselves and their brats. And you dare to call me sanctimonious? You cannot bully and badger or frighten me as you did Thomas and Matthew. It is you who has led us to this sorry state of affairs. It is you who is up to your wig in debt, who has caused this estate to fall down around your shoe buckles. Unless you retrench, there will be nothing left. Edith and Grace won't have a decent cloth to their backs, least of all a modest dowry to attract a suitor worthy of them."

"If you wish your sisters to have dowries, for the servants to have a decent meal, and for these rooms to feel warmth again, then you must and will marry Helen. Her dowry will save us all."

Royston continued as if his father had not spoken.

"You broke our mother's heart, and her spirit. She died from melancholia—"

Lord Salkeld scoffed. "Spare me the medical diagnosis! Your mother died in childbed."

"Yes. After Grace was born, she lost the will to live."

"And if you don't marry Helen, there won't be enough coin to feed your sisters! Is that what you want?"

Royston gritted his teeth. "I won't feel guilty for your sins. And I will not be forced into a marriage with anyone."

Lord Salkeld regarded his only son under heavy lids.

"Don't make your mother a martyr, boy. She knew what she was getting into when she married me. She was just as hardheaded and as hard-hearted. She wanted a title, and she got it. We had an arrangement. And it suited both of us very well indeed. You can have the same arrangement with your cousin. Helen will be made a viscountess, and in return you will receive £25,000. Get her pregnant as soon as you can, and God willing, she will give you an heir within the year. The estate and the title will then have a secure future. And there will even be funds aplenty for Edith and Grace to have dowries worthy of the daughters of a viscount."

"I always wondered if ice ran in your veins. You have confirmed it. You are cold-blooded and calculating, and I want nothing to do with such an arrangement."

Lord Salkeld stuck his tongue firmly in his cheek.

"Is that so? More fool you are because you do not have a choice. You are my heir, and there is nothing you or I can do about it. Your brothers understood this well enough and were reconciled to doing their duty. And part of that duty is marrying, and marrying well, and that means marrying your cousin."

Royston stared back at his aging parent with barely concealed loathing.

"It is true. I cannot change fate. I am your heir whether I like it or not. It was forced upon me by tragic circumstance. But you cannot force me to marry Helen. Just as you cannot force me to give up the practice of medicine. I intend to go on helping the sick, be they human, furred, or feathered, and most particularly if they are beasts of burden. It is my calling."

"*Calling*? God give me strength! Preaching to a congregation is a calling. Captaining a ship or leading men into battle, they are callings. What you describe—tending to and healing beasts, who were put on this earth by God for man to use as he sees fit, as if these creatures have feelings and need succor, is—is—the stuff of—of—*lunacy*! *You* are a lunatic!"

"I don't care what you think. And you are powerless to stop me. I have the small annuity left me by my mother, and I will use it as she intended me to." He made his father a small bow of the head. "If that is all you have to say, I must finish packing. I leave at first light for Lyon and Monsieur Bourgelat's veterinary college."

"To waste your medical training on learning how to heal animals?" His Lordship snorted his contempt. "What rubbish! A better use of your time abroad would be sowing your wild oats so that you know something about women, then come back here and marry and beget an heir—"

"I don't need a lecture on women, and certainly not from you!"

Lord Salkeld glanced past his son and straight at Helen, who stood just inside the door, hesitant to come forward. She gave a little jump of surprise that he was well aware of her presence. He held her gaze but for a moment, as if confirming this, and her fingers tightened in the folds of her floral petticoats. He did not beckon her forward, so she remained where she was. He looked back at Royston.

"Let us be clear. You refuse to be guided by me and give up this preposterous notion of becoming an animal healer to settle and marry your cousin?"

"How many ways must I say it to make it clear to you, sir? There is *nothing* that can induce me to steer away from my course of action. As for marrying my cousin . . . ?" He gave a grunt of disgust. "You hawked her to my brothers as if she were a prostitute and you her bawd. And now you expect me to accept her on those terms, too?"

"I do."

"I do not."

"That is your final word on the matter?"

"I wouldn't marry her under such circumstances if she were the last redheaded gypsy worth a fortune this side of hell! Clear enough?"

Again Lord Salkeld glanced past his son and at Helen. She had slumped against the doorjamb, trembling with sadness, tears spilling onto her cheeks. And again he held her gaze, to make certain she understood. She stared back at him, mute. To her great misery she understood very well indeed.

With an imperceptible nod to her, he scraped back his chair and got to his buckled shoes, saying calmly to his son and heir, "Your feelings and wishes are duly noted. I will say no more on the matter, only that you will rue this day, sir. Mark my words."

Helen did not hear Royston's reply. She fled the room. He unaware she was there. When he tried to say his farewells the next day, she feigned illness. She did not see him again until the commemorative service for her husband, Sir William Dysart. Her knees had almost buckled with surprise at his presence, but she had managed to remain upright. She was Lady Dysart. She was a grieving widow. She was determined to honor her husband's memory with the respect owed him.

Six years had come and gone since that day in Lord Salkeld's book room. She was no longer a silly young girl with stars in her eyes who believed her cousin when he said he would save her from a marriage with his brothers, vowing to whisk her off to Gretna Green to marry her himself when the time was right. That girl no longer existed; the stars had gone out of her night sky.

A week after Royston departed for France, she received a visit from Sir William Dysart, a longtime family friend of the Merediths. Over the course of the next month this widower who was twice her age became a gentle but most persistent suitor. And then one day he came bearing gifts: a string of pearls and a diamond-and-pearl engagement ring—small tokens of his affection—and with them he asked Helen to be his wife.

Encouraged by her uncle, Helen accepted Sir William's proposal. If she gave any consideration to the fact she was marrying her widowed suitor to douse the disappointment at being rejected by the man she loved, it was fleeting. She was young and naive and believed herself capable of forgetting any feelings she may have harbored for Royston precisely because of her youth and naivety. Royston had gone to France to make a life for himself there, and so she was equally determined to make a life for herself anywhere but at Carlisle and the Salkeld household. And so when Sir William vowed to cherish her all the rest of his days, she believed him. What more did a girl require of a husband?

Sir William stayed true to his word, and while her marriage was not an unhappy one, she soon realized she was not in love with her husband. She did her best to be a good wife, and she never let him know her true feelings. But he knew, and had always known. And one day, less than a year into their marriage, he confided he had known all along that she was in love with Royston Meredith. But it did not greatly bother him. She was too shocked to even pretend to refute the claim, and he thanked her for not doing so. What mattered to him was that she belonged to him. She was his wife. All he required of her was that she remain compliant in the bedchamber and remain faithful, in deed if not in thought. He then startled her further by casually mentioning that he had paid her uncle the princely sum of £5,000 to have his consent to their marriage. He would have given Salkeld twice that to make her his, but her uncle was an avaricious fool who grasped at the first offer made to him. Nor did Sir William think much of the son. He could not for the life of him fathom why Royston Meredith had passed up on the chance to marry her, because it was obvious to him—and he had known Royston since he was in leading strings—that the young man was just as in love with her as she was with him. Porridge for brains must run in the Meredith family.

Helen was inclined to agree, and she quickly dismissed such poignant recollections from her thoughts. This was Edith's tea party, and she must not allow Royston's presence to distract her from the occasion. So she searched the crowd with her eyes, wondering what had happened to Grace. Her young cousin had been right behind her just before the double doors were opened by a footman to admit them to the drawing room.

She was about to mention this to her uncle, when she realized Royston was staring hard at her. So hard in fact that she wondered if he had been able to read her thoughts. She stared back, expressionless, and he quickly looked away. In fact he returned to the sideboard, as if wanting to put space between them. Her gaze followed him, thoughts returning to that fateful day in her uncle's book room when he had so vehemently rejected her, and she had a sudden impulse to ask him for an explanation. Surely, with the passage of time, they could talk about it as adults and remain unaffected.

She reasoned it was better to have the question answered now, before Edith's wedding. She could then spend the rest of her time while in Carlisle and at the wedding without worrying about what his response might or would be, speculation gnawing away at her the entire visit, as it had all the way up from London.

She closed her fan and followed him to the sideboard.

Six

Before she could say one word to Royston, the youngest Meredith appeared beside Helen in a cloud of pretty pink petticoats, large, bright eyes full of excitement to be attending her sister's tea party. A tall, thin girl of seventeen, with the family's perfectly arched brows, her exuberance and playfulness reminded Helen of herself at the same age. Although, she had never possessed Grace's audacity of spirit to say and do as she pleased regardless of parental authority.

This was never more in evidence than when Grace went straight up to her brother, and said cheekily, "You look to have the worry of the world on your shoulders, Roy. Had you thought I'd run off to Gretna Green as I have vowed to do on no less than *four* occasions?"

Royston could not hide the smile in his eyes but managed to keep the amusement from his voice.

"No. Not that I don't think you capable of running off. I just don't think there's a boy—and I do mean boy—who'd be silly enough to run off with *you*."

Grace pouted, feigning offense.

"Charlie is not silly. In fact he is very sensible."

"He is. Which is why he won't run off with you to Gretna Green or anywhere else."

Grace included Helen in the conversation by drawing her

arm through hers and bringing her closer, saying conspiratorially, yet loud enough for her brother to hear every word, "I invited Charlie to join us, but he's not permitted into Papa's drawing room because he's the son of Mr. Lawson, our steward. So he's practically a servant, though he is in truth an employee, which is different."

"It is different. What remains the same is, servant or employee, you won't be marrying him anytime soon," Royston stated without heat.

"I do not see what it is about Charlie that has made you take him in such offense."

"You misconstrue me, Grace," Royston said with a grin and a shake of his head. "It has nothing to do with Charlie. I like him. He may marry whomever he pleases, and I wish him well. But you have many more years of growing up to do before you marry anyone."

Grace cocked her head, a glance at Helen. "How many more years?"

Royston threw out a number. "Four. Perhaps five—"

"*Five* years?" Grace hissed. "You cannot mean it!"

"I do."

"In five years I'll be older than Edith is now, and she is about to be married. And no one stopped—"

"You are not Edith—"

"No, not Edith," Grace corrected. "Cousin Helen. No one stopped Cousin Helen from marrying Sir William, did they? You were how old, cousin?" she asked, turning to Helen with an open look. "Seventeen, or were you eighteen?"

Helen suppressed a smile. She was aware Grace knew the answer and was merely provoking her brother, thus she answered her directly, without affront or surprise.

"I married Sir William two months after my eighteenth birthday. You were there, remember? As my flower girl, scattering rose petals here and there, but mostly over the guests."

"Oh yes! So I was!" Grace replied with feigned surprise, keeping up the pretense of lost memory. She giggled behind her fan. "I sprinkled a handful of petals over Edith's head, too, and she was most unhappy because she was flirting shamelessly with one of Sir William's sons." She stared at her brother, all laughter aside. "So if Cousin Helen was permitted to marry at eighteen, and a man as old as Papa—"

"Not quite, Grace, dear," Helen said softly.

"Not quite," Grace agreed. "But, and you will excuse me for saying so, cousin, he was just as fusty as Papa."

"It has nothing to do with age!" Royston stuck in, not a glance at Helen, face flushed with embarrassment to be discussing his cousin's marriage, and Sir William in particular.

"Does it not?" Grace asked with that same look of bemusement that hid her real intent. "Then you should have no objection to your sister marrying the steward's son, for Charlie is only three and twenty, so only five years my senior."

Like Helen, Royston was not fooled. He knew he was being goaded, but he was beyond caring. He needed to set the record straight.

Gaze fixed on Grace, as if Helen were not there at all, he explained patiently, voice lowered so as not to attract the attention of their guests, "Our cousin's marriage was different. She was an heiress. You are not. Sir William was a man of means and position. Charlie is not. And she had a—a choice. You do not."

"*Choice*?"

Grace and Helen blurted out the word in unison, and with the same incredulous disbelief.

Royston looked at Grace, and then at Helen, and for the first time since she'd entered the room, he looked into her eyes, but it was his sister he addressed.

"Why, yes, Helen did, Grace. She chose to marry Sir William Dysart. No one forced her into it, did they, my lady? Just as I would not force Grace into marrying someone she did not want to have as a husband. But as her brother, I can and will counsel my father to stop her marrying before she is of age. Something my father should have done for you. Though . . ." He smiled sadly. "Perhaps he did do so, but you were still determined to marry, and marry well, and then how could he refuse? Sir William Dysart was an eminent and wealthy politician and quite the matrimonial prize."

"*Prize*? You think . . . You think I married Sir William because—because he was a—a prize?"

Shock dried Helen's throat, and she pressed her lips together, unable to go on, though a great wave of words had rushed up into her mouth. But she was circumspect enough to take stock of her surroundings. She was in a drawing room full of guests attending Edith's tea party. It was not the time to continue such a conversation, as much as she wanted to forgo the occasion and drag Royston into an adjoining room and demand he explain himself. Grace had no such compunction.

"You have a strange notion of what constitutes a prize, Roy! Besides, if you'd been here and not in France, Cousin Helen would never have married Sir William at all, would you have, cousin?"

"Behave yourself, Grace, or I'll have you returned to the schoolroom where girls of your age belong," Royston demanded, face flushed with angry embarrassment.

Grace did not wait for Helen's answer. Nor did she heed her brother's warning. What she had to say needed to be said, and she'd been waiting many years to say it. She cared not a jot that they were in a crowded drawing room. Still, she did her best to lower her voice to a hissed whisper.

"You promised to marry her, Roy. You *promised*. You promised to save her from marriage to Thomas and Matthew. I may have been only eleven years old at the time, and no doubt you thought me too young to understand. But I have ears, and I heard the promises you made to Helen, and I was glad of them. Edith was glad, too. We loved our brothers, but we always knew it was you Helen loved. And we thought you loved her just as much! You cannot deny it! And you cannot deny what I heard: you said that you would rather run off to Gretna Green with Helen than allow Papa to marry her to Thomas or Matthew. But you didn't save her because you went off to France instead."

"Grace, I—"

"Grace, please don't upset yourself so," Helen said gently, cutting Royston off and pressing her lace handkerchief on her young cousin. "It doesn't matter. Not now. Not after all these years. We were just children when we made those promises to each other."

When Grace just stood there looking miserable, Helen turned her away from the room, pried the handkerchief from her fist, and gently patted her wet cheeks dry. She spoke to her in a low, soothing voice.

"You must not blame your brother for my marriage. I do not. I married Sir William of my own free will. If I have one regret, it is leaving you and Edith. I had hoped to reside nearby, but—but as a parliamentarian Sir William needed to be in London. And perhaps that was for the best . . ."

She pocketed her damp handkerchief and kissed her cousin's flushed cheek, saying with a glance up at Royston, who was frowning with concern at his sister, "Your brother had to go to France because—because healing is his—his—*calling*. And a young man who needs to concentrate on his career does not need the distraction of a wife. So you see, it all worked out for the best, and here we are! Still friends." She smiled brightly. "Now, we must think of Edith and her wedding and her happiness—"

"*Not matter*? *Still Friends*?" Royston whispered hoarsely, taking a step closer to Helen. "You can be calm and cavalier with your feelings if you please, but don't pretend to know mine!"

He'd been forcing himself not to interrupt Helen's soothing monologue because it was having the desired effect on his sister, and he certainly did not need another scene. Their guests had witnessed enough drama from Grace's entrance and subsequent hollow pronouncements about running off with the steward's son. So he was prepared to let Helen reason with her. But whatever circumspection he possessed evaporated when she had used the word *friends*. And having made his initial outburst, it was as if the dam that had been holding back his feelings finally burst, allowing them to come rushing forward, caution swallowed up in the torrent.

"It matters to me. It has *always* mattered to me that you married someone else—that you chose to marry Sir William. It matters that you had such little faith in my promises—in *our* promises to each other. We may have been children when we first made them, but nothing had changed for me about our future right up until the day I discovered you had married another. Our lives would have turned out very differently indeed had you heeded my words. Had you trusted in me." He regarded his sister, who was staring at him forlornly. "Don't lay all the blame at my feet, Grace. No doubt Helen had her reasons for disregarding my letter. Perhaps it was wrong of me to make such presumptions as I did, because they weren't enough to convince her to wait until my return from France, were they?" Out of the corner of his eye he saw Edith approaching with one of the guests and quickly came to a sense of his surroundings. He bowed stiffly. "You will have to excuse me. I am being a neglectful host." Before he turned away, he said to Helen, "Because we are still friends, I am willing to discuss this further with you. But it will have to wait until tomorrow. And as we'll be stuck in a carriage for several hours, what better way to pass the time! Excuse me . . ."

Grace and Helen watched him step across to Edith to be introduced to her guest, and then both looked at each other, puzzled. They mouthed the same word and in the same incredulous manner.

"Letter?"

Seven

HELEN WAS DETERMINED to take Royston up on his offer and ask about the letter but knew that discussion would have to wait until the journey to Dumfries for Edith's wedding. Thus she put it out of her mind and enjoyed the rest of the afternoon tea. It was a spectacular success, and even Lord Salkeld was able to offer up his congratulations to his daughter and son on a most excellent turnout. Edith was very happy, and that's all that mattered to anyone. And then, just as the guests were taking their leave, Royston was called away to attend to a patient and did not return in time to have supper with the family.

After supper, the cousins sat over their needlework about the fireplace in the sitting room, Helen entering into the excitement of the preparations in place for Edith's wedding at Comlongon Castle, while Lord Salkeld dozed in his favorite chair. And such was the happiness of the two sisters to have Helen returned to them that they remarked it was just like old times, when they were all girls in their teens growing up together. Edith pointed out that one thing about her teens she did not miss was being teased mercilessly by her three brothers. Yet various examples of this teasing provoked giggles. Though when Edith admitted that Royston was always too serious to enter into their brothers' scheming and that he always protected Helen from their playful pranks, there was a moment of awkwardness. But Helen smiled and lamented that she, too, had missed her cousins, even the teasing pranks of Thomas and Matthew, and everyone again fell into easy conversation. That is until Grace voiced what the family knew but which had never been spoken aloud: Roy returned from France a much more serious young man than when he had left. Edith and Grace were convinced the change had everything to do with Helen's marriage to Sir William Dysart.

Helen ruminated about this and the discussion of the previous night while seated at the breakfast table the next morning. She often wondered how different her life might have been had Royston not gone off to France. But she never forgot his words to his father about her: *"I wouldn't marry her under such circumstances if she were the last redheaded gypsy worth a fortune this side of hell!"* Words that still stung after all these years. So while she could wish there had been a different outcome, she was not bitter. She had always preferred to concentrate on the positives of what life had dealt her and so was optimistic about the future and what it might hold and did not dwell on what might have been, which seemed to be what Royston had been doing since he'd returned from abroad.

And then she recalled the fierce sincerity in his tone when at the afternoon tea he had said it had always mattered to him that she had married Sir William. But what did he mean by accusing her of breaking promises they had made to each other? Had he not done that very thing by refusing to marry her when his father had demanded he must?

This brought her thoughts full circle and back to the question of the letter he claimed to have left her before leaving for France. She was wondering where that letter could be and what it contained when Royston entered the morning room, hesitating on the threshold when he saw she was there alone.

He was dressed for travel, in buff leather breeches and top boots, and his riding frock coat, like his waistcoat, was a fine wool of dark blue and had silver buttons. She smiled in greeting, a heightened color to her cheeks the only sign of any awkwardness between them after yesterday's outburst. And when he came into the room, she continued on with her breakfast. She sipped at her tea, nibbled on her toast spread with marmalade, and returned to perusing the newssheet by her saucer.

He went to the sideboard laden with covered dishes, and to one end where the large silver samovar of hot water sat on its pedestal. He lingered longer than was necessary before finally looking over his shoulder and saying as casually as he could, "Would you care for another coffee, cousin?"

Helen held out her porcelain cup. "I would. Thank you."

But when he went to take her cup, his fingers lightly brushed hers, and he fumbled. He would have dropped it had Helen not had a firm grip on the handle.

Royston took a step back with a mumbled apology, and she half rose out of her chair and put the cup into his hand, just as affected by his touch as he was by hers. She quickly turned away to hide her blush and returned to finishing her slice of toast. She stared at the newssheet without reading a word, ears wide open to the sounds of coffee being prepared. He finally set the cup on its dish in front of her and disconcerted her further for having made the coffee the way she preferred, with only a splash of milk, the sugar lump in the bowl of the spoon resting on the saucer, so that she could plop it into the liquid and watch it dissolve.

When she stared fixedly at the cup without a word of thanks, he asked curiously, "Is that not the way you prefer it? Have your tastes changed? Do you want me to make you another?"

She shook her head. "No. Not changed. I've not changed," she muttered, too overcome to say more. When she looked up, he was on the other side of the table, opposite, his plate laden with all manner of breakfast foods. Noticing the Cumberland sausage smothered in cooked apple and onions, she smiled.

"When did your favorite dish become a breakfast staple? Lord Salkeld had only contempt for what he called *farmer's fodder*."

Royston flicked out the linen napkin and spread it across his lap and raised an eyebrow as if in displeasure, but a smile hovered about his mouth. He looked very well pleased with himself.

"A physician who has patients scattered from the town's medieval walls and beyond the River Eden never knows when he will return home from his rounds or when he will next eat. Thus I have prescribed my favorite dish as a means of sustaining my own health and well-being. Cook is very obliging."

"I do not doubt Cook is only too willing to ply Dr. Meredith with whatever his heart desires," she teased him. "You always had a way of overplaying the situation and using to advantage your position to get what you wanted."

He gave a huff of laughter, and the words came out before he could stop them. "How well you know me!" To mask his awkwardness, he quickly took up his knife and fork and concentrated on what was on his plate.

Helen stirred her coffee and returned to reading the newssheet to allow Royston time to eat a good portion of his breakfast before asking in a light tone, "Do you have patients to visit this morning?"

"Not today." He glanced up at her. "But that does not mean I should not enjoy my usual breakfast fare . . ." He ate the rest of what was on his plate, then pushed it aside to pick up his coffee cup. "Besides, Cumberland sausage is justified today, for we have some distance to travel—"

"—to Dumfries?" Helen set down her cup. "I am looking forward to it."

"Truly? I'd have thought travel again so soon after your journey up from London would be the last thing you'd wish to do."

"Surely you cannot think me so feeble! I admit there was little to occupy me on the journey here, which made it tedious. But I have company to Dumfries, so the time will be but an instant by comparison. Though I dare say your father will wish it over before it begins, what with three chattering females for travel companions."

"Ah. I see you were not told."

"Told?"

"I saw Father and Edith off in the carriage at first light this morning."

Helen was surprised. She tried not to sound it. "Oh? They have already left for Dumfries?"

"They have, but they are traveling only as far as Gretna Green in our carriage, which will then return here for you and Grace. At Gretna, father and Edith will be met by Sir James and his men, and it is his carriage which will convey them the rest of the way to Dumfries."

"Dear me! I had no idea an English bride marrying a Scottish lord had to forgo her own carriage and horses at the border. It sounds positively medieval."

Royston laughed. "When you put it like that, it does, doesn't it? With a casting-off ceremony whereby the bride rids herself of all her English trappings and is wrapped in a plaid and taken on horseback to her laird's hilltop fortress!"

"Escorted by a dozen brutish clansmen with thick beards and sporting claymores, and all to the accompanying wail of the pipes."

Royston sat forward. "Oh, I like that! I'm counting on pipes at the wedding, and Scottish dancing."

"I'll be disappointed if there isn't. And so will Grace. But your father . . . He is reconciled to his eldest daughter marrying an invader—for that is what he always called Scotsmen when I lived here."

Royston's smile was lopsided.

"Carlisle has been besieged since before Roman times, and so often by the English as well as the Scots, that my father has no right to direct all his anger at our northern neighbors. Besides, you know my father as well as anyone. His Lordship is easily won over by wealth. Sir James Murray's heritage is overlooked because he is rich. More importantly for me, Edith's intended is a good man. I like him. That he is also a baronet and a distant cousin of the Duke of Kinross, and thus he has ducal connections, impresses my father immensely. What happened at Carlisle in my grandfather's time, when the Murrays were part of the Young Pretender's invading force, was just one more episode of siege, capture, siege, and recapture for this unfortunate town. Their involvement is conveniently forgiven, though never forgotten. Nor should it be."

Helen's brow lifted. "So Sir James Murray's ancestors were part of Bonnie Prince Charlie's army?"

"They were. And it was Sir James's grandfather and his great-uncle, along with the Duke of Perth, who laid siege to Carlisle during the rebellion of '45 and captured it for Charles Edward Stuart. And it was my grandfather, the fifth Lord Salkeld, who assisted the Duke of Cumberland in recapturing the town for the English. It was my grandfather who signed Robert Murray's death warrant. James's uncle, along with many of his fellow clansmen, were strung up on Gallows Hill—"

"The hill just south of the town?"

"The very one."

"Did Sir James's grandfather escape prosecution for his part in the rebellion and capture of the town?"

"He did. But not because he was pardoned. He died of starvation in the dungeon of Carlisle Castle before he could be transported south to London to the Tower to stand trial." When Helen gave a little shiver and grimaced, he added in a less strident tone, "Had he lived, his fate would've been much worse for his family. Dying in that dungeon did him and them a favor. If convicted of treason, he would've been publicly shamed and beheaded."

Helen was quiet a long moment, and then she looked across at Royston and smiled diffidently.

"Sir William's uncle died in the first siege. Cut down by

one of the prince's officers. He had no time for the Stuarts either, and shared his contempt of them with your father. He would have enjoyed toasting the last of the Stuarts dying in Rome this past January. No doubt your father did just that. But I hope with Edith's marriage to a Scot, some of that animosity will be dulled, that he can let go of the past. To harbor such resentment for so long is surely unhealthy . . . It is to the future one must look. I hope he is truly happy for Edith . . . I am, that she is marrying the man she loves, and who loves her. Nothing else matters . . ."

Royston held her gaze. He was well aware she was not only speaking of his father's long-held resentments but of his at her marriage to Sir William, and that the future she spoke of was not only about Edith's happiness, but of her own. He understood. As far as he was concerned it was time to let go of the past, to bury it where it belonged, with Sir William Dysart. He had a sudden desire to talk to her now, here at the breakfast table. He did not want to wait until they were in a carriage trundling along a dreary landscape to Gretna Green. Besides, Grace would be with them, and the opportunity might not present itself. That might mean waiting until they were in Dumfries, or worse, until after the wedding and on their way home. He could not wait that long. He would not.

"Helen, about the letter I left for you when I went off to Lyon—"

"Sir! Dr. Meredith! Sir!"

"Letter?" Helen asked, ignoring the interruption of a servant banging open the door and rushing into the room and straight up to Royston. "You left *me* a—a letter?"

Royston was puzzled by her surprise. He scowled. "I did. You were too unwell to say your goodbyes, and so I could not give it to you in person, so I had—"

"Dr. Meredith! Sir!"

Royston tore his gaze from Helen and glared at the servant. "Five minutes! Only then will I get my bag, and we can be off to—"

"No, sir. You're not wanted to heal. It's not medical, it's—"

"Then it can wait!"

"Go on," Helen urged, hand outstretched across the table, refusing to be distracted. "Tell me about this letter you wrote—"

"Sorry, sir. M'lady. Mr. Lawson said it can't wait," the servant interrupted. "It's about Miss Grace—"

"*Grace*?" Royston and Helen blurted out in unison. The servant finally had all their attention.

"A note was found, sir, and when her maid read it, she ran with it to Mr. Lawson. Mr. Lawson said to tell you Her Ladyship's carriage is all hitched and ready, on account of His Lordship's carriage ain't returned yet. He said time was of the—of the—"

"—essence?"

"That's it, sir! Essence."

"Well?" Royston demanded, hand out for the note when the boy just stood there.

He snatched it when offered and snapped out the single piece of paper with a glance at Helen, who was half out of her chair in anticipation. It took only seconds to read, and then he stared across the table at her, face drained of color.

"What? What is it? Royston? What's happened to Grace?"

"Bloody hell . . ." he muttered in disbelief. "Happened? Grace has run off to Gretna Green with Charlie Lawson."

Eight

"ROYSTON! DR. MEREDITH! Wait! You cannot gallop off after her in this wild way! Think of Grace!"

Helen had picked up her wool petticoats and scurried after Royston when he crushed the note in his fist, tossed it aside, and strode from the room. He was in the passageway headed for the stables when Helen caught at the skirt of his riding frock and held on to make him stop. He did, and spun about so fast that the coat was tugged out of her hand, and so forcefully that she overbalanced and staggered. He caught her before she fell hard against him.

"I am thinking of Grace," he replied patiently, hand still about her upper arm. "Which is why I must leave at once. God knows what start they have, and as the border is just ten miles north, they'll be across it and married over a blacksmith's anvil before I'm astride a horse. I must go."

"Yes, you must. And I am thinking of Grace when I implore you not to gallop off on horseback, a lone rider in pursuit. It will only feed the gossips—"

"As if I have ever cared for what anyone says! If I did, do you think I'd be a healer of animals? As it is, my own father thinks I'm mad. Half of Carlisle agrees with him. The other half ridicule my efforts to educate them to care for their animals as much as they do themselves—"

"More fool them for not believing in you!" Helen

countered fiercely. "And I do not agree that all of Carlisle's inhabitants sneer at your efforts. Sir William certainly did not. Nor did his family or friends. But your father you will never change because he has a rigid mind and no doubt always did, even as a young man. But it is not your father or Carlisle society that worries me, but Grace's future. When she is older, and has the maturity to realize it was misdirected pride that made her act in this impetuous fashion, and all to flout you, she will come to rue her actions this day."

"Is that why you married Sir William?" he asked curiously, finally letting go of her arm. "In a fit of misdirected pride because I went off to Lyon without you?"

Helen blanched. "I beg your pardon, but I did no such thing. I am not Grace, and Charlie Lawson most certainly is not Sir William. And marriage is not something to decide upon while having a fit of any kind."

"I agree. It most certainly is not, which is why, for the life of me, I still cannot fathom why you chose to marry a man old enough to be your father, when—"

"Age had nothing to do with my decision."

"Ha! That's obvious and didn't need to be stated!"

Helen put up her chin, and her blue eyes sparked.

"Nor does it need to be stated that Sir William did not take my red hair in aversion and think it a reason *not* to marry me! In fact he said my red hair was one of my most appealing attributes."

Royston frowned. "Did he? And why wouldn't he? Your hair is glorious. Any man who says otherwise has rocks for brains."

It was Helen's turn to frown. "But—"

"But my concern is not Sir William's likes and dislikes or why you married him, which is fascinating in itself and something I very much want to pursue with you at a more convenient time. But right at this moment I must find Grace and bring her home," Royston continued smoothly, the urgency of catching up to his sister before she and Charlie

Lawson crossed the border into Scotland, where they could marry without parental consent, momentarily overriding the awkwardness of his honesty.

With a quick nod he strode off, Helen so taken aback by his admission about her hair that it took her several seconds to react. When she came out of her stupor, he was off down the passageway and had turned a corner. She followed, but not that way. She dashed through the servant door and along a network of narrow corridors she had used as a child when playing at hide-and-go-seek with Edith and Grace. So when Royston arrived at the stables, Helen was not so very far behind him, coming through the gate from the vegetable garden, which put her a few manly strides away from his back.

Royston had scattered the stableboys with his orders for a horse to be saddled at once. But as the most sturdy and rested of the horses were already hitched to Helen's carriage in readiness to take them to Dumfries, the luggage strapped to the roof and the driver pacing to be off, a heated discussion ensued about uncoupling the carriage and making one of the horses available for Royston's use. It was then that Helen came forward, and mustering her years of marriage as Lady Dysart, she imperiously ordered the stable hands to stand down and told her driver that she and Dr. Meredith would be leaving at once. She then sent a stableboy with a message for her maid that she was to remain behind to await the return of Lord Salkeld's carriage from Gretna Green, which would then convey her and Grace's maid all the way to Dumfries.

And because Royston did not counter Lady Dysart's orders, his servants did as she commanded. She then swept up to the carriage steps and waited for him to hand her up inside. He stomped over and put out his hand.

"Travel by carriage will slow the pursuit considerably," he hissed, not wanting the servants to overhear him.

His actions, however, spoke volumes when he offered her his assistance and then climbed aboard to sit opposite. With the door closed, he gave a knock to the headboard for the driver to set off.

"Which is why, once we have crossed the Eden and are well out of town, you can then take one of the horses and ride like the wind to Gretna Green," Helen explained, well satisfied with herself at having managed to get him inside the carriage. She settled against the padded upholstery. "Taking to your horse here and galloping off at breakneck speed out of town toward the border would only have alerted your servants, your neighbors, and the good people of Carlisle that all was not right in the Meredith household. Questions would be asked—ones you would not want to answer."

Royston sprawled out in a corner.

"You didn't think that perhaps it is a natural occurrence for this physician to sometimes be seen riding at breakneck speed, if the medical crisis calls for it? It happens more often than you know, and as for questions, as I said, I don't care what people think of me."

Helen's eyes opened wide, and she mouthed the letter *O* at the thought of Royston galloping about the countryside with his medical satchel flung over his saddle, giving very little thought to his own fine neck because he was wholly focused on his patient. She gave a little shiver in response to such a mental image of his dedication. Yet when Royston's grin widened, as if he were reading her thoughts, she pouted.

"You may not care what people think of you, but I know you care very much about your sister's happiness. And I know that you want Grace to marry well and be accepted in Carlisle drawing rooms. Thus you must agree that to save her from social ridicule and a lifetime of regret, we must extract her from this potentially scandalous situation in a way that does not draw attention to her. Which means arriving in Gretna Green in a carriage."

"You seem to have formulated a plan . . ."

"Not a plan, but a way of going about the matter to ensure there is no scandal attached to her good name, yes."

Royston folded his arms and said with asperity, "She won't have a name worth having if I can't get there in time to save her from marriage with Charlie Lawson, regardless of turning up in your fine conveyance."

"You will save her. And she won't marry Charlie; well not today, anyway."

"Not ever, if she has any sense. But not today, that is certain. And I do mean to take a horse and ride ahead as soon as we are over the bridge."

"Of course. But promise me once you get to Gretna Green you won't go door-to-door calling Grace's name, or Charlie's, at the top of your lungs."

Royston looked offended. "And why would I do such a thing? I'll head to the nearest publican's house and seek information."

Helen put up her brows as if she didn't believe him. "That's not what you did that day at the fair when Thomas borrowed your slingshot."

"He stole it so—"

"Stole or borrowed. He—"

"—so he and Matthew could harass the travelers' children by pelting them and their ponies with rocks."

"But you didn't just take it back, did you?" Helen replied and could not help a giggle. "You slipped the town crier a groat to wander the fair making pronouncements of a reward for the capture of one Thomas Meredith, slingshot thief."

Royston laughed, well pleased with himself. "Yes. I did. And I'd do it again. Regardless that he was my brother, Thomas was a brute and an ass, and you know it."

Helen smiled thinly. "Yes. He was. And you have always championed those who were at a distinct disadvantage or less fortunate than yourself, regardless of social position."

"When it is the right thing to do. Of course."

"Of course. Gypsy children are at enough of a disadvantage without having rocks hurled at them by two boys who knew they could not be touched because they were the sons of the local peer. You would never use your birthright in such a selfish and destructive manner. In fact you have disregarded it altogether to become a physician . . ."

Royston's smile fell away, and he frowned, suddenly self-conscious, and he took a moment to glance out at the view just as the horses swung right. He grabbed for the leather strap above the window, satisfied when the carriage picked up speed once it had passed through the open gates that proclaimed the Salkeld estate and turned onto the main road heading north.

He brought his gaze back inside the carriage and to Helen, who also had a gloved hand tight to the leather strap above her head. He found her regarding him with a soft smile, and when she quickly looked away he smiled to himself but said seriously, "You must not think my every action was because I am some sort of knight in shining armor come to rescue the poor from the nasty nobles. With two brutes for elder brothers, and me the runt of the litter, I had very little opportunity to fight back. The town crier humiliated Thomas that day, and I was glad of it."

"You were fifteen. Just a boy. Your brothers always resorted to their fists because they could never outsmart you. And they were jealous of your natural affinity with animals, something neither possessed and which galled them because even their own dogs preferred you. So too their horses. Matthew's mare loved you to bits. Surely you realized that—"

"Yes. I do now," he admitted. "You also know that I have always been resolute and selfish. I wanted to become a physician, and I was able to fulfill my dream because my mother left me an inheritance she did not leave the others. Perhaps I should have thought of the family first and handed it over to my father to pay the estate's debts . . ."

"That would have been foolish. Your father would've just accumulated more debt. The five thousand pounds Sir William paid him was swallowed up and gone without a trace. The same would have happened with your inheritance. You made much better use of your mother's legacy by studying medicine."

"You say that with such conviction, my lady."

"Because I believe it to be true." She smiled, head to one side. "Will you not—particularly as we are in the privacy of my carriage—call me Helen?"

He swallowed, the dryness back in his throat. He shook his head and muttered, "No . . . Most particularly because we are in the privacy of your carriage."

"Will you tell me why not? Are we not cousins? Have you not known me since I was thirteen years old? And am I not a respectable widow?"

He huffed on the word *respectable*. He needed to deflect the conversation away from his thoughts, which were decidedly not respectable where she was concerned, for he wanted to throw himself on the seat beside her, take her in his arms, and kiss her—a long, leisurely kiss that left her in no doubts as to his feelings. Instead, he let go of the leather strap and resettled, saying as smoothly as he could, "And who better than a respectable widow and cousin to give Grace the protection she needs once we reach Gretna Green? Is this why we are traveling in this most respectable vehicle through the streets of Carlisle?"

Helen looked out the window in surprise. "Oh! And so we are. I never fail to catch my breath at the sight of the castle dominating the skyline. It has been an age since Sir William and I were last here . . . Oh! And let us pull the blinds—"

"Pull the—"

"—at once! Before we are seen."

Far from doing as directed, Royston remained inert and watched her scramble to the other end of the seat to cover the window with the blind and shut out the streetscape, the heavy gold-and-blue tassel still swinging as she shifted back along the seat to then pull the second blind on the window next to him, leaving them in almost total darkness.

"And now you will have the town talking—about us!" he said with a laugh.

"Nonsense!" Helen countered, and sat forward because she could barely make out his face in the gloom. "This is a new town chariot, so no one knows to whom it belongs. And with the blinds drawn, no one will be able to peer inside and recognize us, or count the number of passengers."

"And why would they do that—Ah! Yes. I see. Those gossips you were talking about earlier. The ones we don't want to rouse suspicion. I'm sure this lovely carriage with the blinds drawn and luggage atop its roof trundling along the high street as fast as any carriage can go that is making for Scotland has not attracted one raised eyebrow or snigger!"

"How smug you are, Dr. Meredith! Silly. It has nothing to do with us. If we keep the blinds drawn, no one will be able to speculate or say for certain who was in the carriage and if Grace was with us or not."

"I concede there is that, but . . ." He grinned in spite of himself. "They may not need to speculate. What if Grace has already been seen, galloping through the town's center on the back of Charlie Lawson's horse. Thus this conjecture and blind pulling is a wasted effort, surely?"

"Oh, and if you were going to elope to Gretna Green, you'd gallop up the high street with your intended on the back of your horse in full view of everyone, would you?" Helen replied, tongue in cheek. "What an ill-conceived plan! And—and—thoroughly *unromantic*."

"*Unromantic*? For a couple in love to gallop off to Scotland on the back of a trusty steed, she with the wind in her hair and holding on for dear life to her beau who is determined to make Gretna Green to have her as his wife or break their necks in the attempt? Ha! If that isn't romantic, I don't know what is! I doubt the couple is thinking of plans or had made any except for one: head for the border with all speed and get married!"

In her annoyance, Helen pulled up the blind to confirm the laughter in his eyes that she heard in his voice.

"Such a scenario is doomed to failure," she replied with a pout. "A true romantic would carefully plan the entire episode to ensure its success. There would be no need to fear breaking their necks. He would have spent hours, days, *weeks*, perfecting his plan of elopement. Much like a military strategist on campaign. Every route. Every contingency thought through to the minutest detail. He wants no disappointments. No last-minute failures. No one stopping them from making it across the border. He must and will marry this woman at any cost, and he will get her to Gretna Green without mishap, because love compels him to succeed."

"Is that what Sir William did to win your hand—campaign? Think of every contingency, every detail, nothing left to failure, all so you would say yes to being his wife?"

Nine

HELEN CAME OUT of her reverie with a jolt. It was not so much the question as the blunt execution in the asking. The tone was so unlike the Royston she knew that she was momentarily unsettled by it. And before she could answer, he relaxed and said with a lopsided grin, "If, for argument's sake, you were executing such an elopement, you'd have organized the exact route beforehand and given directions to my horse well before I was in on the act! Look what happened just now. I was all for jumping astride my mount and off I go, but no, Her Ladyship demands I get in her carriage and trundle off at a more sedate pace and with the blinds pulled. Nothing's changed in that regard since you first came to Salkeld House all those years ago, has it? You are the fiddler and I merely the bow to your strings."

Helen put up her chin and pretended to be affronted, but she had to concede much of what he said was true. Still, her eyes sparked on a memory. "But it was you who suggested we flee to the border that first time your father pronounced he would marry me to Thomas."

"Did I?"

"You did. Naturally, I agreed." She smiled with a lift of her chin. "Which rather refutes your claim that I am the fiddler and you the bow. I dare say, had we fled, you would have taken us on a merry expedition via the Solway so we could look for otters or catch salmon or follow the flight path of those birds you love so much— No! Don't tell me . . . Black. Barnyard. No! It's *barnacle*. Barnacle geese! You loved to watch the barnacle geese flock to the estuary." She rolled her eyes for effect. "And you could talk about them endlessly."

He laughed and shook his head and leaned forward. "What do you mean *could*? I still go to watch them flock. And I can put anyone to sleep within ten minutes of opening my mouth on the subject of barnacle geese migration."

Helen mimicked him by also sitting forward. "And what do you mean *ten* minutes? You exaggerate, Dr. Meredith. Five at most. Admit to it!"

He stared into her bright eyes, and his features softened. "I admit to nothing, my lady, except that I am most impressed that you remembered my favorite bird is the barnacle goose."

"I remember everything about our times together, Royston," she confessed softly, so softly that he wondered if he had heard her say his name at all.

He sat back, and for want of something to fill the awkward moment, because he had so much he wanted to say to her but dared not, not yet, he put up the blind and looked out. She followed his gaze to the moving landscape and let out a sigh of disappointment.

"We've already crossed the bridge . . . And I was so looking forward to the view."

"You can take all the time you want on the return journey," he said conversationally, breathing easy that the awkward moment between them had passed, because he had come within a flea's foot of declaring himself there and then. "I for one am glad we are making excellent speed, particularly when those clouds over there look ominous. The last thing we need is a deluge to turn the road muddy."

"Then it is as well you came in the carriage, and perhaps as we are making such progress, it would be best to remain if you think there is to be a deluge . . ."

Royston pulled the blind up on the other window and looked out. There was blue sky far out to the east, over the Solway, so he thought the rain, when it came, would be short-lived. Which meant he could unhitch a horse and possibly arrive at Gretna Green before the heavens opened. He wished it wasn't so because he was enjoying his carriage ride with Helen. Still, it was Grace on whom he needed to concentrate. Thinking about his sister's elopement with Charlie Lawson made him anxious, and that made his tone harsh.

"I'll wait another ten minutes and then have the driver pull up. We should be far enough out of town by then not to encounter any gossips that may seek to injure Her Ladyship's reputation."

Helen ignored the sarcasm and asked, "Once you've reached Gretna Green and apprehended the couple, what do you intend to do?"

"Whip Charlie Lawson within an inch of his life for his impudence, then send him home to his father with his tail between his legs. He can walk back, which will give him plenty of hours to reflect on the folly of his actions. And Grace I shall throw over my knee and give her a good spanking for her scandalous behavior and extract a promise from her to never run away again."

Helen was dismissive.

"Nonsense! You'll do no such thing. You've never lifted a hand to man or beast—you are too kind and gentle. Your father, yes, he would take a whip to Charlie Lawson and spank Grace with a paddle, too, but not you—"

"—because I'm the mealy mouthed, sensitive runt of the family."

"Better a sensitive runt than an unfeeling, narcissistic bully, which your father was when we were children," she countered stridently. "I should not be disrespectful because he is your father and my uncle, but—"

"—it is the truth. Thankfully, since his last illness has kept him housebound and not very far from the fireplace, he has mellowed considerably. He now offers hollow threats and derisory comments from the comfort of his wing chair."

She was not fooled by his seeming indifference. She was well aware his self-deprecating smile covered a boyhood filled with torment, from his elder brothers and from his father, because he had been a distracted child and they had never understood him or his temperament. She liked to think no one understood him better than she. So with the carriage picking up speed again as the road began to descend toward the River Esk, she gathered up a handful of her petticoats and moved to sit beside him.

"It is my belief, and Sir William agreed with me, that your father took you in dislike because you, of all his children, are most like your mother. You not only resemble her greatly, but Sir William remembered Lady Salkeld as a gentle, kind, and generous soul who had a great affinity for animals, most particularly horses."

Royston took a moment to compose himself, surprised and affected by Sir William's acute observation.

"That is how I remember her, too. And there may be something in what you say."

He shifted to better see her face, acutely aware of her proximity, that the layers of her wool gown bunched against his leg, and that she was close enough for him to breathe in the soft floral scent that enveloped her. He studied her a moment. She had been his closest childhood friend, and they had been secretly betrothed when still in their teens. There had never been any doubt in his mind that when she turned one and twenty they would marry. He would have his medical practice, and they would live in a house in town and raise a family, away from Salkeld House, until such time as he inherited the title and was compelled to take on the responsibilities that came with being a landowner and peer.

He had explained all this in his letter, meant to reassure

her of his intentions and their future while he was away in France, and yet, now, some six years later, he wondered if he truly knew her. Perhaps those hopes and dreams expressed in ink had been his alone and not hers at all? For why else had she forsaken him to marry Sir William Dysart?

The Helen he knew had never worn perfume. But as Lady Dysart she did. Was it a perfume gifted by Sir William? The scent was fresh and lovely, just like her. Jasmine and something else: orange blossom, or was it honeysuckle? And the Helen he knew had never worn a dusting of powder to her cheeks and nose to cover her freckles. He liked her freckles. Did she wear the powder to please her husband because her freckles were not to his liking? And while she had always worn her hair in a coil of braids, he knew that when it was brushed free, her flame-colored tresses reached to the small of her back. She had shown him once when in competition with Edith and Grace, all three had taken out their braids and had him measure the length of their locks and declare the winner. He could not now remember who had won, only that he was mesmerized by the fire and light in her hair and how soft it was to the touch. He wondered if Sir William preferred his wife's hair down her back. Had he brushed it, too . . . ?

Enough.

He tore his gaze from her and snapped around to look out the window without seeing. Why was he tormenting himself with a past over which he'd had no control and which should remain in the past? All his life he had done everything he could not to follow in his father's footsteps of living a life of envy and bitterness, but to have a life that was useful, one that helped people, one that was fulfilling. Yet here he was being just like his father over something that was beyond his ability to fix.

He might not be able to change the past, but he could do something about the present.

It was not Sir William in the carriage with Helen. He was with her, and only he had the power to decide what sort of future he wanted. And the future he desperately wanted was one shared with this woman seated beside him.

Of course he did not begrudge her perfume even if it had been gifted by her husband. And if she preferred to wear a dusting of powder, that too was her right. She had never had the means or opportunity to indulge in such feminine fripperies when living under his father's roof. His father had lavished money on himself, not on his wife or children or his ward. And taking a sweeping glance about the plush interior of the carriage, with its dark-blue velvet upholstery, matching cushions, tassels and fringes to the pull down blinds, he wouldn't have been surprised if this town chariot had been a wedding gift from Sir William to his bride. It was the height of luxury and elegance and very much what he supposed a lady of quality would use when she left the house to go visiting. It was just the sort of gift he would've given her had he the means.

He found himself smiling, pleased Sir William had been a generous husband. And as he continued to glance about the interior, all the bitterness and anger he felt at having lost Helen, at her having forsaken him for another, and at Sir William for taking Helen from him, drained away. He was left with a sense of peace.

Yet with peace came doubt. He wanted Helen and no other, but did she want him? He would be Lord Salkeld one day. What was a title when it came with an encumbered estate and had his father's debts to repay? When he had left her the letter, he had not even had a medical practice, so no means to support a wife and family. No wonder an heiress worth a staggering £25,000 chose Sir William. Age aside, Sir William had been a far better matrimonial prospect. The baronet had wealth, position, and the respect of his peers.

With peace and doubt came revelation. Since his teens he had assumed she would be his. He had also expected her to wait years and years until he made the decision when they should marry. Was that right? Was that fair? Was he just as arrogant as his father, and a presumptuous clod into the bargain? Most definitely.

He looked at Helen then and discovered her comfortably anchored in a plush corner, for the horses were moving at a goodly pace, and the carriage was rocking to and fro. She was regarding him with a smile he knew only too well: she was aware that he was preoccupied with his thoughts, and thus his surroundings were forgotten. A heat came into his throat, hoping she could not read those thoughts. Her reaction to what he said next confirmed that she could not. But he not only surprised her, but himself.

"I'm glad Sir William was a generous and caring husband."

She swallowed and gave a little sigh before saying with a soft smile, "Thank you. He was, but I—but he deserved—"

"He deserved you, Helen. I'm glad you had nice clothes and perfume and a fine carriage to convey you about town," he interrupted, eager to show he had shed any animosity he had harbored toward Sir William. "I hope he indulged you in all the ways a beautiful woman should be indulged and surrounded you with beauty. You deserve nothing less."

She cocked her head, a note of sadness creeping into her voice.

"Is that how you see me now, Royston? As a beautiful woman who should be indulged?"

"No! Yes! You are beautiful, and you should have beautiful things."

"That is the first time you have ever said so, and I accept your compliment. But you did not answer my question."

He moved up the seat to be nearer, and so she could hear the sincerity in his voice.

"It might be the first time I have ever commented on your beauty, but did I not always say you were far smarter than I? If females were able to do anything they wanted in this life, you could be anything you put your mind to. You are clever, and you are good with people. You know just what to say to my father to put him in a better mood—a most conceited, grumbling old fusty breeches, to use Grace's favorite expression. In fact, you have only to walk into a room and everyone around you is in a better mood. That is a skill I do not possess and cannot hope to cultivate. And Edith and Grace adore you. If not for you, I doubt either of them would have applied themselves in the schoolroom. When you married and went to London, they said it was as if all the colors had washed away from their lives. Grace said that rainbows only ever came out when you visited them as Lady Dysart . . ."

He took a breath and to steady the emotion in his voice brushed at a cuff and cleared his throat.

"To answer your question . . . I see you now as I have always seen you—no! How I have always seen *us*. Be it when we were fishing for salmon or watching the barnacle geese, drawing silhouettes of each other with the lamp, or you were helping me solve an equation—we are two halves of a whole." He looked into her eyes. "I told you that many years ago. Do you remember?"

"I do."

"You are the smartest and wisest girl I have ever met," he answered truthfully. "You are also the most beautiful . . ."

His gazed dropped to her mouth and the slight tremble to her lower lip. He felt compelled to draw even nearer, as if pulled by a strong magnet, and was overcome by a feeling of falling from a great height. It was a sensation akin to vertigo, of time slowing, then rapidly speeding up. He had only ever experienced it once before, and with her, years ago. He could not remember where they were or what they had been doing, or why the feeling had come on so suddenly. But what he did know was that from that moment he could not imagine spending his life with anyone but her.

"I still think that," he muttered, leaning in to kiss her. "Nothing has changed. You are wise and you are beautiful—"

"As beautiful as a barnacle goose . . . ?"

He nodded.

She giggled.

That broke the spell.

Ten

ROYSTON TURNED CRIMSON and sat up. Helen quickly dropped her lashes and her smile. There was an awkward silence between them. He because her giggle was a slap of reproach that he dare think he could kiss her. She because she had not given the moment or his sincerity its due.

She desperately wanted to kiss him. But they had never shared a kiss, and before she threw herself in his arms, she needed to be certain he did indeed love her for herself. If marriage to Sir William had taught her anything, it was that men were capable of saying and doing anything to get what they wanted. Yet, in the cool light of day, and in the heat of argument, the truth revealed itself. What Royston had shouted at his father in the study the day before he left for Lyon was forever etched in her memory: *I wouldn't marry her under such circumstances if she were the last redheaded gypsy worth a fortune this side of hell.*

The silence stretched between them, much like the landscape they looked out on from opposite windows as the carriage trundled along a flat and featureless sweep of moorland, made bleak by the heavy clouds blocking the sunlight. Finally, Royston was the first to speak, a knuckle up to the headboard.

"This is a good place to have the carriage pull over. I'll ride on from here."

"You told me two days before you left for Lyon," Helen stated, hearing the lingering note of hurt in his voice and ignoring his statement. "We had just returned from a ride and were leading our mounts around to the stables. You said we were two halves of the same whole, and I believed you."

"Because it was—*is*—the truth."

"If that is true, then how can one half of a soul abandon the other half, as you did me, without any reassurance about the future?"

Royston's hand came away from the headboard. He dropped his arm. He was nonplussed.

"You encouraged me to go to Lyon. You said you believed in what I was doing. And I believed that the care and welfare of animals was just as important to you, or so I thought—"

"It is. It always has been. Sir William met with the gentlemen in coffeehouses to discuss what was to be done about the human disregard for the pain and suffering of our fellow creatures, and I so wished I could join him. If not for my encouragement, I doubt he would've wholeheartedly supported the establishment of a society for the prevention of cruelty to animals."

"Forgive me. I should never have questioned your conviction. I do know that. And it does not surprise me you were able to persuade Sir William to involve himself."

He moved back along the bench to sit opposite her and put out his hand, and when she gave him her fingers, he raised her gloved hand to his lips.

"Just as I should never have expected you to wait for me. Regardless that I made my intentions clear in my letter, three years is a very long time in a young lady's life." He smiled self-consciously. "Particularly for an heiress who could have the pick of any suitor of her choosing."

Helen withdrew her hand yet moved closer, a frown between her brows.

"That is the second, or mayhap the third, time, you've

referred to this letter. But I never knew of its existence until you mentioned it yesterday."

Royston sat up. "Never knew . . . But—I wrote you three pages the night before I left Carlisle. And when you were too ill to see me off, I gave it to Father to give to you."

They both stared at each other, bewildered. And then the same appalling thought dawned on them at the same moment: Lord Salkeld had kept Royston's letter from her. Their eyes widened in horror. Neither needed to say it. Helen shook her head in disbelief. Royston nodded his conviction before saying viciously under his breath, "My own *father*. My God. Of all the scheming, underhanded, outrageous—"

"Perhaps he was trying to protect me from—"

"—from what? From *me*? What did he think I would write to you, other than I loved you and wanted to marry you on your twenty-first birthday, and that I hoped and prayed you would wait for me? Why would he want to protect you from that when all he ever wanted, all he ever cared about, was marrying his niece, an heiress, to one of his sons?"

"But if he thought you did not want to marry me . . . If he thought your letter might contain words that might hurt me, he would keep it from me, wouldn't he?"

Royston threw up a hand. "I suppose so. Why do you always think the best of him when he has only ever thought of one person—himself, and to the detriment of us all?"

"I agree he is selfish and self-serving. But whatever his feelings for you, he has always shown me some regard, possibly because I was worth something to him. Besides which," she added, straightening her back and glaring at him, "after what you said to him in the study the day before your departure, I'm not surprised he kept your letter from me."

Royston's brow furrowed.

"What I said about you in the study? I don't recall anything in particular. What I do remember is that we had a blistering row worthy of a Drury Lane melodrama!" He scowled. "By the by, how do you know what was said in the study anyway, you—"

"I was there. In the doorway. You were so angry you did not notice me."

"Did Father know you were there?"

She nodded. "He sent for me. But I was so distraught by what you said I did not make my presence known. I fled the room, and that's why I never saw you off. I thought you had truly abandoned me."

"*Abandoned* you?"

He was shocked and puzzled. Aside from the distress of witnessing a shouting match between him and his father, he tried to recall what he had said in that heated interview that could have upset her. He did not believe it was anything he did not still hold as true. But it was six years ago, and he had been furious, so it was possible.

"Will you tell me what it was I said that was so hurtful?"

She was eager to do so, but now the moment had arrived she was momentarily overcome. She had been wanting to ask him for an explanation for six long years, but she also dreaded his response, and this despite her husband's remark that Royston Meredith was in love with her and had always been in love with her. Yet why say such a hurtful thing if he did not mean it? Royston was not a man given to throw away comments of any kind. He was earnest and pondered his responses, particularly on matters important to him. Nor did she think him capable of deceit. He was also devoid of hubris and vanity, attributes his father had in abundance and considered qualities. Regarding him now, scowling in incomprehension with the black curls falling across his brow, she smiled and relaxed, curiously uplifted and hopeful by the befuddlement in his eyes. Dr. Meredith was always most handsome when befuddled.

She took a deep breath and held his gaze.

"You said—When your father asked you if you were prepared to settle and marry me, you said no! You—you—

shouted at him: '*I wouldn't marry her under such circumstances if she were the last redheaded gypsy worth a fortune this side of hell.*'"

Royston sat up, the scowl still in place, but he was surprised.

"Did I say those exact words?"

"You did."

"I believe you." He thought about it for a moment. "I understand why you were upset to enter a room to find Father and me shouting at each other. A dreadful business. And you probably took umbrage at being called a gypsy. But the travelers I know are perfectly reasonable people. In fact, when Leonard and his kin are down this way, I often see to his horses and dogs—"

"Royston! I do not care that you called me a—a gypsy, or even that you mentioned my red hair! That is not what upset me." She quickly fumbled in the folds of her petticoats for her pocket, found her lace-bordered handkerchief, and dabbed at her eyes. "I don't know why I am crying," she grumbled, "because I did not think I had any tears left to shed. And now I see that you are not bothered in the least by your words, when I've been consumed by them all this time. You truly meant them! You said you wouldn't marry me, and you didn't!"

"Said I wouldn't marry you? You must have misheard me. Perhaps because you were frightened by our behavior—"

"I may have been frightened by it, but I am not deaf, Royston! You said I wouldn't marry her—*me*—under such circumstances if I were the last—"

"Yes. Yes. I know the rest," he muttered. "And as I recall it Father was doing his best to force me into marrying you before I left for Lyon. And I was having none of that because we—you and I—had decided it was best to wait until my return, and that's what I put in my letter. I wasn't going to let us be forced into anything of his making. I admit I was being stubborn. But you had yet to turn eighteen, and I had yet to complete my studies, and I thought—I thought we had all the time in the world." He smiled softly. "That when we finally did marry, we would then have the rest of our lives—together."

Helen's eyes opened wide with new knowledge. "Oh! So that's what you meant by '*under such circumstances*' . . . Oh dear . . . Oh dear, I fear I did not take much notice of that part of the sentence, and it seems it was the most vital part of all . . . I was—I was so distraught, I thought—I thought you meant you did not want to marry me—*ever*."

To think she had misinterpreted his meaning and had held to that conviction for so many years made her suddenly ill, and she slumped against the upholstery, face in her hands. Royston scrambled to sit beside her and gathered her to him. They stayed that way for a long time, both oblivious to the fact that the horses were slowing, the driver bringing the carriage to a standstill in the middle of the road. Nor were they aware that a great deal of activity and noise had erupted around the carriage.

"Oh, Helen . . . Oh, my love . . ." he murmured, kissing the top of her hair and leaning his cheek there. "And here was I thinking you had abandoned *me* by marrying Sir William. And all the while you believed I had forsaken you. Are we not a silly pair of geese?"

Helen pulled a little out of his embrace. "As silly as those who believe the barnacle goose is born out of driftwood."

"Ha! So you remember me telling you about that ridiculous myth? I am sillier," he stated firmly, "because I should have set aside my stubbornness and listened to my father for once and married you before I left for Lyon. Can you forgive me?"

"And you me for not waiting for your return?"

"There is nothing for me to forgive . . ."

As he murmured this he lowered his mouth to hers, his kiss gentle, a mere brush of his lips against hers. It was reverential and invited her to respond if she so wished. And Helen most certainly did wish it. She had been waiting so many years to kiss him that she had never thought this day would ever arrive. And so she clung to him as if he might suddenly disappear into the air, and pressed her lips to his on a sigh of contentment and joy. And when they finally sat back to take a breath after a long, leisurely kiss that left no doubt as to their feelings for each other, they smiled shyly and hesitated to put their feelings into words for fear of ruining the moment.

Nevertheless the moment was ruined. Not by them, but by forces beyond their control. Such was their preoccupation with each other that they were blissfully unaware not only that the carriage was no longer moving but also that they were being watched.

A face had appeared in the window while the couple was in the throes of a passionate kiss. A long nose pressed to the glass, and when the couple sat back, with eyes only for each other, the owner of the long nose rapped on the pane to get their attention.

The carriage door opened, and the long nose intruded into the interior.

"*Bonjour, madame et monsieur le médecin.* You are being robbed. Please to step down at once. *S'il vous plait.*"

Eleven

THE COUPLE WAS too shocked to move. Helen's first thought was not about being robbed, or for their safety, but that she had completely forgotten the primary reason she and Royston were heading north into Scotland—to save Grace from an imprudent match. Having their carriage held up by highwaymen meant delay, and they might not arrive at Gretna Green in time to rescue her young cousin from marriage to Charlie Lawson.

Royston's first thought was to think himself a complete dunderhead because in the rush to get to Gretna Green he'd forgotten his pistol and his sword, and now he was wondering if he had also left behind his medical satchel, and he never went anywhere without that, ever. And with this interruption to a most wonderful moment shared with Helen, his second thought was for her safety and coming between her and this ruffian. The last thing on his mind was saving Grace.

And with the urgency to protect the woman he loved came action.

The highwayman had barely ended his pronouncement when Royston leaped up and hurled himself at the nose peering through the doorway. He may not have had his pistol or his sword, but he still had fists. With an energy fueled by the necessity to protect Helen at all costs, Royston threw himself at the intruder.

Caught off guard, the highwayman failed to defend himself from such a physical onslaught. Royston thudded into him, instantly winding him and knocking him off his feet. He lost his footing, staggered back and into midair. With arms flaying, he fell out of the carriage.

And because Royston had launched himself with all the energy he could muster, he could not now stop himself. Inertia took over. When the highwayman stumbled backward, Royston fell out of the carriage after him.

Helen rushed into the open doorway, and in time to see the highwayman hit the ground with a sickening thud, and then Royston land hard on top of him, both men left sprawled out in the dirt, inert. Taking a sweeping look about, she saw that the carriage was stopped this side of the redbrick bridge that spanned the River Esk. A line of wagons and caravans hitched to mules and followed by men, women, and children on foot, was slowly making its way across the bridge to this side of the river. The dinging of rattling pots and pans and metal utensils hanging from the sides of the wagons proclaimed their vocation as traveling tinkers.

With no room for passing traffic, Helen's driver had been forced to pull up the horses to wait for the bridge to clear. And on any other day, had she not been worried for Royston's welfare, she would have enjoyed watching the colorful procession and taken in the majestic view. Here was the very spot where the Young Pretender and his volunteer army had crossed this fast-flowing river without benefit of this bridge, built a decade after the Stuart prince's failed attempt to reinstate his bloodline to the English throne. But this was no time for taking in the scenery or for historical reminiscing. Helen quickly returned to the present. There was a more immediate and personal conflict taking place on this very spot below her feet.

Those travelers first across the bridge surged forward at the sight of Royston and the highwayman grappling with each other in the dirt by the carriage and four. But rather than break up the fight, they formed a semicircle around the pair and cheered them on. Not even the driver of Helen's carriage made a move but just stood there, aghast.

Helen clomped down the carriage steps but with no real plan of action. She just knew she had to do something to help Royston. She was about to enter the fray by pounding on the highwayman's back in the hopes of distracting him enough to give Royston the advantage, when the two men suddenly and inexplicably stopped fighting and stared at each other.

Royston had his fist raised, about to plant it into the highwayman's face when he froze. The man was not putting up a struggle. In fact he had raised his hands in a gesture of capitulation, one to his face to shield it from being struck. What stopped Royston in mid-punch was the man's convulsions. But he was not ill. He was laughing, and so hard his whole body shook. It was then that Royston took a good look at him. He blinked.

"Leonard? *Leonard.*"

"*Oui, mon cher ami.*"

Royston instantly scrambled off the man, stuck out his hand, and helped him to his feet.

"Bloody hell, Leonard! I almost knocked your front teeth down the back of your throat!" Royston declared, brushing the dust from his riding frock coat and buff breeches. "What the devil are you playing at?"

The highwayman continued to chuckle. He lost his French tongue, dropped the accent, and said in a lowlands burr, "Had y'fooled, didnae, doctor!"

"Fooled and a fool," Royston huffed, and then he grinned.

The old friends then shook hands and laughed.

Royston looked about, saw the smiling faces of Leonard's kin, returned their smile, and put out his hand to Helen, who was now regarding him with a curious half smile, though the scowl remained between her brows. When she put her hand in his, he drew her closer and introduced her.

"Lady Dysart, this is Leonard, an unrepentant rogue, but most definitely not a highwayman. And this is his family of travelers."

Leonard made Helen a sweeping bow and showed her a toothy grin.

"The pleasure is all ours." He glanced slyly at Royston and slapped his shoulder, saying to Helen, "And this is the best physician on both sides of the border. He looks after my animals and my people, and in that order. One cannot put a price on a good milking cow."

"And in return for my services, Leonard's wife, Deidra, kindly shares her recipes for herbal medicinals," Royston explained to Helen. "Which I value as much as Leonard does his milking cow." He looked to Leonard again. "How's Alice's lion?"

"*Lion*?" Helen asked, surprised, and found herself ignored.

Leonard pulled a face and shrugged. "More kitten than cat now he has half a tail. But the wound has healed better than expected, and he's still alive, thanks to you. We were hoping you'd take a look at him at the fair—Alice!" He looked about him. "Alice? Alice! Show your ferocious beast to Dr. Meredith."

A girl of about nine years old came forward holding a tabby cat. She smiled shyly at Royston, who had gone down on his haunches to greet her. But when Royston addressed the cat and Alice tried to move her pet from her shoulder, Lion was having none of it and clung tighter, draping himself over Alice's thin shoulder, head halfway down her back.

"So you do remember me, Lion," Royston said soothingly as he gently stroked the cat. He winked at Alice and continued to address Lion. "Don't you worry yourself. I won't be cutting or cauterizing you today. In fact, by the look of this most magnificent stub," he added, gently inspecting what was left of Lion's tail, "your personal physician did a splendid job in patching you up. The wound has healed very nicely. So you may indeed continue to call yourself Lion."

When Alice giggled, Royston chucked her under the chin with a smile and stood.

"He saved Lion's life," Leonard confided in Helen. "Silly puss ran under a wagon and got his tail mangled. It was lucky the doctor was with us. We thought there was no chance he'd survive the injury, but the good doctor, he knew better. With one swift stroke of his hot knife, the mangled tail was no more. A few stitches and a bandage later and Lion was saved, for my eldest."

Helen winced at the mental image of Royston removing the cat's mangled tail, but she quickly found her smile, knowing the little girl still had her precious pet. "Your daughter and Lion are inseparable."

"They are. Very much so. Will you stay and share a bowl of broth with us before you continue on your way?" he asked, addressing them both.

"On any other day we would accept, willingly. But Lady Dysart and I must press on to Gretna Green."

Leonard's bushy eyebrows shot up. He glanced at the smart carriage, with the luggage strapped to its roof, and then at the couple, and his face split into a grin. This was an elopement! He couldn't have been happier for his friend the physician.

"Of course! I see how it is. Go! Go, my friend, and quickly." He dared to slap Royston's back. "I wish you and your good lady all the best, and if your plans permit and you are returned from your honeymoon in time to take in the Carlisle fair, I will be disappointed if you do not stop by. My family and I will want to share a dram and drink to your health and happiness!"

"It's not—we're not—" Royston started to explain, feeling the heat in his face.

"Thank you, Dr. Meredith and I will not want to miss the fair. I always enjoyed it as a girl," Helen managed to say smoothly, and in what she hoped was a light tone, asked, "Did you see a couple on horseback pass you in the last hour or two, heading toward Gretna Green?"

"A couple on horseback?" Leonard shook his head. "The road has been quiet this morning."

"Perhaps they cut across country—" Helen began to postulate and was interrupted.

"Too treacherous for man and beast," was Leonard's opinion, and Royston agreed with him.

"Then perhaps they have not come this way yet and are in hiding somewhere—they could very well be under the bridge out of sight—and are waiting for Lord Salkeld's carriage to pass through the village on its way to Dumfries?"

Royston laughed, not to dismiss Helen's hypothesis but because he believed it a possibility. "Just the sort of hide-and-go-seek game Grace would indulge in all to add to the adventure! Perhaps Leonard has a paddle I can borrow," he teased, only half jokingly, then turned and stuck out his hand to his friend. "We must away. And yes, Lady Dysart and I will most certainly call on you at the fair, thank you."

Leonard shook his hand and then folded his arms over his chest and said thoughtfully, "We did not see a couple on horseback, but Lord Salkeld's carriage, it was coming into the village as we were leaving it. I remember, not because it was your father's carriage but because your sister, she leaned out the window to wave to us, and to blow Alice kisses."

"*Edith* was leaning out the window—"

"—*blowing kisses* to Alice?" Royston finished Helen's sentence for her, just as incredulous.

"Not Miss Meredith," Leonard corrected. "Miss Grace. Do you forget she was with you when Lion lost his tail? She was a great comfort to Alice."

"Yes. That does sound the sort of thing Grace would do, in both instances," Helen agreed.

"But how is *that* possible when Grace has eloped with Charlie Lawson on horseback?" Royston hissed in her ear.

"She can't be on horseback and in Father's carriage at one and the same time!"

Helen had a sudden thought. "Do you know, Dr. Meredith, if anyone can be in two places at the one time, it is your sister Grace." And on that cryptic comment she picked up her petticoats and bustled back to the carriage, where her driver was waiting to help her up the steps.

Before joining her, Royston turned to Leonard with a quizzical frown.

"How did you know I was an occupant of the carriage when you held it up?"

Leonard grinned. "I didn't, my friend. But I'm glad you were, and it is evident, so too is your ladylove. Now go marry her and be happy! And when next you see Miss Grace, give her a kiss from Alice and Lion."

Twelve

IT WAS ONLY a short drive from the Esk bridge over the border into Scotland and the tiny village of Gretna Green. But for Royston and Helen, who sat silent and looking out at the flat, uneventful landscape and the heavy sky from opposite windows, it seemed an eternity, where every turn of the wheels could be counted. They had so much to say to each other, and yet the interruption by Leonard and the subsequent short interval by the bridge only seemed to bring into sharp relief the misunderstandings that had parted them six years ago.

Royston felt an idiot for allowing his intractability and prejudice against his father to dictate his behavior in not marrying Helen before he left for Lyon. While Helen was incredulous that she had allowed herself to misinterpret Royston's heated words to mean that he did not love her at all and never meant to marry her.

But the past was in the past, and as she stared out the window, biting her lower lip in thought, she decided there was nothing like the present to settle their future one way or the other. She must be brave and unconventional, and as it was a leap year, she was well within her rights to ask him to marry her. But before she could muster all her courage to put the question to him, he startled her with a simple one of his own, one that was unexpected but did not surprise her. What did was the suppressed ferocity in his tone.

"Did you—did you *love* him? Did you love Sir William?"

She slowly turned from the view to look at him and kept her voice level.

"Why is that important to you?"

"It is not important to me, but perhaps you think it is important to you? Because you did not—you did not love him?"

Helen frowned. "You said you were glad Sir William was a generous and caring husband . . ."

"I am. And I still hold to that. And you assured me he was a good man, a very good man. But then you began to say something about what he deserved, and in my earnestness to assure you I hold no ill feelings toward him I interrupted you. But now I wonder what it was you wished to tell me . . . That perhaps you did not feel you were deserving of him because you did not love him." His features softened when her scowl deepened. "I am not explaining myself well, am I? I hope—I hope you realize that you need not feel any guilt for not being in love with him. That good men are subject to the same impulses as us flawed creatures, lust and avariciousness amongst those."

Helen lost her frown, and she smiled tremulously. "I am well aware of that—now."

She put her gloved hand on the cushion beside her in invitation, and he readily accepted. Settled beside her, he caught up her hand and looked into her eyes.

"If we are to be happy for the rest of our lives, then we need to divest ourselves of these heavy cloaks of guilt, here and now. Mine is the easier to discard because I have only ever loved you, have never married, and could easily have gone to my grave a bachelor physician. But you have the added burden of a first marriage, and to a good man who treated you, I suspect, as his—for want of a better term—*ornament*."

"Please, Royston, must we talk about—"

"Just this once, and then never again. But if you truly do

not want to confide in me, then so be it. I will not ask a second time. We will consign your first marriage to the pages of history where it belongs—as long as you are able to leave it there, content and untroubled."

Helen nodded, as if that was what she did indeed want, and then she startled Royston by confessing, "I married him because when I thought you did not love me and had no intention of marrying me, it mattered little who I married, only that my husband be a good and kind man. And Sir William was both. But I—I could not understand why I did not grow to love him. I never stopped loving you, but I supposed that if he loved me, I should have been able to love him in return. And then, one day, the answer came to me." She paused, eyes widening, and breathed deeply, surprising herself by voicing her innermost thoughts. "He had married me to please himself." She dropped her gaze to their fingers entwined, face hot, then bravely lifted her lashes to look at him. "And that is all he wanted from me: to please him. I was to be a compliant wife, in every sense, and in every way. Do you—do you understand?"

Royston nodded, a sudden lump in his throat.

"Yes. Yes, I do."

Helen gave a little sigh and nodded, unaware the carriage was slowing.

"I knew you would. And you are right. I was an ornament. Proudly displayed to friends and family as an object of beauty. Royston, Sir William bought me. He paid your father five thousand pounds to have me as his wife. He bragged he would've paid your father my entire dowry if that had been demanded of him."

Royston looked down at her hand in his and toyed with her fingers, needing a moment to gather his thoughts and to allow his anger to subside. But he was not surprised. He knew his father too well, and men of Sir William's vintage and reputation more often than not always got what they wanted.

And having gathered his thoughts and formulated what he wanted to tell her, he spoke with a fierce sincerity, leaving Helen in no doubts that he spoke from the heart.

"I don't want a—a compliant wife. And I certainly don't want an ornament. And your dowry was only ever a hindrance. In truth, I'm glad you no longer have it. I want to marry my best friend. I want to share my life—with you. Everything else will work itself out if we are honest and open with each other. I love you, Helen. I always have and always will." He gave an embarrassed laugh and pushed a hand through his black curls. "But enough of what *I* want—tell me, what is it that *you* want?"

Helen gave a watery chuckle and swiftly kissed his cheek. "What do *I* want? I thought you'd never ask!"

They both laughed and smiled at each other. With her eyes never leaving his, she took a deep breath and held his hands. She was giddy by his admission and by the question she was about to put to him. She was also apprehensive, though she was confident she knew what his reply would be.

"I love you, too. I always have and always will. Royston Ivo Meredith, will you marry me?"

His smile widened into a grin.

"Is this a leap year by any chance?"

"Aye, it is, Dr. Meredith. And if you decline my proposal," she added in mock haughtiness, "custom dictates you buy me a new gown and a pair of kid gloves as recompense for my disappointment. And as I will be exceedingly disappointed, I'll demand a very expensive gown and the softest kid gloves you can find!"

He shook his head sadly. "The lengths a widow will go to, all to catch a husband—"

"You mean for a new gown and gloves? Why of course! A lady must look her best at all times. Particularly in her widowhood." Her eyes widened on an idea. "Perhaps I should ask several gentlemen to marry me, so that by the end of the year I will have a complete wardrobe—"

"No you won't! Because the first gentleman you ask will say yes, leaving you without a gown and with no gloves!"

"Oh? I see . . ." She pretended to be disconsolate. "That wasn't very well thought out of me, was it? I should've asked others first and you last."

"You are much mistaken if you think I would be the only gentleman who would say yes to a proposal of marriage to Lady Dysart. In fact I'd wager my medical satchel they'd all jump at the chance to marry you!"

Distracted by the shouts greeting the carriage as the horses were pulled up in front of the first inn in the village, Helen glanced out the window before turning back to Royston, to say with a bashful smile, "Does that mean Dr. Meredith accepts my proposal?"

He returned her smile and leaned in to kiss her forehead, and there he remained, so close that his every word was like a caress.

"You must know—surely you must know my answer. It is yes. I will marry you. I have loved you since I can remember, and I have wanted to marry you for almost as long as that, too. I often imagined how this day would be, but never did I imagine it would be as perfect as this. I have waited a long time for us to be married, and it would be my very great honor to be your husband."

Helen threw her arms around his neck, and he gathered her to him and murmured into her hair, "My best friend. My helpmate. My one and only love . . ."

They sealed their engagement with many tender kisses interspersed with utterances of love and devotion, but their reverie was cut short, as their passionate kiss had been earlier interrupted by Leonard, by an urgent rapping on the window-pane.

The couple turned as one in their embrace as the carriage door was wrenched open.

"Sir! Lady! Be quick! Mistress says she cannae wait."

The couple looked at each other and had the same thought, but it was Royston who voiced it.

"Grace!"

Thirteen

ROYSTON AND HELEN hurriedly followed the boy into the inn, the surroundings of little consequence. Such was their apprehension and dread that Grace and Charlie Lawson might already have married, that neither noticed Helen's carriage wasn't the only one pulled up at the inn. There were in fact two other fine conveyances and their teams of horses. On the door of one was the coat of arms of the Viscount Salkeld; the other had the family crest of the Murrays of Comlongon Castle.

The inn was snug and warm and filled with the inviting smells of hot stew and fresh bread. Accompanying this most welcoming of mingling aromas was a constant murmur of cheerful conversation, punctuated with the occasional laugh, coming from the taproom.

Sidestepping servants fetching and carrying for their esteemed guests, the boy finally stopped at the entrance to the inn's best parlor. Here he bowed and retreated, leaving Royston and Helen to enter the room unannounced and upon a scene they were least expecting.

Brightly lit, the candles supplied by its titled occupants, the room had a good fire in the grate, and a small gathering was standing about in comfortable conversation as if at a soiree.

Helen wondered if the boy had led them to the wrong

room; Royston certainly did, thinking they had been deliberately misdirected to give the young couple enough time to marry in some other part of the inn or perhaps in another part of the village altogether. He was about to find a servant, or better yet, the publican, when who should break through the cluster of gentlemen and ladies but his youngest sister.

"You're finally here!" Grace announced, bringing all conversation to a halt and directing eyes at Helen and Royston. She rushed up to Helen and hugged her. "I'm so happy you brought Roy with you!"

"What the devil are you playing at, Grace?" Royston hissed, wholly fixed on his sister, not a look at the rest of the occupants who all wore welcoming smiles. "Have you any idea what we've been through to get here? The—the worry. The idea that you could run off in such a—a thoughtless and—and uncaring—"

"Oh, it wasn't thoughtless," Grace countered, unabashed by her brother's angry concern. She smiled cheekily, a glance at Helen. "It was exceptionally well thought out and executed. Though I cannot take *all* the credit. Papa and Edith played their parts, and so, too, did Charlie. Though I wish Papa had allowed Charlie to bring me here on his horse rather than be stuck in a carriage for endless miles. I had no notion of how dreary the landscape is between Carlisle and the border from inside a carriage. If we hadn't seen Leonard and his wagons to divert us—"

"No—*notion*? *Dreary*?"

Royston's fury at his sister's seeming total disregard for her person, that he and Helen had spent several hours bumping about in a carriage in an agony of apprehension as to her welfare, made him deaf to the fact she had traveled not on horseback but with their father and sister. As to the other persons in the room, he saw no one. He was about to launch into a brotherly lecture when he was completely disconcerted by Helen. Far from joining him in his anger at Grace's outrageous behavior, Helen was shaking with laughter.

"My dear Lady Dysart, I trust your mirth is your show of relief at finding my sister unharmed, and I can only hope, unwed."

"Don't be a fusty breeches, Roy!" Grace demanded with a pout. "If you must know, I am not married and don't intend to marry for many years yet!"

"The first sensible thing I've heard about you all day! And I am not a fusty—"

Helen lightly kissed Royston's cheek. "You are, my love," she said quietly. "But I shall make it my life's mission to see that Grace has no cause to call you fusty ever again."

"Am I? And will you?"

"Papa! Edith! See! See! Do you *see*?" Grace demanded, turning to the gathering with a bright smile. "I *told* you that all they needed was time alone together to fall in love all over again."

Royston barely heard his sister's declaration. He was staring at Helen, her kiss and accompanying smile draining away his angry concern. And with the loss of anger came contrition for his outburst at Grace, when all he truly cared about was her safety and well-being and that no harm had come to her. He turned and opened his arms to her, and when she readily stepped into his embrace, he hugged her to him.

"Forgive me, Gracie. Forgive me for being a fusty breeches. I was worried about you. We were worried. You gave me—*us*—quite a scare."

"You haven't called me Gracie since before you went away to Lyon." She hugged him tighter. "I am truly sorry for making you worry. But there was no other way, because I do love you, and we all so want you and Helen to be happy—together."

"Do take a look about you, Dr. Meredith," Helen said at his shoulder. "I think you'll find that while we have been preoccupied with saving Grace, our journey was orchestrated by Grace to save us! Is that not so, Edith?"

Edith had crossed the room on the arm of a tall young

gentleman of sandy complexion. She introduced her fiancé, Sir James Murray, to Helen, then explained, "The trickery of an elopement was indeed Grace's idea. Papa, Grace, and I, with Sir James's support, agreed that Grace eloping with Charlie Lawson was about the only circumstance that would get you both dashing to the border together. And we hoped and prayed that if you spent time alone, you would sort out your differences and see that you belong together, forever."

"Be thankful I was outvoted and we settled on a carriage ride for the two of you to come to your senses! I wanted to lock you up in Carlisle's keep," Lord Salkeld drawled from his chair by the fire. He put out his hand to Helen, and she readily went over and took it in a firm grasp. He smiled up at her with damp eyes. "I am exceedingly happy you and my heir are reconciled."

"And I am exceedingly happy you are, Uncle," Helen replied, her eyes also filling with tears. She glanced at Royston, who had come to join them, then addressed them both. "My only wish is that I still had a dowry to bring to the marriage, to help Royston and the estate."

"I'm glad you no longer have it. No one can say I married you for your fortune," Royston stated.

"And no one can say I used my fortune to marry a title. You are the finest physician in Cumbria, which is a far better reason to be proud of you and to want to be your wife."

"I take it you have asked her?" Lord Salkeld enquired of his heir.

"Papa! Of course he has!" Grace exclaimed, rolling her eyes. "We all knew it as soon as they walked in here. Roy only gets that silly look around Helen, and that's been missing for years! But it's back now, isn't it? And Helen has a way of smiling at Roy that Edith says is a private smile ladies keep for the men they truly love."

Everyone in the room laughed at this summation, but no one refuted it. Yet Royston was able to wipe their smiles away when he said, "In point of fact, I have not asked Lady Dysart to marry me—"

"But you *must*, Roy!" Grace burst out. "You simply must! You love her. She loves you. You always have. You must be together—*forever*. Tell him, Papa! Edith!"

Helen squeezed Royston's arm. "Stop being a tease. We are engaged—"

"—because I did not have to," Royston continued smoothly, a wink at Helen. "Helen asked me, and I eagerly accepted."

There was a sudden collective intake of breath.

"Oh yes! This is a leap year!" Grace announced with awe.

Edith sighed. "That is far more romantic and fitting, for both of you."

It was Lord Salkeld's turn to shock everyone.

"Helen, my dear, I do not know where you got this notion you do not have a dowry. Sir William bequeathed you fifteen thousand pounds on condition you marry Royston Meredith. And as you know only one Royston Meredith, as did he, then I take it he meant my son."

Helen and Royston stared at each other.

"I'm sorry. I had no idea," Helen apologized. "I was not at the reading of Sir William's will. His family preferred I not be there."

"It makes no difference to me, if it makes no difference to you. But it will make a difference to the estate, and we can give generously to the society for the prevention of cruelty to animals. And I do not doubt Sir William knew that we would honor his legacy and do just that."

"That is very fitting," Helen agreed with a smile.

"Of course, as my dear wife, you will hold the purse strings and distribute this largesse as you see fit. Without the interference of others. Isn't that so, Father?"

Lord Salkeld waved a thin hand. "I am too old to argue with any of you anymore. Do as you see fit. But do get married first."

Royston made his father a respectful bow and took hold of Helen's hand.

"Helen and I wish to marry as soon as possible after Edith's wedding."

"Oh no, that would never do," Edith announced, and with a smile up at her fiancé, said, "We have decided that you can attend our wedding only if you are already married."

"But, Edith. Your wedding is the day after tomorrow," Helen said with surprise.

"All the more reason to be married today," Lord Salkeld stated. "Here. Now. At Gretna Green. I have no other reason for being here. Neither do my daughters, or Sir James." He looked at Royston and then at Helen. "Do you?"

Royston and Helen stared at Lord Salkeld and then at each other, and they were instantly taken with the idea. Both could only shake their heads and then nod eagerly. Which was enough for everyone to applaud the couple and put into action the final part of their elaborate scheme to see these cousins finally wed. Grace was flower girl, Edith Helen's attendant. Sir James acted as Royston's best man. Lord Salkeld walked Helen to the other end of the inn to the anvil over which runaway couples were married. And there before family, these childhood best friends and sweethearts, Royston Ivo Meredith and Helen Meredith Dysart, were married by the publican of the Gretna Green inn. A most conventional wedding ceremony conducted in the most unconventional of ways and settings.

Author's Note

Societal attitudes toward animal welfare began to change in the final quarter of the eighteenth century and were rooted in the intellectual climate of the time. Parliamentarians, social reformers, and members of the clergy met in coffeehouses to discuss what was to be done about the harsh use and maltreatment of animals in hauling carriages, scientific experiments, and cultural amusements. The first meeting debating the prevention of cruelty to beasts of burden and animals in general was held at Old Slaughter's Coffee House in St. Martins Lane, London. This society of like-minded gentlemen eventually became the Royal Society for the Prevention of Cruelty to Animals (RSPCA), granted royal status by Queen Victoria in 1840.

Lucinda Brant is a *New York Times* and *USA Today* bestselling author of Georgian historical romances and mysteries. Her award-winning novels have variously been described as from "the Golden Age of romance with a modern voice" and "heart-wrenching drama with a happily ever after."

A graduate of the Australian National University and post-graduate of Bond University, Lucinda has degrees in History, Political Science, and Education. When not writing and researching, Lucinda loves watching BBC period dramas, Sci-Fi, and classic murder mysteries. Visit her 18th Century world on Pinterest: http://pinterest.com/lucindabrant/

"Quizzing glass & quill, into my sedan chair & away! The 1700s rock!"

Visit Lucinda's Website: LucindaBrant.com
Follow her on Twitter: @LucindaBrant

Fools Rush In

-JULIE DAINES-

One

RICHARD POURED HIMSELF another glass of wine from the bottle, then pushed it away. No amount of drink would settle his mind. He leaned forward, resting his elbows on the wobbly table of the coaching inn. The list of marriage prospects he had to choose from was dismal. Hung, drawn, and quartered would be a welcome escape from being forced to spend the rest of his life with any one of those ladies.

Harriet Herbert: a widow with four children under the age of six. All of them boys who would make the hardest prisoners in Newgate look like gentle lambs. Dorothea Fortescue: a spinster with spectacles thick as an oak beam. It always gave him the feeling of staring at a beetle through the wrong end of a telescope. Lady Cecilia Finch: a beautiful young woman who believed the world revolved around her. She also believed the world was flat and that reading was only for women who could not get themselves husbands.

Dismal indeed. If he did not so desperately need his inheritance from his aunt, he would have tossed all prospects of marriage into the fire. Let them burn up in a puff of smoke. Ash was all that he had to live for anyway.

What did it signify? He downed his glass and refilled it with the last of his bottle. Any chance of a happy union had ended a year ago with the death of his dear Eliza. He may as well draw straws and accept his fate.

"Eliza!" came a harsh voice from the table behind him. "Stop it this instant."

Richard spun around. A young woman sat in a pale-green dress, her head hanging low. She dabbed at her eyes with a limp handkerchief as her shoulders shook. Not *his* Eliza, of course. Why must every third girl have that name, tormenting him, teasing him, calling up hope that could not be?

A woman with graying hair sat across from her. "You're making a scene." The inn was fairly empty, and the older lady's words carried.

The younger lady pressed the handkerchief against her face in some sort of effort to hold back the waters. It only made her shoulders shake harder.

This was how far his life had sunk. Listening in on the conversations of crying women.

The girl, Eliza but not *his* Eliza, lifted her head, and her gaze fell directly on Richard.

He tried to look away, but her eyes caught him. Huge gray eyes, the exact same color of *his* Eliza's, rimmed in red and utterly forlorn.

She blinked at him a few times. Richard turned away, back to his empty bottle and his lonely prospects.

The older woman scolded Eliza again. "Adolphous Barrington is a good match. You could scarcely hope for better."

"He is twice my age," bemoaned Eliza. "He has rheumy eyes and a belly like melting butter. His bald head calls to mind some sort of pockmarked pumpkin. He is the most boring man ever born. Every time he speaks I want to puncture my ears with knitting needles."

Richard snorted. At least she wasn't afraid to speak her mind. It seemed he and this new Eliza were in the same boat. A boat that would anchor them to a partner they despised. A lifetime imprisonment. Hung, drawn, and quartered was looking better and better.

"I would rather be hung, drawn, and quartered than have to marry that man," cried the Eliza behind him.

Richard spun around again. Who was this woman?

"Hush!" The older lady smiled at a serving girl who'd brought a tray of tea and cake to their table. "Thank you, miss."

The serving girl gave her a nod and hurried back to the kitchen.

"Don't exaggerate," the older woman said. She must be her mother. "Mr. Barrington is a gentleman with money, a house in the country and in town, and connections in all the right places. You will be the envy of the *ton*."

If Eliza's description of this Mr. Barrington was anything close to accurate, he doubted she would be the envy of anyone.

Eliza wiped her eyes and glared at her mother. She opened her mouth to speak but caught Richard staring again. She redirected her glare at him, and he turned around, caught like a fool eavesdropping. Even so, he kept perfectly still to better hear the conversation going on at the table behind him.

"Mr. Barrington will be here any minute. Now dry your eyes and make yourself presentable."

Richard gave them a sideways glance. A new wave of tears streaked Eliza's face. Her handkerchief was already saturated, but she pressed it to her reddened eyes anyway.

"How can I, Mother, when you are sending me to my death?"

The mother sighed, long and heavy. "You will thank me later, when you are living a comfortable life in the best society. All the finest of everything at your fingertips."

Richard well understood the girl's desperation. Family was often the greatest hardship one had to bear. He was facing a similar dilemma. He could get what he so desperately needed only at the expense of his happiness—marriage to an unwanted companion. It was indeed a high price to pay.

The mother swallowed a bite of cake and checked a watch hanging from her chatelaine. "Go and take a turn in the garden. Dry your eyes and recover yourself. Your face is splotchy. Mr. Barrington will be here to collect you in a few minutes."

Eliza's chair scraped back with a screech, as if every movement she made punctuated her protests. "I will *never* be recovered."

Then she strode away and out the rear door into the inn's little garden.

Richard stared after her.

He understood her completely. He was not a romantic man, but was it too much to ask to spend life with a person he could at least call companionable? Interesting? Lively?

There was a way to solve both of their problems. It was preposterous. Vulgar, even. And more than likely would land him in Newgate along with the Herbert boys.

But she had Eliza's eyes. And really, that was enough for him.

He downed the last of his wine and followed Eliza but not *his* Eliza out into the garden.

Two

ELIZA SHOOK OUT her handkerchief in attempt to dry it. It had completely lost its absorbency. If her father had been here, she would never have been forced to marry such a buffoon. He would have fixed everything.

Barely twenty and her life was already over. She picked up a switch of willow and used it to decapitate a clump of daisies. She turned to attack the dog roses behind her but collided with a pillar of buckskin breeches and a dark-blue coat.

"I beg your pardon," she mumbled, turning on her heels in the opposite direction.

The pillar's hand caught her arm, spinning her around until they were face to face. Eliza looked up and immediately recognized the man that had been so interested in her and her stepmother back inside the inn. She opened her mouth to call for help, but there was an earnestness in his eyes that stopped her.

He stared at her without speaking, his hand still wrapped around her arm. She waited for an explanation, but his silence continued.

"The eavesdropper," she said.

That seemed to bring him around. He let go of her arm. "Miss Eliza," he said, "I couldn't help overhearing your situation."

Of course not. Since he'd practically fallen off his chair trying to listen.

"I . . . That is . . . What I mean to say . . ." He glanced over his shoulder, then pulled her behind a large box hedge where they were no longer visible to the main part of the inn. "I know this will sound untoward, but hear me out."

She gave him a nod.

"You and I have a similar predicament. That is to say, marriage prospects that have been chosen against our wills. Am I correct is this assumption?"

Eliza could not answer for Mr. Eavesdropper's circumstances, but yes, he had correctly understood hers. She gave him another nod.

He pinched his mouth together, then pressed on. "I propose . . . a proposal. I think we can be the solution to each other's predicament."

Eliza's mouth dropped open. Either he was willing to kill Mr. Barrington for her or he was offering to marry her. She hoped it was the first, but unless going to jail would solve his problems, it seemed likely he meant the other thing.

"We need not actually marry," he quickly added. "I suggest we merely play the part long enough to post the banns, discourage your Mr. Barrington, and collect my inheritance from my aunt. Then we part ways before actually having to wed."

Eliza's mind spun. Could that actually work? Could she even trust this man? He was tall and well-enough looking. A crop of dark hair atop his head. Brown eyes the color of roasted chestnuts. Finely attired. It seemed he could have his pick of women.

"You appear to be a man of means," she said. "How is it you are forced to marry against your will?"

He glanced over his shoulder, as if the source of his problem trailed behind him. "It is not exactly against my will to marry, per se. I have an aunt—"

"Is she here?" Eliza followed his gaze but saw no one.

He shook his head. "No. She—"

"Is she deceased? If you look for the dead, you will be followed by ghosts." Wang Mei had taught her that. Leave the dead alone, and they will leave you alone.

He blinked a few times, then shook his head again. "My aunt is not dead, but my father is, and he was rather old-fashioned. I am desperately in need of my inheritance. An inheritance that cannot be surrendered to an unmarried man."

Most men in fine clothing with financial troubles were chancers and cheats. They squandered money faster than snowflakes melted on your hand. "Are you a gambler? A drinker, perhaps?"

"Nothing of the sort, I assure you."

"Eliza," her mother called from the inn's door. "Mr. Barrington is here."

So soon? She wasn't ready. She would never be ready. She dove behind the buckskin man, clutching his coat to keep her hidden even though the box hedge already had them well concealed.

"It is Mr. Barrington," she whispered. "He is here to take me away. He will not take no for an answer."

"It is your choice," he said. He sounded awfully confident for a man proposing marriage to an utter stranger. Eliza could barely breathe, and her knees had gone limp, yet his hands hung calmly at his sides.

They wouldn't actually have to marry, he'd said. Just keep up the pretense long enough to drive Mr. Barrington away and collect his money from his aunt. A few weeks, at most. La, how her head ached. She was too tired to think.

All she knew for certain was that any man would be better than Mr. Barrington, even if he was a chancer and a cheat.

"Miss Barnes?" called a gruff and rattly voice. Mr. Barrington. She shuddered at the very sound of it.

"I agree," she blurted out. "I accept your proposal."

Three

RICHARD LET OUT a long puff of air. Until that moment, he never thought she would accept him. Now, suddenly and by his own doing, he was responsible for this Miss Barnes. What had he been thinking? All because she had *his* Eliza's eyes.

"All right then." He pulled her out from behind him, taking her hand and wrapping it around his arm, for she seemed on the verge of collapse. He stepped out from behind the box hedge, dragging her with him.

A stout, watery-eyed man was coming down the path toward them. Eliza tightened her grip on Richard's arm. He prayed she would not faint, for then their charade would be up.

"Miss Barnes, there you are," said the man who could be none other than Barrington. She had not exaggerated his repellency. No mother with any amount of love for her child would try to force a match with this man. "My coach is waiting. Are you ready?"

Barrington's eyes widened as he finally seemed to notice Richard's hand on Eliza's. Eliza's mother approached now as well, her mouth dropping open.

"Mother," said Eliza with a squeak. "Mr. Barrington." She gave the man a quick curtsy. "I'm afraid I've been keeping a secret. I hope you will forgive me, but I shan't be able to accompany you. I am already engaged to . . ." She glanced up at him. He'd never told her his name. "This man."

Mrs. Barnes and Mr. Barrington's heads turned in unison, their eyes landing on him hard. They stared, her step-mother's eyes blinking like moth wings, Mr. Barrington's glistening with watery seepage.

Richard bowed. "Richard Arden, at your service."

They did not respond. Richard couldn't even be sure they were breathing.

"I'm sorry we haven't had the chance to meet before now."

Still nothing from the stunned pair in front of him.

"I apologize for any inconvenience our secret plans may have caused."

Mrs. Barnes's mouth moved, but it took several tries for words to come out. "Secret plans?"

Eliza nodded. "Our engagement. We couldn't mention it before because of his aunt."

Richard nodded. That was a convincing lie. At least she was quick on her feet.

Barrington now found his voice. "Impossible. She has been promised to me. It has all been settled. I'm here even now to take her back with me to Slough."

"Sir." Richard wrapped his arm around Eliza. "She is a woman, not some item to be traded and bartered."

Eliza's head snapped up, searching his face. He squeezed her closer, and she covered her mouth while tears rolled down her cheeks. Again. Or perhaps he should say still.

"Now look what you've done," Richard said to Barrington. He patted Eliza's hand. "There, there, my dear."

"I . . ." Barrington fumbled for words.

"Impossible," said Mrs. Barnes, returning to the steely woman sitting behind him in the inn. "Nonsense. Eliza is engaged to Mr. Barrington. She couldn't possibly have a secret engagement elsewhere. 'Tis absurd."

No more help seemed forthcoming from the girl weeping

in his arms, so Richard carried on as best he could. "We met some time ago, and our love was immediate," he said. "We've only been waiting for my aunt to . . . pass away. She did not approve."

"What cause could your aunt have for not approving of Eliza?" asked Mrs. Barnes with a huff.

"Oh, it wasn't Miss Barnes she didn't approve of, it was her connections." He gazed pointedly at her mother. A laugh slipped out from Eliza.

Mrs. Barnes eyed him. "Where did you meet?"

Eliza's head came up, and she dried her face. "We met at the midwinter ball at the Ealings'. In London."

Richard nodded. Another good lie, for anyone could be met in London. "Yes, at the Eastons'—"

"Ealings'."

"Ealings'," he corrected.

Mrs. Barnes pursed her lips. "If that is true, then why did she cry for three days straight at the prospect of marrying Mr. Barrington?"

"What?" Barrington's eyes jerked to Mrs. Barnes.

"My aunt died only this morning," Richard said. "I'm sure the uncertainty of it all was distressing."

"Where is your mourning?" Mrs. Barnes was too perceptive.

"He was away on business," Eliza said. "He hasn't had time to go home and dress properly."

"Two minutes," bellowed a man into the courtyard. "Coach to Oxford departs in two minutes."

"This is all very sudden." Mrs. Barnes removed a handkerchief from her reticule and wiped her brow. "Secret engagement or not, we have already made arrangements with Mr. Barrington, even before the midwinter ball. He has prior claim."

"But you cannot tear apart our love," Eliza cried.

What she did next proved fully her desperation to escape marriage to Mr. Barrington. Eliza but not *his* Eliza grabbed the lapels of Richard's coat and pulled him close, kissing him with more determination than he was prepared for.

She smelled of rosebuds and lavender, and her lips pressed upon his with surprising softness despite her sudden attack. The black look coming from Mrs. Barnes dimmed to nothing. Mr. Barrington's shouts faded away. Something stirred in his chest that he had not felt in a long time. His hand slid to her waist. Then suddenly it was over.

Eliza pulled away, her face red as a royal robe. He must have been equally flushed, yet she cast her mother and Barrington a triumphant look. Barrington's head was also red, but his was born of rage.

Eliza must have noticed the danger rising in Barrington's puffy face. "My dear," she exclaimed. "We will miss our coach." She took Richard's hands and pulled him away.

He stumbled to catch up, but he could not force his thoughts from the touch of her lips.

She led him through the inn and out into the yard. The stagecoach was still there. The footman opened the door as they approached. By habit, Richard handed Eliza in, then loaded himself up after her. There was barely room for them in the crowded box, but they squeezed in. The door closed, and the coach pulled away with a jerk.

Richard watched the inn disappear from view. And there, in the coaching yard, was his own horse and phaeton. But no, he was instead sitting in a public coach on his way to Oxford next to a woman he did not know. A woman who was now twisting the strings of her reticule while silent drops of tears landed on the pale-green fabric. Astonishing that she had any left.

"Miss Barnes?" he asked quietly.

She shook her head.

Richard let it go. A lot had happened in the last quarter hour. He himself needed time to let it settle. He'd never done something so impetuous in his entire life. By the distress of his companion, neither had she. It had been his idea. His doing. And now he had brought on this latest wave of tears.

If she didn't want to talk, so be it. But there must be something he could do. The other passengers were staring. Some of them casting dark looks, as if he'd been cruel to her. He extracted his handkerchief from his coat pocket and handed it to her. She took it and dried her eyes.

She held tight to his handkerchief, looking down at it rumpled between her hands, until her head began to nod. He waited until she was all the way asleep, then gently tilted her head to rest on his shoulder.

A hawk-nosed lady sat across from him, glaring at him like he was a highwayman—or worse.

"She had an argument with her mother," Richard explained, to clear his name.

The woman folded her bony arms and turned her gaze toward the window, directing a sidelong glance at Richard every mile or so to make sure he was behaving. Eliza slept for the duration of the two-hour trip.

When they came to a stop at a coaching inn on the outskirts of Oxford, Richard nudged her. "We have arrived."

Four

ELIZA OPENED HER eyes. A woman with an angular face and hooked nose was watching her. Eliza glanced around. She was in a coach—a public one, her head leaning against a man. She jerked her head up as the memory of her circumstances returned.

What was his name, this man who'd saved her from Mr. Barrington? She'd forgotten. Her pulse raced at the recollection of what she'd done. Kissing him and dragging him onto the road to—where was it? She'd just taken the first means of escape she could find, not caring one straw about the destination. And he'd come along without question.

She looked up at him at the same moment his eyes turned to her. He smiled, his brown eyes warm. It seemed he was about to ask her something, but as he glanced around the coach he changed his mind.

"We are here," he mumbled.

She nodded. The door to the coach opened, and he climbed out first.

As soon as he was out, the woman across from her grabbed her hand. "Are you in trouble, young lady?" The woman's eyes flashed at Mr.—Allen, was it? Something with an *A*. "If he is a cruel man, I know a place you can escape."

In truth, Eliza had no idea what kind of man she was with. All she knew was that he had to be better than Mr.

Barrington. "On the contrary," Eliza explained, "he has saved me."

Mr. A reached his hand in to help her out. Arnold, perhaps? She placed her hand in his and climbed down the steps. It seemed they'd gotten here in the blink of an eye. Strange, as she always had such a difficult time sleeping. Their housekeeper used to make her a special tea to help her sleep, but it worked only occasionally. Eliza was used to the dark circles under her eyes. Perhaps it was those in combination with her tears earlier that led the woman to wonder if she was in trouble.

Mr. A led her apart from the rest of the passengers. "How are you faring?"

Eliza smoothed the creases out of her dress. "I am well, thank you." She tried to give him back his handkerchief, but he waved it off. He must think her the biggest ninny.

"We can take a few moments here," he said. "Let us go in and get something to eat, and we can discuss our next plan of action."

She nodded, though her stomach was so tightly coiled she doubted she'd be able to eat a bite of anything.

He offered his arm. Whether trying to keep up the pretense of a respectable couple or because he worried she might faint, she could not say. Either way, she took it because her head spun and she had real concerns whether her knees would carry her into the inn.

He went straight to the innkeeper and asked for a private room to dine in. The man took them to a quiet room in the rear of the house. Mr. A ordered some wine and two plates of whatever they were serving that day. The innkeeper dipped his head and left.

"Sir—"

"Miss Barnes—"

"Please," he said, motioning for her to go first.

But now she didn't know where to begin. An apology for the kiss? No. She dared not mention that out loud. An apology for dragging him to Oxford? Yet another cause for embarrassment. Appreciation for saving her from Mr. Barrington? It was never wrong to start with gratitude.

"Sir," she began again. "Let me say again how grateful I am to you for saving me from Mr. Barrington. I would have killed myself by now if I'd had to go away with that odious man."

His eyebrows went up. "I sincerely hope you are never driven to that extreme. And in return, let me apologize for my unconventional methods. But you are a quick thinker, and I believe it all worked out in the end."

By *unconventional methods* he probably meant her kiss. Nothing had been more unconventional than that. It had seemed necessary, at that moment, to convince her stepmother and Mr. Barrington. Still, she would not be the first to bring it up with this man. Nor would she soon forget the press of his hand on her waist nor the way his lips felt against hers. She withdrew a small fan from her reticule and fanned her face.

He pulled a chair from the table. "Won't you sit?"

"No, thank you." She could not possibly be still. Not while thoughts of her foolish kiss swarmed her mind. Her stomach pulled tight like tanned leather. She paced the perimeter of the tiny room while he watched, his face unreadable.

He had done what he'd promised. Now she must fulfill her end of the bargain.

"You have helped me, Mr.—" Ah. His name. As if she needed this uncomfortable situation to get worse.

He smiled. "Richard Arden." He pulled the chair out again. "I know this is all rather strange, but I beg you, do not make yourself uneasy."

"Mr. Arden." She sat, merely because to refuse his offer again seemed wrong. "As I was saying, you have fulfilled your part of our agreement; now it is my turn. What must I do to help you secure your inheritance?"

The door to their little room opened, and a serving girl

entered with a tray of food. She carried it to the table and deposited her load, arranging everything tidily. She looked up at Mr. Arden fluttering her long, dark lashes. Shameless girl, flirting with a man right in front of the woman he was engaged to. Even if it was a pretense, the servant did not know that.

"Will that be all, sir?" the girl asked, grinning at him.

"Yes, yes. You may go." Eliza shooed her from the room and closed the door firmly behind her. She turned to find Mr. Arden staring at her again, undoubtedly sizing her up, trying to decide what kind of woman he'd gotten mixed up with. For was that not the same thing she was doing to him—trying her best to make out his character.

Certainly he would be concluding that she was a half-wit. And not without reason. She'd spent half the journey in tears, and now this. "Uh. The fewer people who see us the better," she said, as if it explained her behavior.

"Do you really think we were followed?" he asked.

Eliza dropped back into her chair. It was difficult to say what lengths Mr. Barrington would go to. "I think it possible. Mr. Barrington may look harmless, but he has a mean streak. He is greedy. And he does not like to be made the fool."

Just thinking about it caused sweat to break out across her forehead. She fanned herself again. Mr. Arden poured her a drink and pushed it across the table. She took a sip. Hopefully it would help steady her nerves, which at the moment were ready to snap.

She turned back to her original question. "What can I do to fulfill my end of our agreement?"

He stabbed a potato and held it up on his fork. "I suppose we must go to my aunt and tell her of our plans to marry." He popped the boiled potato into his mouth and chewed thoughtfully.

Would they be able to fool his aunt? They'd done pretty well in front of her own stepmother. Perhaps it would require another kiss. She glanced up and felt the heat rush to her cheeks again.

"Her estate is in Lancashire." He forked another potato, leaving it dangling on his cutlery. "Now that I think on it, perhaps I'm asking too much. Perhaps this is not a fair trade. It is at least a two-day journey from here to there."

Two days. That was indeed a lot to ask. Then the return trip. And probably a day at his aunt's home in between. But what would she do if not this? She could not go home, not until it was certain she was clear of Mr. Barrington. If she showed up too soon, she would have accomplished nothing, and Mr. Barrington and his great pumpkin of a head would be back, pounding on her door, demanding that which he thought was his.

Her stepmother would be of no help, pushing her out the door to the highest bidder. No. If the pretense was going to work, she had to stay away longer.

"On the contrary," she said. "Your part is not finished yet. If I am to be truly free of Mr. Barrington and my stepmother, I cannot turn back now. I cannot return home, and if not to your aunt's, I have nowhere else to go."

He ate the potato. "I did not know she was your stepmother."

"Let me assure you, Mr. Arden, had that been my mother, I would never have been forced onto Mr. Barrington."

He looked up at her. "I understand what you mean quite perfectly," he said quietly. Then he went back to his meal, leaving his revelation hanging, like a half-finished tapestry, revealing only a small portion of what must be a much bigger picture.

He seemed to be turning things over in his mind, for his eyes were far away. He ate without seeming to care what he was putting in his mouth. Finally he gave himself a little nod and said, "We can travel onward today, to make sure we are not followed. Then we will stop for the night."

Seemed like a good plan. Above all, she did not want to run into Mr. Barrington again. So wherever Mr. Arden was going, that was where she was going. "I agree."

"Very well." He stood and opened a small drawer in a writing table. He set the paper and ink in front of her. "Write to your stepmother and explain that you are with my aunt or cousin and wish not to return home just yet."

"But won't that alert them to our whereabouts?"

"Do not mention a location. They already know we got on the stage to Oxford, so a postmark from this inn should not be a problem."

But still, it seemed a letter was inviting Mr. Barrington to track her down.

"It should be made clear," Mr. Arden said quietly, "that you and I are not traveling together. Alone."

Ah. Of course. How could she be so slow? He was worried about her reputation once all of their little act was ended. "You are right," she said, taking up the goose quill pen.

"I'll go settle with the innkeeper and see what time the next coach north is leaving. You should eat to keep up your strength."

While they'd been talking, he'd wiped his plate clean. She'd barely eaten a bite. But he was right in this too. If they were to continue on the road, who knew when the next meal would be. He excused himself and left the room.

She quickly penned an explanation to her stepmother. Then she tucked into her meal, finding herself more hungry than she thought. Every chance to put distance between herself and Mr. Barrington loosened just a little the tightness in her stomach.

If she never saw either of them again, she would count herself blessed. Eliza glanced over her shoulder. What would Wang Mei say if she heard such a thought? *Do not wish death upon anyone, or they will become your enemy in the next life.*

"I don't wish them dead," she said aloud. "I just want them out of my life."

"Who do you want out of your life?" asked Mr. Arden from the doorway.

Eliza's head spun around. "No one," she stammered, but

he'd be a fool if he could not guess. "That is to say, I think you already know."

He let out a small laugh, deep and soft like a goose-down bed. "But you do not want them dead."

She nodded. "Wang Mei says if you wish someone dead, they will come back as your enemy in your next life and be the cause of great sorrow."

"Wang Mei?" He crossed the room in two strides and sat down at the table beside her.

"Our cook." She drained the last of her cordial. "She says that all life must have balance. She calls it yin and yang. If the bad people in my life are taken away by death, the balance will be upset, and I'll be too happy. So in my next life, those same spirits will become a great torment. My life will be overly sorrowful to fill the balance."

"Your next life?"

"Wang Mei is from China," she explained.

Eliza loved to listen to the old woman ramble about her beliefs. She couldn't always understand what Wang Mei was saying, but it still fascinated her. After her mother died, her stepmother forbade her from fraternizing with Wang Mei. Of course, she was the best cook in the county, so it was acceptable to eat her food, just not to talk to her. That never stopped Eliza, though. She found her way to the kitchen often enough.

"Well," he said, "Wang Mei has some very interesting ideas." He picked up the letter. "Is this finished?"

"Yes. Do you think it will do?"

He cleared his throat and read. "Dearest Mother." He glanced up, then continued. "By the time you receive this, I will be in London, staying at the home of my beloved's sister, the wife of a marquess." He looked up again. "I will not say her name because I do not wish to be found, but she lives in a castle with a deep moat, so do not think to follow me. You will not get in. The last person who tried fell into the water and was dragged away by an enormous catfish."

Five

RICHARD LOWERED THE letter. "Dragged away by a catfish?"

"My stepmother cannot swim, and she hates dark waters more than anything. I thought it might scare her away. Do you think it's too much?"

Too much? It was hard to know where to begin with what was too much about this letter: a sister married to a marquess or the moat of man-eating fish.

He finished reading. "I am only thinking of your safety. I will contact you later when our plans are finalized. Yours etc., Eliza."

It was the most strange and unexpected letter he had ever read. He had half a mind to secret it away in his pocket as a memory of this very strange and unexpected day. But, it had a purpose and must be sent to her stepmother regardless of its questionable believability.

"It will do," he said. "Get it sealed and give it a direction." He gave her a sealing wafer from the writing table's drawer. She folded the letter and affixed the wafer, adding her stepmother's name and location on the front.

Richard took the letter from her. "I'll give this to—"

"Hush!" Eliza cried.

"What?"

"It's Mr. Barrington."

Richard listened. A gruff, raised voice came from the front of the inn. "Are you sure?"

"I would know that voice anywhere, so oft it has haunted my nightmares. It is the sound of death."

Richard couldn't help smiling despite the lady's distress. She certainly felt things very deeply. If it was Mr. Barrington, they'd best be on their way.

"Wait here," he said. "Close the door after I leave and turn the lock."

She gave a little nod. All color had drained from her face, and the smile she'd finally found as she spoke of her Chinese cook and the giant catfish was long gone. Instead her lips pinched tight, and she pressed one hand on her stomach as if her meal were threatening to come back up.

Richard wanted to throw a fist at Barrington. What had the man done to cause such panic in this woman? Hers was a face of true and utter fear.

He leaned forward and took hold of her hand. "Miss Barnes, we have an agreement. I fully intend to keep my end of the bargain, so please do not worry. I will not let him take you."

She lifted her eyes to his, and in them he saw both hope and despair. Yin and yang, just like this Wang Mei woman had said. 'Twas the same look he'd seen in his Eliza's eyes just before she died. For his Eliza, the despair had won. He'd not let that happen to this Eliza.

He gave her hand a gentle squeeze. "I promise."

"Thank you," she whispered. Her mouth transformed from a tight line to the bud of a smile. Lips full and soft, as he'd discovered back at Tetsworth when she'd kissed him. He wouldn't complain if Barrington provoked her into another kiss. But no. Best to leave without being spotted.

He stood. Also best to keep some distance from her, if her smile was going to stir up his blood. This was only a temporary agreement. And once she was clear of Barrington and Richard had his inheritance, she would certainly be anxious to part ways.

He left, closing the door behind him, and waited to hear the lock click into place. *Good girl.* From their private sitting room, he walked down the hall and peered into the public room. Sure enough, Barrington was there, grumbling at the innkeeper, spit flying from his mouth as he spoke. Richard had given the innkeeper a few extra shillings to keep his mouth shut, but when Barrington reached for a stash of banknotes, Richard had to question the innkeeper's price for silence.

The bell in the yard clanged, and the sound of carriage wheels clattering across cobblestones shook the ground. A coach had arrived—a big one by the sound of it. He turned and went out the back into the coaching yard where the ostlers were working on changing a set of four on the mail coach.

"Is this coach going north or south?" he asked.

"North, sir."

They could wait here. If he sent back to Tetsworth, he could have his own carriage here by nightfall. It would mean spending the night in Oxford. The clouds overhead had darkened considerably in the short time they'd been in the inn. If the weather turned, his open-topped phaeton would not be suitable to travel in with a lady.

"Hold two seats, please," he told the ostler, tossing him a gold coin.

The ostler tugged at the brim of his cap.

Richard hurried off. In a matter of minutes, they'd have the horses changed, and the mail coach would be on its way.

In the back hall, the door was still closed to their sitting room. He knocked softly. "Miss Barnes?" he whispered through the door. "It's me, Richard Arden."

The latch clicked, and she opened the door. He reminded himself that the look of relief crossing her face was not for him but for the lack of Barrington.

"Let's go. We can catch the mail coach heading north."

She peered down the hall, where the sound of Barrington's voice still filled the public room.

"Sir," he heard the innkeeper say. "I beg you to calm down."

Richard grabbed the letter and rushed Eliza the other direction. When he glanced back, he caught sight of Barrington pulling a revolver from somewhere in his waistcoat. *What the devil!* No wonder Eliza was so scared of him. He really was a beastly man.

Richard nearly pushed Eliza out through the door. The ostlers had the horses changed. The one he'd spoken to before held the door open for them, and Richard lifted Eliza in before she had a chance to get her foot on the step. Richard handed the ostler the letter and a coin, asking him to post it, then leaped in and pulled the door closed. He sat beside her, turning his head away from the glass window.

He felt Eliza's body shaking beside him. He looked down, expecting to find her in tears again. But she was laughing. She looked up, her eyes bright from the burst of exertion.

The bell clanged, and when the coach lurched forward, she fell into him. In all his life he'd never fled from anywhere, let alone taken a mail coach. Since he'd met this woman, twice he'd made a clandestine dash for a departing coach. It was quite exhilarating.

He smiled back at her. "We made it."

The coach was once again filled to the brim, including the several passengers stacked on top. Whoever was willing to pay the highest price got the seats inside the carriage. Those who could not rode on top. The whole thing was stacked so heavily, every corner Richard feared it would tip.

When he looked away from Eliza, he noticed a man sitting diagonal from him grinning at them.

The man tipped his head. "How do ye do?" The man's cheeks were flush. Seemed he'd already been deep into his cups before boarding the coach. "Runnin' off, are ye?" His grin broadened. "This be the way ta Gretna Green."

"On the contrary," Richard replied. If anyone thought that, her reputation would be ruined. Truly, if anyone recognized them or learned their true names, she might never recover her good name, even with the letter to her stepmother. In any case, he wouldn't be caught dead eloping to Gretna Green. "This is my wife," he said. "We are on our way to visit my aunt."

"'At's what they all say." The man waggled his brows.

By now, every occupant was staring at them, wondering, he was sure, if he had despoiled this innocent girl.

"Don't see no ring," the drunken man added.

Eliza curled her fingers, hiding them in her lap.

If this is what it came to, Richard had little choice. He reached into his waistcoat pocket and removed a ring. One that had belonged to his grandmother, then his mother, and which he had planned to give *his* Eliza.

"My dear," he said. "You left this at the inn. You mustn't be so careless."

He took her hand and slipped it on her finger. Everyone in the coach gasped. It was no ordinary ring. A clear blue sapphire surrounded by a ring of diamonds glittered on Eliza's hand.

She stared at it. Then up at Richard. He gave her a tiny nod, hoping she would overcome her shock and play along.

She blinked at him several times. "S-sorry, my dear. You know how forgetful I can be."

"Blimey!" crooned the drunk man.

"I'll say," added the woman next to the drunk.

"What ya doin' in the mail coach?" asked the man sitting on the other side of Eliza. He couldn't take his eyes of the giant gem.

"Our barouche sprung an axle," said Eliza. "And we couldn't wait for repairs."

The drunken man laughed lewdly, implying things that caused Eliza to blush.

"We're trying to get back to our son," Eliza said.

Richard choked and then coughed. What was she thinking?

"We left him with our aunt while we went to London." Eliza turned to the woman. "He's only just a year, and I miss him so." She dabbed at a tear in the corner of her eye. She was better than any actress from the West End.

The woman nodded sympathetically. "You poor dear. What's his name?"

"Thomas—" she said at the same time Richard said, "Henry."

The woman looked from Eliza to him, then back to Eliza.

"His name is Thomas," Eliza said. "But his father likes to call him by his middle name, Henry, after his father who died taking a fall from a horse just before our little Thomas Henry was born."

"Ah," said the lady, turning her sympathy to Richard. "Sorry for your loss."

"Thank you," he said. This new Eliza kept surprising him. He found himself drawn to what she'd say next.

"We would have named him Henry, after my dear husband's father." She spoke loud so that all could hear over the racket of the wheels over the road. "Save that was the name of our first child. Sadly, he didn't live past a few hours." She looked up at Richard with saddened eyes.

Richard swallowed down his laugh. "There, there, my dear." He put his arm around her, and she settled close.

"Sir," Richard said sternly to the drunken man. "I must beg you to stop dredging up these sorrowful memories for my wife. Really, you are too cruel."

Every eye in the coach turned on him, angry and outraged. The woman beside the drunk tsked loudly.

"I ain't done nothin'," the drunk said.

Rain now streaked the windows, and it was falling harder by the minute. Between that and the sound of the coach rattling over the dirt track, talk inside was almost impossible.

Richard leaned close so she could hear. "Our son?"

She stretched up to reach him, her mouth only inches from his ear. Her breath brushing his neck. "What was I supposed to say when you slip this giant stone on my finger? It's like I'm wearing the moon. I might as well put an advertisement in the *Times* for a highwayman to come and steal it."

"You could give it back." His arm still draped her shoulders. He thought of moving it but thought it best to keep up the show. At least that's what he told himself.

"It's fine for now," Eliza said, admiring the ring on her finger. "But why are you carrying around something like this?"

A fair question. Since his Eliza had left him, it had been locked up safely at his home in Berkshire. "I was on my way to London to sell it when our paths crossed."

"How could you sell such a beautiful thing?" Eliza whispered into his ear.

Such a beautiful thing. He lifted his arm from her shoulders, trying to create some distance between himself and her soft lips. *'Tis naught but a charade.* He must never forget that all of this was nothing more than a means to an end. She was not *his* Eliza.

The coach rattled on through the pouring rain, its pace getting slower and slower as the storm worsened. The wind blew across the fields, swaying the top-heavy coach so hard that Eliza grabbed his arm, certain they were going to tip.

There was a bump and a jolt. Then the coach came to an abrupt halt. Eliza and the man sitting beside her flew out of their seats onto the laps of those sitting across from them. Richard pulled Eliza off; the carriage was at such an angle that the one side had to fight to keep from falling on the other.

"I'll see what has happened." Richard kicked the door open and climbed out. It took some effort as the carriage was halfway tipped.

The two front wheels of the mail coach were buried axle deep in a slog of mud. The driver descended from his perch.

"Can you get it out?" Richard asked. The postillion joined the driver, both of them soaked through and looking very grave.

Eliza came up beside him.

"You'll be drenched out here," Richard said. "You should wait inside the box."

She shook her head. "I don't trust those people."

He appreciated the implication; she trusted him. He took off his coat and draped it over her shoulders. She pulled it close around her. They had brought nothing with them. He had a coat, but Eliza had no wrap beyond her shawl and a light spencer.

The driver was shaking his head. "It'll take another team to help pull this out."

The four that had been pulling the coach had already been working for a good twelve miles through rain and mud. The sun was already on the cusp of the western horizon. Daylight—what little there was trying to crawl through the black clouds—was fading fast.

The postillion unhitched the lead horse. He climbed on and set off to find help.

"How far to the nearest town?" asked Richard.

"Milcombe's but a mile or two that way." The driver pointed up the road.

"Fancy a walk?" he asked Eliza.

Six

THEY'D BEEN SLOSHING through the mud for nigh on an hour. It was pitch black, and the rain still fell in torrents. Eliza had never been this wet in her entire life. Mr. Arden held her shawl over their heads like a waterlogged umbrella. It helped a little.

He was in his shirtsleeves, gallant knight that he was, letting her wear his coat. He must have been freezing, but he didn't complain. Nor would he take his coat back.

"Are you sure this is the right way?" she asked.

"I believe so."

He didn't sound as confident as she'd hoped. A mile or two, the coachman had said. It was impossible to tell how far they'd gone because the night was so dark and the going so slow. It seemed they should have been there by now. Her shoes weighed like stones on her feet so caked were they with mud.

A few of the other passengers followed them—the husband and wife that had been sitting next to her, and someone from up top. The rest had chosen to stay at the mired carriage and wait for rescue. She wondered now if waiting would have been the better choice. But sitting in the rain doing nothing seemed rather pointless. Mr. Arden had also seemed eager to move on.

"Do you think Mr. Barrington will continue following us in this storm?" she asked.

"I doubt it," he said. "One would have to be a fool to come out in weather like this."

"Or desperate."

That's what had brought them to this point. Mr. Arden had been so desperate for his inheritance that he'd agreed to take her away from Mr. Barrington. She was a complete stranger to him. He must have been very desperate.

He laughed softly. "Desperate indeed."

She should apologize for causing this mess. But it had been his idea in the first place. In hindsight, perhaps it would have been better had she refused him. But then she would now be the wife of Mr. Adolphous Barrington. The thought made her shiver.

"You are cold," Mr. Arden said. "I'm sure we'll be there soon. We'll get you warmed up by a nice fire." He put his arm around her and pulled her closer, trying to share his warmth with her even though he was the one without a coat. He must have been ten times colder than her.

Light flickered up ahead, little glowing squares of yellow seeping out of someone's window. At last a sign of civilization.

"Almost there," he said. He sounded just as relieved as she was.

After another quarter mile or so, they paused outside the door to an inn, scraping the mud off their shoes before entering. The innkeeper must have heard them, for the door opened, and a stout man wearing a black apron came out.

He looked up and down the dark road. "Did the mail coach finally come in?"

Mr. Arden greeted the man. "No. It's still mired a few miles from here. We walked, along with the couple following behind us." The husband and wife had not kept up.

"Right then. You'd better come in and get dry. My Molly's got plenty of warm stew."

"Thank you, sir," Mr. Arden said as he wrung the water out of her shawl. "We'll be needing two rooms for the night."

The innkeeper glanced from Mr. Arden to her, then gave a nod. "Right away, sir."

Eliza followed Mr. Arden into the inn. A huge fire blazed in the hearth of the public room. She went to it directly, leaning close. Never before had a fire been so welcome. Mr. Arden stretched his hands out near the flames.

She slipped her arms out of his coat and gave it back. "Thank you."

The coat was twice its weight from being wet. Rivulets of water rolled off it. It was completely ruined, making it no different from all the clothes they were wearing. Her muslin dress was brown up to the knees. She was fairly certain she'd worn holes in her stockings from walking with all the grit that had seeped into her boots.

She looked up to find Mr. Arden watching her. His hair was matted to his forehead, his face still damp. His shirt clung to his shoulders, showing a strength in them she'd not noticed whilst he was wearing his coat.

It then occurred to her that while Mr. Arden wore the damp and disheveled look very well, it might not be as charming on her. Her hair had come unpinned. The brim of her bonnet, heavy and wet, hung low and crooked over her face. She pushed it up, but it immediately drooped again.

Mr. Arden chuckled. He tried to fix it, but like the rest of her wardrobe, it was ruined.

"I don't think it will recover," he said, his eyes bright with amusement as he took in her appearance.

She couldn't help laughing as well. A clap of thunder rattled the inn. Eliza jumped at the sudden force. This only caused her to laugh harder. Soon Mr. Arden was doubled over, letting his deep laughter roll across the room, warmer even than the fire.

"We look like we've just survived Noah's flood," Eliza said, wiping tears from her eyes.

"Feels like we did."

The innkeeper appeared with two mugs of steaming

mulled cider. He stared at them, their clothes steaming as they dried. Both of them fighting to regain composure.

"Would you like to change first?"

Eliza looked up at Mr. Arden. Neither of them had a stitch of clothes to change into. All they'd brought were the clothes on their backs. This was her fault. She had a trunk full of dresses she'd left behind in Tetsworth. Likely he did too.

Mr. Arden shook his head, his lips pressed tight to keep in more laughter. "Our trunks have yet to arrive," he said.

"Very well." The man set the mugs on the nearest table and went back to the kitchen.

The husband and wife from the carriage arrived, the wife cursing her husband up one side and down the other for getting them into such a mess. The husband took his upbraiding in grim silence. They looked even worse for wear than Eliza and Mr. Arden.

What a relief that Mr. Arden was a pleasant man and not grim like the husband—or angry, like the wife. Eliza sipped her drink, wrapping her hands around the earthenware to share its heat.

The meal was hot and delicious. Simple fare that warmed the soul. Perfect for such a night. Mr. Arden had secured her a room on the upper level and one for himself next door. By the time the husband and wife from the mail coach also got a room, the little inn was full.

Mr. Arden opened the door to her room for her. A number four was painted on the door in red. She stopped before the threshold.

"What is it?" he asked.

"Would it be too much to ask to trade rooms?"

"Uh . . . not at all. If you wish."

"Wang Mei told me four is a bad-luck number. You have no idea how many times she has cautioned me against anything to do with that number." She leaned closer to keep her voice from carrying. "Mr. Barrington has four children.

And he was the fourth man to pay me suit. And he has four carriages. He owns four vessels for shipping. And he—"

"Yes. Fine. It would be my pleasure to take the bad-luck room." He stepped down the hall and opened the door with a red three, painted by someone with a terrible hand. "Is this better?"

She would feel much more at ease in this room. "Thank you."

He bade her good night, and she closed and locked the door. The room was small but well kept. The bed soft and inviting. Fatigue hit her fast and hard now that she was alone. It seemed like weeks since she'd left Tetsworth with Mr. Arden this morning.

She pried off her spencer and hung it over the back of a chair to dry. Then she wiggled her feet out of her half boots. They would be two sizes too small by the time they dried in the morning. Next her stockings. They were not as bad as she had feared.

She stretched her arms over her shoulders to unhook her dress, but only the top few buttons could be reached. She tried going the other way, around her waist, but they were too high. She wedged the dress higher and managed to undo a few more. Why did this frock have so many buttons? Before now, she had always had Betsy to put her in and out of complicated garments.

What to do? If the thing wasn't soaking wet and filthy, she would have simply slept in it. She could go downstairs and ask for a scullery maid to be sent to her room. Or she could ask Mr. Arden for help. As if kissing him and dragging him away had not been shameful enough.

She opened the door to her room and listened. The mail coach must have been rescued, because many voices climbed the stairs from the public room. She could hear the innkeeper apologizing that all the rooms were full and doing his best to make them comfortable in the main room. Mr. Arden must have paid a goodly sum for their rooms.

Her feet were bare. Her dress wet and muddy and halfway undone. She could not go down there. Leaving her only one choice. *Never again will I buy a dress I cannot get out of myself,* she vowed. To think how much worse her predicament would have been in room number four. This was bad luck enough.

She checked that the corridor was clear. This would make her humiliation complete. Once more she considered sleeping in her filthy dress. But she would be cold all night. Swallowing the last of her pride, she knocked softly on his door. He might already be asleep, if he was half as exhausted as she was.

There was no answer. She knocked again. "Mr. Arden," she whispered with her mouth pressed against the frame of the door. "Are you awake?"

The latch clicked, and the door cracked open. Mr. Arden stood in his long white shirt and breeches. "Miss Barnes? Is something wrong?"

She checked the corridor again, not wanting to be caught in this state of undress with a stranger, even if everyone here believed him to be her husband.

Color rose to her face, burning and hot.

Mr. Arden mistook her flush. "I beg your pardon. I would have fully dressed, but everything is wet."

At least she wasn't the only one. "I . . . need help . . . getting out of my dress."

He leaned closer. "What?"

She tried again, a little louder, her cheeks still on fire. "I need help getting out of my dress."

Seven

RICHARD SWALLOWED HARD, choking in the process. He coughed a few times. "Of course," he said, though his mouth was dry as bone dust.

He crossed into her room and closed the door. If anyone in London found out about this, she would be ruined. How had he let Eliza get into so many compromising situations? Never, never did he imagine this was how his rushed proposal would turn out. Then again, it had all happened so fast, he hadn't had time to give the eventualities much consideration.

She turned around, presenting her back to him. She'd already made some progress on her own. One of the buttons had torn the fabric, attesting to how desperately she'd tried to accomplish the task herself before asking for help.

He swallowed again and set to work. This was not his Eliza, he reminded himself. He unclasped the first button, his fingers brushing her skin. A little shiver rippled down her back. Nor was he actually engaged to this Eliza. He undid another button, thankful now that her underpinnings separated his fingertips from her bare flesh. Everything was a farce. He undid the next button. And the next. She still had his ring on her finger, but it was all for show. Another button. Four more to go.

In truth, he'd met this Eliza only twelve hours ago. Even so, he felt as if he'd known her for months. He fumbled with another button. Who in their right mind made a dress with so many abominable buttons? And each one the size of a pinhead. Impossible to undo unless the undoer had hands like a child. Certainly they weren't meant for a man's hands.

"There," he said, stepping back.

She quickly spun around, removing her bare back from his view. But the front wasn't any better. Her soft, gray eyes looked up at him.

"Thank you," she said with the mouth that had been on his twelve hours ago.

His gaze went from her lips back to her eyes. Then back to her lips again. He was on dangerous ground; why weren't his feet moving?

A thud came from the public room below. The other guests getting rowdy with drink. The noise loosened his stubborn legs.

"Good night." He didn't wait for a response but hurried back to his room, closing and locking the door—number four. Bad luck.

He collapsed onto his bed. What was wrong with him? All the reasons why he did not have feelings for this girl recounted in his head. Any affection he imagined she felt for him was all for show. A charade. To keep up the pretense until they each fulfilled the requirements of the other. She was not his Eliza.

Richard gazed at the ceiling, sleep far out of his reach. The creaking of her bed frame sounded through the wall. She'd gotten her dress off, likely laid it out to dry, then climbed into bed.

He pressed his ear against the wall, hoping to hear her breathing slow as she fell asleep. He could hear nothing through the layers of plaster and board. Just as well, for he had no right to try and listen. To eavesdrop yet again on her private moment.

All too soon the sun shone through the window. He had managed to get a few hours of sleep, despite the fact that Eliza was sleeping only a few feet from him on the other side of the wall.

Richard did his best to brush the filth from his clothes. Looking back, perhaps they had left Tetsworth with a bit too much haste. He had offered her safety, and thus far he had managed to make her cry, get her on the run from Barrington, and drag her through miles of rain and mud, all while putting her reputation deeper and deeper at risk.

He scraped the dried mud off his boots and donned his hat. Today he would do better. He would remember that she was not his Eliza, and he would not let himself get carried away. All would be proper and correct. He gave himself a nod of determination, then opened his door.

Eliza stood with her hand poised, ready to knock. She looked beautiful this morning.

Five seconds and already he'd failed.

"Good morning," he said, tipping his head. "I hope you were able to warm up enough to get some sleep." The entire bottom half of her dress was stained and the brim of her bonnet askew. They both looked like they'd just come from a week's worth of farm labor. There was nothing to be done about it.

"I never sleep," she said.

"Never?" He recalled how she'd not opened her eyes nearly the entire journey from Tetsworth to Oxford, her head bent against his shoulder. He would suspect her of feigning sleep had she not been snoring.

"Not well, at least."

"I'm sorry to hear that. I hope tonight we can find better accommodations to suit your needs."

She smiled. "It has been an affliction since childhood, so I am used to it. Wang Mei says it is a sign that I see ghosts."

"You see ghosts?" Who was this woman?

She shook her head. "'Course not. I've never seen a ghost in my life. But if I did, we would know why."

"Right." Richard missed the connection between insomnia and ghosts, but clearly her Chinese cook believed in one. He didn't know what else to say about it, so he moved on. "If you're feeling well enough, let's see what we can muster for breakfast."

"I am well." His mother's ring was still on her finger.

She noticed his eyes drawn to it. "Shall I return this?" she asked, slipping it off.

"No. Best you wear it while we are traveling together."

She put it back on, and it sparkled brightly against the rest of her bedraggled attire. They would not be able to present themselves to his aunt until they acquired a new wardrobe.

She started down the hallway, and Richard followed behind. The buttons on the back of her frock were all fastened, so she must have found someone working at the inn to help her. He wouldn't have minded if the job fell to him again, but this was for the better. Proper and correct.

This inn was too small to have private rooms, so Eliza and Richard sat in the common room. Most of the occupants had already left on the recovered mail coach.

"There is a stagecoach leaving here to Birmingham in a half an hour," Richard explained. "From there we can hire a post chaise and complete the journey with no more need for public transport." He would be relieved to get her away from prying eyes. "Also, in Birmingham we can acquire some new clothes."

She nodded as she spread preserves across a piece of toasted bread.

"Unless you would prefer I take you back. After last night, I wouldn't blame you if you decided this was all too much for you."

"Last night?" she looked up at him, her eyes wide.

He should have been more specific. "The storm and the mud."

"Oh. That." She let out a breath. "Pff. What is a little weather?"

"It's not too late for you to back out of our arrangement." He'd already put her through too much.

She poured some cream into her coffee and stirred, taking a long time to answer. "If a person backs out of a contract, that person will be unfairly shackled in their next life."

Richard had heard about rebirth of the soul. It was a common belief in those from the Far East. This was the first time he'd met an Englishwoman who seemed to accept it. "Did Wang Mei tell you that?"

"Yes. She is very wise." Eliza pushed her empty plate to the side. "But you know, this is the second time you've offered to let me out of our arrangement." She blew on her drink to cool it and then took a sip. "I can't help but wonder, Mr. Arden, if you are the one who wants out."

"Certainly not," he said, probably too eagerly. Traveling with Eliza was the most fun he'd had in a long time—even if he was forced to do so on public coaches. She was bright and charming. Delightful. It would all be over as soon as he secured his inheritance and found a way to keep her out of reach of Barrington; until then, he would not give up a second.

She grinned and her eyes lit up. "Good. I'm having the best adventure. And I don't want to do anything that will come back to hurt me in my next life. As I said, if I go back now, it will be straight into the hands of Mr. Barrington. I'd walk from here to Scotland in a sea of mud to get away from him."

It always came back to Barrington. For a moment, Richard had thought she might be thinking of him as more than simply a means to an end. But no. She was a woman of her word, dutiful to her promise and desperate to be free of Barrington.

The bell in the yard rang, signaling the coach was ready to leave. They climbed aboard, taking their usual seat with Richard by the window and Eliza beside him.

It took them the whole of the day to get to Birmingham.

Eliza took turns sleeping with her head leaning on his shoulder or talking with the other passengers. It seemed there wasn't a person on earth with whom she could not easily converse. With Richard's ring on her finger, no one questioned why they were traveling together. Still he would be glad to have a private carriage for the rest of the journey.

Richard secured rooms in a coaching inn on the edge of the city. In the morning he would take her in to the shops where they could get changes of clothes. But for now he bade her another good night. He went to his room and waited in case she needed help again with her buttons, but she did not come knocking.

Eight

Eliza lay on her bed, her eyes wide open. As usual, she'd been awake most the night and finally had risen before dawn. A maid had come up to help her dress, and now she waited, ready to go. Two more days, Mr. Arden had told her, until they reached Windley Mills, the home of his aunt.

He had kept himself aloof yesterday. Always cordial, but careful as well. First the kiss, then her dress. How could she blame him for setting some barriers? He probably thought her the most wanton woman in the country.

She held up her hand, letting the morning sun catch the sapphire of Mr. Arden's ring. This was her favorite thing about it, the way it caught the light, sending blue sparkles dancing on the walls and ceiling. It must be worth a fortune. Yet he'd said he was on his way to sell it. A family heirloom. He must be desperate for his inheritance from his aunt. He didn't act like he was low on funds, though, spending whatever was needed to get them rooms, food, and coach fares.

There was a soft knock on her door. "Miss Barnes?"

She stood and smoothed her dress, which used to be a lovely pale green and now was the color of stable muck.

In the hall stood Mr. Arden, his face as handsome as ever even though his clothes were in no better condition than her own.

"I thought we should get an early start if we are to stop at the shops before continuing north."

"I am ready." She grabbed her bonnet off the wall hook and followed him out.

"Did you not sleep again?" he asked.

"A little." No need to burden the man any more with her poor sleeping habits. She usually kept a book by her bed to pass the long nights, but as with all of her belongings, it was somewhere in the trunk she'd left in Tetsworth.

They took a quick breakfast, then he led her out to the coaching yard where a yellow post chaise waited. Mr. Arden lifted her in, then sat down beside her. The postillion called out, and the team was off, pulling the carriage quickly and neatly out of the yard. It was nice to be just the two of them for a change.

"Our first stop is Dickerson's for a change of clothes. I'm sure even the ready-made garments will be better than what we have now." He laughed. "The place was recommended by the innkeeper's wife. She said we'd be able to find what we need."

Eliza could scarcely wait to get rid of her stained dress. It took only a few minutes for the carriage to come to a stop in front of a shop displaying clothing, hats, and gloves in the front window.

A little bell tinkled as Mr. Arden pushed the door open. A man in a clean apron came forward. "Good morn—" His words caught as he took in their appearance. "May I help you?" He sounded as though he thought they'd wandered into the wrong shop. Or perhaps even the wrong part of town.

Mr. Arden stepped forward. "We are in need of a new wardrobe," he said as if the man were half-witted to need to ask.

The shopkeeper stared at him. He needed more explanation than that to accept such riffraff.

"We are traveling, my husband and I." Eliza flashed him the enormous ring. "But we were set upon by highwaymen."

Mr. Arden's eyes snapped to hers. She forced a tear out. It was a talent she'd always had, to cry on demand. It had gotten her out of many a punishment from her father. It had also gotten her anything she wanted—at least until her stepmother came along. Then her father had promptly died, leaving her alone with her stepmother.

"Our trunks were lost," Eliza continued. "You can't imagine how we have suffered."

"Of course," the man said, motioning for them to come deeper into his store. "Mrs. Dickerson," he called. "My wife will come and help you, Mrs. . . . ?"

"O'Connell," she said. Mr. Arden looked at her again. "Amelia O'Connell. And this is my husband, George."

"George O'Connell, at your service," Mr. Arden said, and it sounded very much to Eliza like he was trying not to laugh.

A thin woman came shuffling out from the back storeroom. She hurried over and took one look at them, and her mouth dropped open.

"They were set upon by a highwayman," her husband explained.

"Oh, you poor dears," said Mrs. Dickerson.

"Highwaymen," Eliza corrected. "'Twas more than one man. Had it been only one, let me assure you my husband would have made short work of him; but it was a whole gang. Armed, they were, with pistols and sabers."

Mr. Arden was hit with another fit of coughing. He might need to see a doctor, so often he seemed to suffer.

"We barely escaped with our lives," Eliza continued. "As you can see, we traveled miles in the rain and dark and mud before making our way to The Rose and Crown."

"Yes, my dear," Mr. Arden said. "Let's not bore them with the details."

"But this is far from boring," exclaimed Mrs. Dickerson. "What a fright you must have had. Come along—I'll get you fixed up directly." The woman motioned for her to follow.

"Get whatever you need," Mr. Arden said, as he walked toward the men's clothing side with Mr. Dickerson.

The selection of ready-made dresses was better than she thought it would be this far from London. Eliza found a pretty muslin with blue trim that fit her well enough. She also needed a new bonnet, petticoat, boots, and pelisse. Should she be worried about the amount of money she was spending while Mr. Arden's funds were tied up?

He'd said to get whatever she needed, and she really did need these things if she was to play the part of his future wife once they reached Windley Mills. Truly none of what she had been wearing was salvageable, save her stays.

She could always pay him back later. She had funds of her own, just not with her at the moment. With that in mind, she also chose a lovely pelisse in light blue. It fit her a little large, but it could be altered later. It was warm and soft, and that's what she needed for this journey into the north country. Besides, she always thought blue set off her eyes better than any other color. After a full day in filth, she wanted to look her best for Mr. Arden.

She came out from behind the screen to find Mr. Arden settling the bill at the counter. He wore a smart dark-blue coat, buckskin breeches, new boots, and a fresh hat. It seemed he'd had more success in finding something to fit his build than she had, for he looked taller and stronger than ever.

"You're all set, dearie," Mrs. Dickerson said.

Mr. Arden looked up, his smile growing wider the longer he looked at her. The blue pelisse was already paying off.

"Doesn't she look better?" Mrs. Dickerson gave Eliza a spin.

"Beautiful," Mr. Arden said. "Come along, Mrs. O'Connell." He offered her his arm, and Eliza slipped her hand into the crook of his elbow.

They bade the Dickersons farewell and returned to the waiting chaise.

As soon as they were settled and on their way, Mr. Arden turned to her. "Highwaymen?"

"Well they needed some kind of explanation. We looked like gutter rats."

"You could have told the truth."

The truth that they were pretending to be married to help each other get what they wanted? No, she couldn't tell them that. "The truth is so boring. Since we are already acting, we might as well make it good." She looked up at him, but he was already watching her. Suddenly the chaise seemed very small, as they sat there, jostling into each other while it rattled along.

"It is a little shocking, is it not, how well you tell your lies?" Mr. Arden asked. "What would Wang Mei say about that?"

Perhaps she had gotten carried away with the Dickersons. And the others. But he didn't really seem to mind. For all his talk, she could see the smile on his lips and tugging at his eyes.

"Wang Mei would say that each life we live plants the seeds for the next, so we must be careful what we sow." Eliza had tried to follow this advice, hoping that the better she was here, the better her next life.

"Do you really believe that you will be reborn into another life? As a new person?" he asked.

"Wang Mei believes it." Wang Mei had been teaching Eliza her beliefs since she was a child. It might be true, it might not. "Who can ever know for certain what will happen after we die? It sounds nice, though, don't you think? To have a second chance at a better life. It would be terrible if all our efforts here were wasted because we ceased to exist when we die."

"They won't be wasted," Mr. Arden said. "They are what will get us into heaven."

Then heaven would be the end. She preferred the idea that her efforts here could build her a better life in the next go-around. Of course the vicar informed her she was a heathen and a pagan. He probably would have banned her from church had it not been her father paying his living.

In the days they'd been together, Mr. Arden had managed to learn most everything about her, but she knew very little about him—aside from his need for his inheritance and that he also had lost his mother. She assumed his father had also passed on, otherwise there wouldn't be an inheritance.

Which reminded her. "Thank you for the clothes. When things are settled, I can repay you for the expense."

"Think nothing of it." He smiled. "You look lovely, so the pleasure is all mine."

He had been throwing money down without apparent thought throughout this whole journey. If he was so desperate for his inheritance, should he not be more frugal? She twisted the ring on her finger. He must be in great need of funds to sell this family heirloom.

"Mr. Arden, may I ask you something?"

He nodded. "Of course."

"How can you so easily spend money if acquiring your inheritance is so urgent?"

He gazed out the window. Perhaps the question was too personal. After all they'd been through, she thought they had a bond at least of friendship. Maybe she assumed too much.

After a deep breath he said, "It is not that kind of inheritance."

"What?"

"The inheritance I'm after is not money."

"A house, then?"

He shook his head. "No."

"What is it?" Eliza could think of no other form of inheritance.

"It is my sister."

"What?" His sister? What kind of inheritance was that?

"My parents died when she was young. Too young, they thought, to be left in my care. She was passed to my Aunt

Beatrice Arden. My aunt gave her a roof, clothing, and food, but not love. In return my aunt receives a stipend set aside from my father's will. I have tried many times to get little Lucy out of there, but my aunt will not relinquish her, for then she would lose her allowance."

Eliza had never heard of such a thing. Was it even possible to hold a child as chattel like that? The law couldn't possibly be on his aunt's side. "But how can that be? What makes you think your aunt will hand her over if you show up with me?"

"It is specified in the will that when I marry, I will be a suitable guardian for the child. My father was very old-fashioned. He believed a woman was needed for the proper raising of children."

"So by law, you can take Lucy away once you are married."

He nodded. "Exactly so."

"Where will you take her?"

"To my home in Berkshire."

"But won't your aunt want her back when she finds out you are not really married?" It had been his suggestion to fake marry, but if parting ways meant he had to give his sister back, what was the point of all of this?

"If I must, I will take her away. Perhaps to the continent for a while, until my aunt loses interest in the child."

Suddenly it seemed the stakes of their little charade were much higher. A child's happiness was at risk should Eliza fail in her role. She twisted the ring on her hand.

"Why sell the ring, then?" Eliza asked. "If you are not in need of money, why sell such a beautiful piece? It has been in your family for generations."

"It carries memories I no longer want to keep."

Memories of his mother, perhaps. Or of another woman. If that was the case, Eliza didn't want to know. For her, the ring carried a different set of memories. Of a quick kiss in the courtyard of an inn. Of his fingers as they brushed the skin of her back. Of his eyes, right before he made a hasty retreat from her room. Those were the memories she wanted to keep, at least for the few more days she would be wearing the ring.

Nine

RICHARD PULLED THE carriage blanket higher over Eliza's lap. She had told him thrice now that she never slept, but for the past two days she'd spent most of the time in the carriage asleep, her head leaning against his shoulder.

He wasn't complaining. Her rose-and-lavender scent curled around him, her lips slightly parted as she slept. If she truly did not sleep well at night, it was good that she could get some rest in the carriage. He was unsure if it was a compliment that she was comfortable enough with him to sleep, or if he was too boring to keep her awake.

They neared the village of Ingleton. A turn from here would take them to Windley Mills in a quarter hour's time.

"Miss Barnes," he said, giving her a gentle nudge.

Her head came up.

"We are almost there."

A look of panic flashed in her eyes.

"There is nothing to worry about. No matter what happens, it will be fine." He'd been working on removing Lucy from this place for the past seven years. If it didn't work, he would be no worse off than he was now; but if it did, he would get his sister out of the place she hated.

"Lucy," Eliza said, as if she were going over the things he'd told her in her head. "Ten years old. Brown hair. Butterflies and birds."

She was putting in a tremendous amount of effort for a girl she'd never even met before. Eliza had really taken Lucy's plight to heart. It only added to her attractiveness.

The carriage came to a stop in front of a stone house spread out wide and low, just like his aunt. Even the lawns were manicured to look stern. His aunt had never married. Richard had hoped her childlessness would have created a loving bond between her and Lucy, but it did not work out that way.

Richard exited the carriage and lent his hand to Eliza. She stepped out the same moment the door to Windley Mills opened and Lucy came running out.

"Richard!" The girl ran straight to him, leaping at the last moment into his open arms. He caught her and squeezed her tight. "Why didn't you tell me you were coming?"

Richard winked at Eliza as he said, "It was a spontaneous decision." He set Lucy down. "I wanted you to meet Miss Barnes."

Eliza gave Lucy a lovely curtsy, and Lucy did the same. "Hello," Eliza said.

Lucy took in Eliza's stunning eyes, more blue now against the color of her pelisse, and smiled. "Hello."

Richard's aunt came out of the house next. "Aunt Beatrice," he said.

The woman marched over, her heavy legs scuffing loudly on the graveled drive. "Richard. What brings you here with no warning?"

"I'm here for Lucy." No sense beating around the bush. The less time they had to spend here the better.

Aunt Beatrice looked from Richard to Eliza and then back to Richard again. Her face lost a few shades of color. She took Lucy by the wrist and pulled her close. Lucy flinched at the pain, and Richard wanted to grab the child and run.

"You are not married," his aunt said.

"I am engaged to Miss Barnes."

Eliza, always good at playing her part, acknowledged his

aunt with another deep curtsy, then walked over to Richard and slipped her hand lovingly around his arm, making sure the sapphire-and-diamond ring glittered in the last of the evening sun.

"It is a pleasure to meet you, Aunt." She looked up at Richard as if he was the most important man in the world to her. Lud, how that woman could act. "My Richard has told me so much about you. And about Lucy. But he said Lucy was a child, so I did not recognize her at first when I saw this beautiful young lady."

Lucy's eyes lit up.

"Engaged is not the same as married."

"Aunt. It is not as if Windley Mills is conveniently located. We are getting married next week in Berkshire and departing immediately for a tour of the continent. Lucy will be accompanying us, but there is not time to travel here and back between the wedding and our tour."

He hated fighting over the child in front her. Just one more insult to Lucy's little life that had already been so awful.

Eliza, still with her hand on Richard's arm, bent to Lucy's level. "Miss Arden, I hear you are quite the entomologist. Won't you show me your butterfly collection?"

Lucy pried her arm out of her aunt's grasp. "Yes!" She took Eliza by the hand and hurried off with her into the house.

Aunt Beatrice planted her fists on her hips. "The will states not until you are married. What if this girl dies like the last one?"

He should have known she would bring up the other Eliza.

"Thank you, Aunt, for that cruel reminder." He could not get Lucy away fast enough. "Miss Barnes will not be dying. She is in perfect health." If he really wanted to win this argument, he had to speak his aunt's language. "I am prepared to offer you one thousand pounds to spare me the inconvenience of having to return here to collect her."

His aunt's eyes flashed with interest.

"We are getting married. That much is inevitable. And if I have to return to Lancashire for Lucy, I will instruct the bank to withhold your final payment to cover the cost of travel and our delay."

She did not answer.

"It is your choice. You can take the thousand pounds or lose all of Lucy's final payment."

He had no intention of leaving without the child no matter what his aunt agreed to. But his aunt was stubborn, and letting her believe she had some choice in the matter might make things better for everyone.

"We will be leaving in the morning." He bowed to his aunt. "I will go and instruct Mrs. Hale to get Lucy's things together."

Richard strode into the house and up to the small room in the attic that served as both the nursery and Lucy's bedchamber. Richard himself had paid for a governess for the child, but after a few years Aunt Beatrice had announced she would no longer tolerate strangers living in the home and took to teaching Lucy herself.

Richard found out later that little teaching, if any, actually took place. Instead, Lucy spent her time waiting on her aunt. Not quite a servant but certainly not a member of the family. As the years passed, more and more signs appeared that his sister was being treated cruelly. Every time Richard came to visit, he observed Lucy doing her best to please her aunt and getting nothing in return but pain.

When he became engaged to the other Eliza, he'd thought at last the problem was solved. But then she died, and he was back at the beginning again.

He entered the nursery and found Eliza sitting in the narrow window seat, Lucy close beside her as they bent over her collection of butterflies. He paused in the doorway. It was a scene he would be happy to see for the rest of his life.

Eliza looked up at him and smiled. His breath caught. She

had never looked so lovely, sitting with his sister, bringing the child a moment of happiness she so rarely got.

She was not his Eliza, he reminded himself for the thousandth time. This was all an act, and it would be over soon. Too soon, but over nonetheless. The thought soured his mood.

"Dinner will be served in half an hour," he said. "I have business to take care of. I'll see you then." He left, closing the door behind him, resting his forehead against it. How rashly he'd proposed this game back at the inn at Tetsworth, not knowing how painful the ending would be.

He found Mrs. Hale and asked her to pack a small trunk of Lucy's things. He would send for the rest later, once he was safely and finally away. Then he took a turn around the garden to cool his thoughts until mealtime.

Lucy and Eliza arrived right on time for dinner holding hands.

Aunt Beatrice took one look at Lucy and said, "The child eats in the kitchen."

Lucy's face fell. She cowered behind Eliza.

"She eats with us," Richard said. "Bring another place setting," he told the maid holding a tureen of soup.

The maid's face went pale. She looked at Aunt Beatrice, then at Richard, unsure who to obey.

Richard didn't give his aunt a chance to counter. "Do it now," he demanded.

Aunt Beatrice's face hardened, but she gave the maid a nod.

The maid set the soup on the table and scurried to add the extra place setting. Richard put Lucy on his side of the table, shielding her from his aunt.

"Who are your family?" Aunt Beatrice asked Eliza, after they'd all taken their seats and the rest of the simple meal had been placed.

"My father is Fitzwilliam Barnes," Eliza said. "Cousin to the Duke of Norfolk."

Richard choked on his cutlet and had to wash it down with a swallow of wine. Another of Eliza's tales was coming.

His aunt stared at her, looking at her with more interest than she'd shown before.

Eliza smiled at Aunt Beatrice. "Every year for Michaelmas we used to go there, and my father would join the hunt. Until three years past when the duke was angry at my father for besting him." Eliza turned to Lucy with a wink. "The duke is not the most accomplished hunter." Lucy laughed, and Eliza went on with her tale. "He challenged my father to a duel."

Eliza put her napkin on the table and leaned forward, ready to awe her captive audience. Truly this woman had missed her calling in life when she did not enter the theater.

"They met at dawn while the mist was still rising off the river. Ten paces, they marched. Then turned. My father didn't fire. He was sure the duke would cry off, seeing as how they were related. My father thought it was all for show. But no. The duke's pistol went off with a bang, and my father was shot."

Aunt Beatrice gasped, showing all the horror Eliza could've wanted. Her tales always inclined toward the morbid. Perhaps her life really had been a dreary one. Lucy was listening with her eyes wide.

"Killed by his own cousin," Eliza said. "A duke, no less."

"My dear," Richard said.

Eliza looked at him.

He nodded toward his sister. "The child."

Oh, she mouthed with a nod. "After my father died, we have not been back since for fear we will lose another family member."

"Eliza." These were not stories for someone so young.

"I had to tell the end." Eliza gave him an exultant look. "I will say no more." She turned to Lucy, "I beg your pardon, Miss Arden."

"Oh, I don't mind." Lucy clearly admired Eliza.

Richard downed the last of his wine. Lucy had already formed an attachment. How could he blame her when he was suffering similar symptoms? He did not look forward to when he must explain to Lucy it was all for show and Eliza would not be her sister. He didn't want Lucy's heart broken when it all came to an end. His only hope was that Lucy would be pleased enough to be out of Aunt Beatrice's house that she would forgive him the deception.

Ten

MR. ARDEN SCOOTED his chair from the table. "Come, Lucy. Let's go see how Mrs. Hale is getting on with packing your things."

Lucy's eyes shot to her aunt.

Eliza stood as well. "Yes. Let's go pack you up." She took Lucy's hand and followed Mr. Arden out of the room.

Lucy had expressed doubt while they'd been alone in the nursery that her aunt would actually let her go. Eliza had assured her that Mr. Arden was very serious about taking her away and wouldn't be leaving without her. The girl's eyes had filled with hope.

The bruises on the side of Lucy's head and on her arm had not gone unnoticed. After living with her stepmother for so long, Eliza had a good eye for the hurts inflicted by those meant to protect. She would do all she could to help Mr. Arden save this child. Lucy was delightful, so it was easy to want the best for her.

The housekeeper had a small trunk ready to go when they entered the nursery. Lucy dug through it, taking out a few things and adding some more. When she was satisfied, she turned to Mr. Arden and gave him a nod.

"Perfect. I will have Thomas load it first thing in the morning."

"Am I really leaving here?"

"Indeed you are," Mr. Arden said.

Eliza had never seen such a bright and lovely smile as the one Lucy gave her brother.

"And you will be my new sister?" Lucy asked Eliza.

After all the stories she'd told, the answer to this child's earnest plea was too much. Eliza's eyes went to Mr. Arden's. How could she tell this girl that in a few days they would never see each other again?

"That's right," said Mr. Arden, though he did not meet his sister's eyes. "But first you must get a good night's sleep, and in the morning we can begin our new life together."

Lucy gave her brother a hug, then one for Eliza. She reached under her bed and pulled out a tattered cloth doll.

"I have to keep it hidden from Aunt Beatrice."

"We will be sure to bring this with us," said her brother.

They left Lucy tucked nicely in bed, a smile on her face. Outside, Mr. Arden closed the door to the nursery.

Eliza's dinner sat heavy in her stomach. Poor Lucy was caught in the middle of their game. "How can you lie to her like that?" she whispered.

"After the Duke of Norfolk, you are hardly one to censure," he said.

"Telling made-up stories to adults I will never see again is not the same." The others, save perhaps his aunt, would never even know the difference.

"What else would you have me do?" he asked. "Once we leave here, we will have both gotten what we have wanted."

Meaning it would be time to part ways. He always found a way to remind her that this was a temporary arrangement. This afternoon, when he had found them in the nursery, he seemed almost displeased that she was giving his sister so much attention.

He was probably right. She need not try so hard to be liked by Lucy, adding to the hurt the child would feel when all was finally revealed to be a farce. She would be more careful tomorrow on the journey home. Keep her distance.

The dull rumble of voices came up from the drawing room. Mr. Arden stared down the stairs for several moments but made no move to go down.

"I have no interest in sitting with my aunt and her neighbors. The fewer people that see us here the better, anyway."

Eliza concurred. She was not in the mood to play the part of betrothed any longer tonight. What started out as fun now felt like tearing away little pieces of her heart. "I'm tired, Mr. Arden. I would like to retire."

"Of course." He directed her down the hall to a small room at the opposite end of the house as Lucy. "Mrs. Hale has prepared this room for you." He opened the door for her but did not move away.

"Thank you."

Still he did not step out of the way. He just stood there on the threshold, watching her. He reached out and took her hand, tilting it back and forth as he studied his ring on her finger.

"Miss Barnes," he said at last, but nothing more followed.

"Yes?"

"I wonder . . ." Again he did not finish.

She wanted to step closer. She wanted him to look at her the way he had the night after the storm. When he took his eyes off the ring and raised them to hers, it was there for a moment, that burning. Then it was gone.

"I hope you can sleep well tonight," he said, clearing the path to her room. "Good night." He turned to leave.

"Mr. Arden."

He turned back.

Now it was her turn to be at a loss. Why had she called him back? What did she want to say? She could not say what she wanted to say. Not after his many reminders that nothing was real and all would be over soon.

"I have enjoyed this journey with you." Then she turned and closed the door so he wouldn't see the color in her cheeks or the longing in her eyes. He had enough to worry about without her adding to his concerns. Perhaps after they were clear of Lancashire and Aunt Beatrice she would try again to tell him how she felt.

Eleven

RICHARD LAY IN his bed, his eyes wide open. He'd gone to the stables and worked it out with Thomas. A carriage would be ready for them first thing in the morning. Lucy was packed and ready. He and Eliza had no luggage to worry about.

Three more days with Eliza, and then they would be home. Would it be safe for her to return to her stepmother? Or perhaps he could find a place for her to stay among the women of his neighborhood. To give Barrington more time to cool his heels. He would gladly let her stay at his home, but that would put her reputation on the line. He'd already compromised her enough as it was.

The clock on his mantel ticked. The tree outside his window thumped in the breeze. Truly this was the longest night of his life. He'd come so close to telling her how he felt. In the end, he'd lacked the courage.

I have enjoyed this journey with you. What had she meant? That it was not as horrible as she'd been expecting, or dare he hope her feelings were not completely impartial? There were times when he thought her sentiments were sincere, but it was so hard to tell in this charade what was real.

He sat up, giving up entirely on sleep. It was early, not even light. But before he'd made a conscious decision, he was dressed and standing in front of Eliza's bedroom door. She was always awake at this time, as her insistent insomnia kept her from sleeping. He would just see. See if he could muster the fortitude to tell her how he really felt. If she refused him, then at least he would know the truth from the farce.

He knocked softly on the door. "Miss Barnes? Are you awake?"

There was no answer.

"Miss Barnes?"

Still nothing. Of all the times for her to finally fall asleep. He glanced down the hall. Not even the servants were up yet. He was such a fool. Such a fool, but he could not help himself.

He cracked the door open. "Miss Barnes?"

All was quiet. He should leave, but he didn't. He crept in.

Her room was empty. Her bed was unmade, but there was no other sign of her. Perhaps she'd gone in to Lucy during the night. The sapphire ring rested on her bedside table. She must have removed it to sleep. He slipped it into his waistcoat pocket, then hurried to the nursery.

Lucy was sitting on the narrow window seat where she'd been reading with Eliza just the evening before. She glanced up when he pushed the door open, tears glistening on her cheeks.

"Lucy, what is wrong?" He crossed to her and lifted her into his arms even though she was getting far too old to be held. "Why are you not asleep?"

She didn't complain about being held. "I'm not leaving with you," she said.

"Of course you are. Everything is prepared, and we will be off as soon as it's light." And as soon as he could find Eliza.

She sniffed, and he felt her body quiver. "But Miss Barnes already left."

He sat down on the bench and put her beside him. "What?" Had Eliza changed her mind? She'd sounded sure yesterday. Or had she? *I have enjoyed this journey with you.* Had she been telling him goodbye? "Lucy, why do you say that?"

"I was too excited to sleep. So I was sitting here waiting

for morning." She wiped her eyes with her sleeve. "I saw Aunt Beatrice and a man put Miss Barnes in a carriage. Then they drove away."

Richard's blood drained to his feet. "What man?"

She shrugged her shoulders. "I never saw him before. He was old. With a big belly."

Barrington. It had to be. That black-hearted boor. "And Aunt Beatrice went with them?"

She shook her head. "She went back in the house."

Richard ran his hands across his face. Barrington had found them. Richard never imagined he would track them all the way to Lancashire. Aunt Beatrice would have been only too happy to push Eliza into his carriage and let him take her away. Then Richard couldn't get married, and his aunt would continue receiving the allowance.

Lucy burst out with a sob. "What if it was the duke? What if he has come to fight in a duel?"

Eliza and her tales. He gave Lucy a hug. "I can assure you it was not the Duke of Norfolk."

Poor little Lucy would be trapped here even longer. Maybe forever. Where would he ever find someone like Eliza, willing to travel with him this far north with a fake engagement? Nowhere. Another woman like Eliza Barnes did not exist. He'd have to choose Harriet Herbert and her four unruly boys. Or Dorothea beetle eyes.

He patted Lucy on her back. "Don't worry. I'll bring her back." And he would make it so that Barrington could never get his hands on her again. "Can you wait a few more days while I go after Miss Barnes?"

Lucy nodded.

Aunt Beatrice rarely rose before ten. Richard pounded on her bedroom door even though it was barely dawn.

"Open up, Aunt Beatrice. Or I will break this door down."

There was no answer from the other side.

"I will give you to the count of five." He counted loud enough to be heard three counties away. "One. Two."

Lucy watched with eyes wide and a speck of a grin. Richard suspected she was hoping to see her aunt's bedroom door kicked in. A few servants peered from the end of the hall with the same sort of eagerness in their eyes.

"Three. Four. Five." He stepped back to get some momentum, but the door swung open. Little Lucy's shoulders fell.

His aunt appeared, a shawl around her night shift and a mobcap askew on her head. "How dare you come to—"

"Unless you are going to tell me where Miss Barnes went, do not open your mouth."

Aunt Beatrice's mouth snapped shut.

"I know she went with Barrington. And I know why."

His aunt's eyes widened.

"Where did he take her?"

Aunt Beatrice said nothing.

"Where is he taking her?" Richard stepped closer so that he was towering over her. "Aunt?"

She glared at him, a tactic she used so frequently it had no effect on him whatsoever. "I do not know," she finally said. "I do not know where they went."

Eliza must be beside herself. To be free of Barrington was the one thing he had promised her, and he had failed. Every time he pictured that man's filthy eyes on her, Richard's blood boiled. He clenched his fist, tempted to throw it at his aunt, but he would save it for Barrington. Besides, he would never hit a woman, even if she were a witch.

"Mark my words," he said. "If anything happens to her, you will regret that you were ever born. And in your next life, there will be hell to pay."

He strode out to the stables. Barrington was from Slough, he thought Eliza had said. All the way back down past Oxford again. It would take four days for Barrington to get there.

Three, perhaps, if he pushed hard. Once Barrington got Eliza home, how long until they would marry?

He hadn't ever thought to ask about the specifics of the arrangement between Eliza and Barrington. Had they already posted banns? Perhaps he had a special license. Either way, Barrington would rush the whole thing. He would want the marriage as quickly as possible if he thought there was any chance she'd run away with Richard again.

Twelve

ELIZA HAD BEEN trapped in Mr. Barrington's carriage the entire day. She'd spent the first several hours screaming, but Mr. Barrington kept clapping his hand over her mouth. The disgust of his balmy palm on her lips was the only reason she was now sitting still.

The afternoon was getting on, and still he pushed on. When they'd stopped to change horses, Mr. Barrington let her out only to relieve herself, then forced her straight back into the coach. Her head rattled from traveling the unkempt roads of the north country.

Now she was resigned. Mr. Arden had done his best to save her from this fate worse than death. But in the end, she still wound up in the clutches of Mr. Barrington.

She considered again throwing herself from the moving carriage. With her luck, she would just end up crippled *and* married to the pumpkin head. Though perhaps if she was crippled, he would no longer want her, so maybe the idea wasn't so bad. She leaned her head against the glass and watched the dirt track roll by beneath the carriage wheels. She could easily open the door and tumble out.

In the end, she lacked the courage. She'd spent most of the early morning staring out the rear window, waiting to see Mr. Arden riding after her. But when she saw the direction Mr. Barrington was taking her, her hope died. Mr. Arden would have ridden south, toward Slough. Toward Mr. Barrington's home. But Mr. Barrington was taking her north, across the border. Mr. Barrington wanted a quick wedding. And there was nowhere quicker than across the border into Scotland, where anyone could marry anyone, no license needed.

Blast her and her weak heart. Weak because she dared not throw herself from the carriage, and weak because she'd let herself form an attachment to Mr. Arden.

The carriage rattled as it crossed the River Sark, marking the border. Only a few minutes left until she would become Mrs. Barrington. Worms crawled through her skin at the thought of it.

She closed her eyes and tried to fill her mind with something better. Mr. Arden, and the stunned look on his face when she'd kissed him way back on the first day of their adventure. The way his hand pressed against her waist, as if he'd wanted it to last longer. His chestnut eyes hungry as she turned to him once he'd helped her with her buttons.

She shook her head. These thoughts did not make it any easier.

The carriage came to a stop, and Eliza's heart dropped from her chest. She was out of time.

"Remember, not a word, or Mr. Arden dies," Mr. Barrington reminded her for the nine hundredth time since he'd shown up at Windley Mills. He had told her that he had two expert marksmen standing by if she put up a fuss. Whether it was true or not, she wouldn't gamble with Mr. Arden's life. He had given her a glimpse of a dueling pistol he had tucked away as if to verify the threat.

Mr. Barrington opened the door to the carriage and dragged her out.

They were in front of a smithy. She'd heard about people getting married in such a place. Here in Scotland, all you needed were witnesses and a willing couple. Eliza was most certainly not willing. But again, if there was any chance Mr.

Barrington did have Mr. Arden in his sights, she would not risk it.

Even if she put up a bigger fuss than Napoleon, Mr. Barrington would offer enough money that the smith would look the other way. Why else was this such a booming business for the folks of Gretna Green?

Mr. Barrington smiled at the man who came out of the forge. "We wish to be wed."

The blacksmith looked long and hard at Mr. Barrington, then over at Eliza. He had a keen eye, it seemed, for he grinned and said, "One hundred pounds."

Mr. Barrington scoffed. "I'll give you fifty." Even fifty was an exorbitant price.

The blacksmith turned and walked back toward his shop.

"Seventy-five," called Mr. Barrington.

The blacksmith paused but did not turn around.

Mr. Barrington glanced over his back as if he expected Mr. Arden to come galloping across the Sark any moment. Eliza knew better; if he bothered at all to come after her, he would have ridden south, toward Slough. Toward where it all began.

"Very well. A hundred," Mr. Barrington conceded.

The blacksmith turned with a genial smile. "Right this way." He opened the door to his shop and let them in.

A young girl was carrying a bucket of water and looked up as they entered.

"Go fetch Thomas and Jack," the blacksmith said.

The girl set the bucket down and ran off. "Uncle Thomas," she called as she disappeared out a back door.

The blacksmith wiped his filthy hands on an even filthier cloth, then reached out. "Martin Halcrow."

Mr. Barrington looked at the man's dirty hand for a moment before shaking it. "Adolphous Barrington." He motioned toward Eliza. "And this is Miss Barnes."

Eliza did not give Martin Halcrow any acknowledgment.

She couldn't even look up or she would fall apart, utterly and completely.

"You all right, miss?" Mr. Halcrow asked.

She nodded, knowing full well she would never be all right ever again. Her fate was sealed, it seemed. And all the fussing in the world would only put Mr. Arden in danger. Maybe even Lucy.

"It'll cost ye an extra ten guineas if'n the miss don't want to," Mr. Halcrow informed Mr. Barrington.

La! What kind of business was this? Shouldn't the blacksmith be a gentleman and rescue the damsel in distress? He certainly had arms thick enough to wrestle a dragon to the ground.

Two men walked into the shop with a paper. A marriage certificate, to make it all official. And it would be. No matter that she was standing on straw while a horseshoe cooled on the anvil. No matter that the man officiating wore a tanned leather apron. In the eyes of the law, they would be married.

Mr. Halcrow asked them their names, and one of the other men—Thomas or Jack, she knew not which—wrote it on the certificate. Then he asked if they were each there of their own free will.

Mr. Barrington spoke up quickly. "Yes, yes. We are both here of our own free will."

"Why don't you let the lady speak for herself?" called a voice from the door of the smithy.

Eliza spun around. Mr. Arden stood on the threshold, breathing heavily as if he'd run here from Windley Mills on foot. He wore no hat, and his hair was a wild mess, but he'd never looked better.

He frowned at her. "Mrs. O'Connell, what are you doing here?"

"Mrs.?" asked the blacksmith.

Never had the sight of another human being brought her such joy. "Mr. O'Connell," she said. "You came for me."

Mr. Barrington grabbed for her, but she leaped away and

ran straight to Mr. Arden. He opened his arms and caught her, holding her tight. She was saved. Once again, Mr. Arden had given her back her life. Good thing she had not thrown herself from the carriage—she would have regretted very much being crippled right now.

"Now see here," Mr. Halcrow said, pointing a finger at Mr. Barrington. "Ye can't marry a married woman. Not even here."

"She's not married," Mr. Barrington growled.

"And she will never be married to the likes of you." Mr. Arden led her a few paces away. He let out a long breath, then smiled at her. That beautiful smile that melted her to her bones. He leaned close and whispered, "I know this will sound untoward, but I propose a proposal."

She laughed softly. It was those words that had saved her the first time around.

"Miss Eliza," he continued, "I believe we can be the solution to each other's predicament."

"And what predicament is that?" Though she already knew it was his sister.

But he did not mention Lucy. He pressed his fist over his heart. "There is a piece of me missing, and I think you might have it. When I found you gone, it hurt."

Her eyes flew to his. Was he in earnest? So much of their time together had been an act, by now the lines were mixed and blurred. Was this part of the charade to keep her from Mr. Barrington, or did he mean what he had said? All traces of humor were gone from his face, so perhaps this was real.

One way to find out. "Do we have to marry?" she asked.

He held his hand out, holding the beautiful ring between his forefinger and thumb. "I'm afraid this time we do."

She looked down at his ring, then up at him. It was no longer a game. It was real. "Wang Mei always says things are better in pairs. I accept your proposal." She put the ring on her finger; she had felt bare without it.

"But she is mine," Mr. Barrington bellowed. "I have the prior claim."

Mr. Arden did not even look at Mr. Barrington. He grabbed her hand and went straight to the blacksmith. "Sir, how much for a wedding?"

The blacksmith sized up Mr. Arden, then Eliza again. "Fifty pounds."

"What?" Mr. Barrington's face was scarlet now. Even the bald patch on the top of his head had turned from pumpkin orange to bright red. "This is preposterous."

The witnesses and Mr. Halcrow had been standing by, waiting for things to resolve. They must be used to this, conducting marriages with couples of dubious connection. Some must be truly in love, as she was with Mr. Arden. Considering they didn't blink an eye at her and Mr. Barrington's situation, they must have also seen other couples with less of a romantic attachment.

"You should go now, Barrington." Mr. Arden let go of Eliza and walked over to him. "You'd better be off."

Mr. Barrington's rheumy eyes hardened. "And what if I don't." From under his coat, he pulled out the pistol.

Quick as a blink, Mr. Arden swung his fist so hard the smack echoed in the little workshop. Mr. Barrington flew back and landed in the straw with a thud. He did not move, but a little groan escaped his mouth. His firearm lay in the straw. Mr. Arden picked it up and tossed it to the blacksmith.

"Perhaps you should hold on to this," Mr. Arden said.

Mr. Halcrow set it on a shelf behind him, among his tools. The blacksmith stared at the body on the ground for a moment, then said, "All right then, let's start all over. Thomas, fetch a new certificate."

Thomas did, and their names were added accordingly. Mr. Halcrow asked again if they were there of their own accord.

"Yes," she said without hesitation. For things were working out now better than she had ever imagined. When they'd left Tetsworth, she'd been assured they wouldn't have to marry. Much had happened since that day, and how quickly her heart had bound to Mr. Arden.

The blacksmith finished the ceremony and handed them the certificate. He tossed the old one with Mr. Barrington's name into the fire. Thomas and Jack lifted Mr. Barrington from the straw and escorted him out.

"Felicitations on your happy day," Mr. Halcrow said. He picked up a large piece of metal that appeared to be some sort of carriage spring and went back to work.

And that was that. In less than ten minutes she was a married woman. Married to a man she barely knew, yet after their long journey together, in many ways she felt she knew him better than anyone.

"Come," Mr. Arden said, holding her hand and guiding her out of the blacksmith shop.

Mr. Barrington was climbing into his coach, still flanked by Thomas and Jack. He did not look back at Richard and herself. The carriage door closed, and Mr. Barrington's driver snapped the reins. He was gone. Hopefully forever.

Her stepmother would be furious. There was nothing she could do about that now. The deed was done, and Eliza had no regrets.

Thirteen

When they were a good twenty-five paces from the blacksmith shop, Richard stopped. This was the outcome he'd been hoping for, but he really hadn't given Eliza much choice in the matter. Just because his heart was sure did not mean hers was. Though she had seemed to agree to the marriage readily, she was very good at acting. Perhaps she'd only been putting on a show for Barrington and the blacksmith.

"Miss Barnes," he began, then corrected himself. "Eliza." He wasn't really certain what it was he wanted to say. That he was sorry for ever putting her in such a position in the first place? That he hoped she did not regret what they had done? That he wanted to take her in his arms and kiss her until the world around them faded away?

He settled on, "Are you all right?"

"I am very well," she said. "You saved me again."

Just because she was saved did not mean she was happy. What was done was done. He had plenty of time in the future to make her happy. Right now, the evening was coming on, and Lucy waited for them.

"You must be exhausted. Still I have to ask if you can go a little longer."

"Lucy," she said, already knowing his thoughts.

He nodded. "The moon is bright, and I think we can make good time if we travel at night."

"We should not leave her there a moment longer than needs be. I never sleep anyway, so we might as well get going."

We. The way she said it warmed him through and through. The two of them together. This was not the most romantic way to spend their wedding night. But their relationship had not been a conventional one from the start.

"Lucy is very worried about you," Richard said. "She is convinced the Duke of Norfolk is the man who took you away and that your life is danger."

Eliza laughed. "That would have been preferable over Mr. Barrington."

The horses where changed, and they set off again, back on the road to Windley Mills. Barring any more mishaps, they would arrive late morning. He helped Eliza into his aunt's phaeton and took the reins.

He handed Eliza a blanket. "It will get cool during the night."

She shook it out and spread it across her legs and Richard's. They crossed the River Sark, back into England. Eliza's head slowly lowered onto Richard's shoulder. Her long lashes closed over her cheeks tinged with pink from the night air. Richard pulled the blanket higher to cover her shoulders.

She slept most of the way. Richard was glad she could get some rest, but he was beginning to doubt her claims of insomnia. Either he was the most boring person on earth or she had exaggerated her difficulties sleeping. Or, if he might indulge his vanity, perhaps she felt secure enough to drift away only with him.

Either way, he would not complain. He put one arm around her and pulled her close, her head tipped on his shoulder.

Darkness came and went, and the morning sun was reaching noon when he guided the trap into Windley Mills. He caught a flurry at the nursery window, and almost before he could bring the phaeton to a stop, Lucy came running out.

She skipped Richard altogether and went straight to Eliza. "You're back!"

"I am. I would never leave my sister." Eliza's fingers ran across a new bruise on the child's cheek. She looked up at Richard, a fire burning behind her gray eyes. "We are leaving within the hour."

Richard couldn't agree more.

Aunt Beatrice lurked in the doorway.

He sent a runner into Ingleton to fetch a hired post chaise. As soon as it arrived, they loaded up Lucy's belongings and were on their way yet again. Lucy tucked snugly between himself and Eliza, a huge grin on her face.

It took them three more days before they reached Richard's home in Berkshire. By the time they did, he was thoroughly and utterly sick of traveling. Eliza must have been as well. For Lucy, it was all a grand adventure.

The carriage came to a stop, and Lucy was the first to spill out. His housekeeper, Mrs. Hampton, came out to meet them, followed by his butler, Mr. Weston. Richard had sent word ahead that he would be arriving today with his sister and his new wife. He could only imagine the shock that must have rippled through his household. Even he, never in his life, imagined a wedding such as the one he'd just had.

"Welcome to Whitestone," Richard said, holding Eliza's hand while she descended the carriage steps.

Eliza gazed up at the house. It was probably not as grand as Mr. Barrington's. Or even perhaps the one Eliza had lived in before he had carried her off to Scotland and back. But it was warm and bright and home. He prayed desperately that she would be happy here.

"It's lovely," she said. "It's perfect." She hooked her arm around his and followed him as he made the introductions to his staff.

"Mrs. Hampton, Mr. Weston, allow me to present my wife, Eliza Arden."

Mrs. Hampton showed them to the dining room where a hearty meal was spread out. It was so good to be finally home. Lucy ate and ate, until her head began to nod and Richard worried she might fall asleep in her pudding.

"I'll see her to bed," Eliza said, rising from the dinner table and taking the hand of Lucy, who had nearly fallen asleep in her boiled potatoes.

He waited awhile, sipping his brandy at the table, then climbed the staircase to Lucy's room. A real and proper room for the young lady she was becoming. The door was ajar, and through it came the voices of Eliza and Lucy. Richard paused to listen.

"What if Aunt Beatrice comes here to get me?" Lucy asked.

"Even if a hundred Aunt Beatrices come, they could never take you away. Your brother would never allow it. Neither would I."

Richard peeked in to see the smile on Lucy's face.

"Now be brave because you are safe."

Lucy nodded.

"The more courage you show in this life, the fewer trials you will have in your next life, when you are born again. That is because you will have already proved your strength."

What would the vicar say if he heard this conversation?

Richard pushed through the door. "You *are* very strong and very brave," he affirmed. "And Eliza is right, you are safe now."

Eliza laughed. "Eavesdropping again?"

He shrugged. "It's a habit I can't seem to break." He placed a kiss on Lucy's forehead and tucked the covers up under her chin. The exhausted child was already asleep by the time they closed the door. He guided Eliza to the other part of the house.

"This will be your chamber," he said, not quite daring to meet her eyes. This was their first night alone since the hasty wedding in Gretna Green. They'd either been traveling or

Eliza had shared a bed with Lucy at the coaching inns along the way.

"It's very nice." Eliza looked around the room, at everything in it except Richard. He must not have been the only one feeling unsettled at that moment.

His ears burned as he said, "And I will be right through here if you should need anything." He pointed to the adjoining door leading to his bedchamber.

"Thank you." She seemed very interested in the weave of the carpet.

"Well then." He took a step toward her.

She must be so tired from travel. She'd not gotten a full night's sleep in all the time he'd known her. He placed a finger under her chin and lifted her head, his eyes drawn to her lips. Instead he placed a kiss on her forehead, just as he had done to Lucy. Though this didn't feel anything like kissing Lucy.

"Good night. I hope that you will be happy here." He forced himself to step away.

Once through the door and into his own room, he went straight to his washstand, splashing cool water on his face. He took off his coat and tossed it over the back of a chair. He would give her time to settle in. And time to sort out her true feelings for him.

Was she here only to escape Mr. Barrington? Perhaps it was only her sympathy for Lucy? Maybe he should have offered her a way out besides a wedding when he'd found her at the smithy in Gretna Green. He would have taken her away from Barrington even if she had refused marriage.

There was a knock on his door. Not the door to the hallway but the door leading to Eliza's room.

He wiped his face with a towel and pulled the door open. Eliza stood there, her cheeks red, her eyes on his, glowing like silver moons. How beautiful she was. He marveled again at the strange events that had led to this remarkable woman standing in his bedchamber.

His wife. He could still scarcely believe it.

She was his. His Eliza.

"Mr. O'Connell," she said. "I can't seem to manage the buttons on the back of my dress."

Julie Daines was born in Concord, Massachusetts, and was raised in Utah. She spent eighteen months living in London, where she studied and fell in love with English literature, sticky toffee pudding, and the mysterious guy who ran the kebab store around the corner.

She loves reading, writing, and watching movies—anything that transports her to another world. She picks Captain Wentworth over Mr. Darcy, firmly believes in second breakfast, and never leaves home without her verveine.

Visit Julie here:
Website: JulieDaines.com
Facebook: https://www.facebook.com/julie.daines.7

A Lady of Scandal

-Heather B. Moore-

One

Lady Bridget Wilde's marriage lasted four hours. In that fourth hour, it ended quite abruptly with a resounding finality when her husband, Lord Anthony Wilde, the son of the Earl of Marsden, shot himself. On accident, of course. In the middle of a rather rambunctious wedding party that took place *after* the first wedding party where all the respectable folk had been in attendance. The second party was the one in which pistols were fired into the air after each round of drinks.

Ironically, when Anthony first collapsed to the ground, his friends had roared in laughter. Some of these particular friends hadn't been at the wedding but had been only too happy to show up for the wedding-party-after-the-wedding-party.

It was Bridget who saw the blood first. She had never been the type of woman to faint, but seeing her new husband upon the ground with a bullet wound to the neck made her feel like she was about to faint. Which she promptly did.

When Bridget was revived by a kindly older gentleman who must have seen many days upon the battlefield, since he wasn't fazed by either blood or death, Bridget sat up, only to faint again.

Upon her second revival by the same kindly older gentleman, Bridget gripped his steady hand and said in a voice that only he could hear, "Is my husband dead?"

"I am not a physician, Lady Wilde." The gentleman handed her a mug of something strong to drink.

Bridget took one swallow of the flavorful stuff, grimaced, and handed it back. She scoured the room, looking for Anthony, and saw that he'd been laid upon one of the banquet tables. Men had gathered around him, and Bridget could only assume one of the men was a physician.

"I want to see him." Bridget tried to stand. It was quite a feat to move at all with the volumes of skirts that made up her wedding dress—something that her Aunt Harriet had insisted upon.

The gentleman extended his hand and helped Bridget to her feet.

"I would strongly advise against seeing your husband right away," he said. "Come with me, and we'll wait outside where the air is fresh."

"I want to see him now." Bridget tightened her grip on the gentleman's hand. She felt the hysteria rise, but she was determined not to faint.

"Lady Wilde . . ." The gentleman's voice trailed off when a man with a cropped beard and spectacles turned from the circle surrounding Anthony.

"Are you Lady Wilde?" the man with the spectacles asked.

"Yes," Bridget whispered. She'd been Lady Wilde for less time than it took to stew a Cornish hen.

The man cleared his throat and pushed the spectacles farther up his nose. "I regret to inform you that your husband has died."

Bridget didn't faint a third time. Nor did she move or react in any way. This was not real. This was something no one could have ever dreamed up or planned. Some young widows might consider this the most tragic day of their lives, but Bridget considered it a miracle.

Lord Anthony Wilde, her husband of four and a half hours, was dead.

And Bridget was free.

Two

HUGH WILDE, THE oldest son of the Marquess of Crawton, waved off his valet before Mr. Simon could say a word. It had been a long day, and Hugh had no desire to read through one more piece of correspondence.

Mr. Simon nodded in his dutiful manner. He left the missive on the credenza, which was actually a large scuffed table. This drafty manor lacked the civil furniture Hugh was used to.

Hugh adjusted the thick wool rug about his legs and took another sip of his brandy. The roaring fire in the hearth was taking an age to warm the room, and he wondered why the housekeeper hadn't thought to light the fire hours earlier. It was freezing in Scotland. How did these people live up here year-round? They were a hardy lot, the Scots were. Hugh supposed that he'd get used to the temperature differences if he lived here long enough. As it was, a month had been plenty, and he hoped to finish up the remainder of his business early next week and return home to his father's estate with a full progress report of their Scotland property.

At first, Hugh relished the opportunity to be on his own for a few weeks, to get away from the *ton*'s gossip about whom he might choose for a wife. Ever since his thirtieth birthday, he could practically see the mothers of the debutantes sharpen their painted nails. Hugh didn't embrace the endless social events during the Season. He'd rather spend time with a few friends, discussing politics and things of a more intellectual nature, instead of wooing young misses in the ballroom. But these long nights with only his valet for company had worn on Hugh.

He could, he supposed, visit the local pub again. But when he visited during his first week, all conversation had stopped as soon as he had crossed the threshold. One could have heard a mouse sneeze, the silence was so deafening.

So here Hugh sat, drinking alone. And there, on the table, was another letter from home. Even from his chair, Hugh recognized the fine-milled envelope and his father's seal. Eyeing it more than once, he finally decided that his mind wouldn't let him rest until he read the contents of the letter.

He set his glass of brandy on the side table, heaved himself to his feet—these Scottish chairs were all too low for his long frame—and ambled to the wide table. He picked up the letter, broke the seal, then turned it toward the light of the fire to read his father's hasty scrawl.

In fact, the handwriting was so rushed that Hugh could barely make out the words. And when he finally pieced them into sentences, every part of him went numb. The letter fell from his fingers and drifted to the floor, where it settled onto the aged wood, forgotten.

"Simon!" Hugh bellowed.

The door burst open seconds later, and a harried Mr. Simon came in, mouth agape.

It wasn't often that Hugh called for his valet in such a manner, but the contents of the letter from home had just upended his entire life.

"We're leaving tonight," Hugh said sharply. "Ready the carriage at once!"

"Yes, my lord," Simon said.

When the valet left to notify the driver, who also acted as groomsman and man of all work while on their visit to Scotland, Hugh bent and picked up the letter. He walked closer to the fireplace again and reread the words. This time, though, he didn't yell for Simon. This time, Hugh let the tears fall.

His cousin Anthony, to whom he was as close as any brother he might have had, was dead.

Three

One year and three days later

"YOUR SISTER *MUST* start her Season this year," Aunt Harriet said, looking down her rather long nose at Bridget. "You are the widow of Lord Anthony Wilde, the heir to an earldom, and you must take your place in Society. Your mourning period is over, and you are no longer confined to wearing widow's weeds. Besides, my feet and ankles are in too much pain to act as Phoebe's chaperone. All that traipsing about will overtire my poor swollen feet, and I will surely have a stroke. You would not wish that upon your poor aunt, would you?"

"Of course not," Bridget murmured and looked away from Aunt Harriet's long nose and piercing gaze. The woman could get a wild dog to obey her, but right now, Bridget didn't want to deal with her aunt's insistence about Phoebe.

What was wrong with waiting one more year until the girl was eighteen? As it was, Phoebe acted such a child sometimes, so throwing her into the jaws of the *ton* felt like Bridget was offering a kitten to a tiger.

Bridget exhaled and closed her eyes. The morning meal was over, and she sat with her Aunt Harriet in the drawing room while they waited for Phoebe to fix her hair. They were about to set off to do some shopping.

Harriet put a hand on Bridget's shoulder, a rare show of

affection. "I know you have grieved over losing your husband, my dear. But it is time to move on. Think of your sister and her future."

Bridget literally bit her tongue to keep from letting loose a retort. First of all, she didn't grieve over being Anthony's widow; no, she had in fact loathed him. And all she had thought about, for years and years, *was* her sister Phoebe.

After their parents' deaths, Bridget and her younger sister had been taken in by Aunt Harriet and raised under her watchful eye. Which meant that Bridget was always finding ways to protect her errant sister, and Bridget had become more like a mother to Phoebe than a sister.

Bridget had put off her first Season as long as she could. But when Aunt Harriet threatened to have Phoebe come out first, Bridget had finally relented, and at the age of nineteen, she entered Society. Bridget decided she'd find a husband, then bring her younger sister to her new household, where they could create their own life away from the ever-critical eye of Aunt Harriet.

But when Bridget captured the attention of the legendary rake Lord Anthony Wilde the first week during her first Season, her aunt had flown into action.

"Lord Wilde will be an earl someday, and he will provide well for you," her aunt had said.

"He's said to have mistresses all throughout London," Bridget had argued.

"Pish posh," her aunt had said. "No man is *that* virile, not even one as handsome and well-built as Lord Wilde."

"Aunt Harriet!" Well-bred ladies never spoke of such things, and most likely ill-bred ladies did not either.

"He will please you on your wedding night, that is for certain, and then you'll be free of him while he returns to his mistress," Aunt Harriet continued as if it were perfectly normal to speak of such private matters as marriage beds. "You will have money, an assured place in Society, and freedom."

Bridget had felt sick at her aunt's plan. She wanted to marry, she wanted to protect innocent and impetuous Phoebe, but *Lord Wilde*? She'd rather marry one of the older gentlemen and not a famed rake. At the very next event, she purposefully avoided all eye contact and chances at conversation with Lord Wilde. Yes, he was devastatingly handsome with his dark, wavy hair, deep green eyes, and generous lips that quirked at the slightest amusement. Yes, he made her laugh, but there wasn't that connection she thought should be there with a true love match.

Lord Anthony Wilde didn't love her; he was merely a flirt, and she was the newest debutante. He didn't see a future wife in her—although she did have a nice dowry left to her, it wasn't a fortune like some women. Lord Wilde had plenty of wealth to call his own.

Bridget had been proud of herself for avoiding Lord Wilde at several events until the musicale at the Arringtons'. Bridget had fetched a glass of punch during an intermission and thought she heard the whimper of a small child coming from one of the corridors. She knew Mrs. Arrington had a young son, and Bridget wondered if he'd escaped the nursery. Perhaps his nanny was looking for him. Bridget stepped into the corridor and followed the sound until she reached the library.

The sound had stopped. Perhaps the child was inside the library? She pushed open the door. Several candles had been lit, and although there were deep shadows near the bookcases, there was no evidence of a child. Bridget walked into the room a few paces, scanned the corners, then turned to leave.

A dark form shifted in the chair near the door. Bridget flinched in surprise, then quickly recovered herself. "Oh, excuse me," she'd said to the man who sat with his legs stretched out. He seemed to be in deep thought, or even half-asleep. Perhaps he was an older man, tired of the musicale and in need of rest. "I didn't see you there."

When he lifted his head, she saw that it was Lord Anthony Wilde.

Oh no. She explained her reason for being in that part of the house, then quickly made her exit . . . Only to run into Mr. and Mrs. Arrington. She was so surprised that she actually stumbled backward, into the arms of Lord Wilde, who had apparently decided to rise and follow her out into the corridor. Nothing else could explain why he was there to catch her fall.

Yet Mr. and Mrs. Arrington didn't see it that way. It was their home, and something untoward had happened in their library. By the time several members of the *ton* had come down the corridor, smelling a scandal as a dog smells fresh meat, Bridget was in tears.

Her predicament would have been made worse only by the arrival of her Aunt Harriet. Which of course happened. Harriet came upon the scene and called out Lord Wilde in such a way that Bridget's father probably heard it in his grave two counties away.

Bridget married Lord Anthony Wilde three weeks later, not even waiting for his close family members to travel to the estate for the celebration. Anthony hadn't even waited for his cousin Hugh to return from his travels to Scotland, even though they'd been raised like brothers as they grew up on neighboring estates and went to school together. Bridget had found out the reason for Anthony's haste later.

"There you are!" her aunt said as Phoebe came into the drawing room.

Phoebe was all ruffles today, pink and white, and it only made her look like an eleven-year-old girl. Yet Aunt Harriet had said that ruffles were all the rage, and so Phoebe must oblige. They would be out and about in the London streets, and Phoebe needed to be seen and noticed. Phoebe's blonde curls and blue eyes made her look like a painted china doll, especially so now because her pink dress brought out the rosy blush of her cheeks.

Bridget had once been as young and innocent as her

blonde, blue-eyed sister; although Bridget's hair was a darker blonde and her eyes more gray than blue, it was plain they were sisters.

Aunt Harriet rose to her feet, her gaze sweeping over every inch of Phoebe with a critical eye. "We haven't got all day, you know. The invitations are already starting to come in, and I will be responding in the affirmative that I'll be bringing both of my nieces." At that point, she looked at Bridget, as if challenging her to argue.

But Bridget knew she was defeated. Last Season, she'd been in mourning, and this Season, Harriet was determined to make a match for Phoebe. Upon Anthony's death, Bridget had been offered the dower house at the Glenwood Estate, but she'd declined. Bridget didn't want to live on the same property of her deceased husband's family. His parents had made no secret of their dislike for Bridget.

Bridget had never dreamed that Anthony would propose, right then and there in front of Mr. and Mrs. Arrington and their guests. She was left with little choice but to accept his suit, since she could not very well publicly turn him down.

It was perhaps the only honorable thing Anthony had ever done in his life as far as she could tell.

Bridget had spent the year out of Society, trying to forget all that had led up to her fateful marriage and Anthony's death. But her time was up. Although her own tale was a tragic one, she could still find hope in Phoebe's future.

Oh, Phoebe, Bridget thought as she watched her sister pull on her new gloves. The girl was sweet, guileless, and Bridget would do anything to protect her from the scoundrels of London. She didn't want her younger sister experiencing the embarrassment that Bridget had.

Bridget stood and held her hand out to her sister. "Are you ready to take on the *ton*?" she asked with a smile she didn't truly feel. "We must have you the best-turned-out debutante in Society."

Four

"YOU ARE TO play a ballroom dandy, then?" Jeremy drawled as he stretched his legs before Hugh's cheery library fire. It was early afternoon, but the driving rain outside contributed to the need to light the fireplace of the family town house in London.

Hugh had been friends with Jeremy, Earl of Lansing, since their school days at Eton. The man had always been extremely perceptive, even in his youth, which today was annoying Hugh.

"I wouldn't go that far," Hugh said. "My cousin Walter has infringed upon my parents long enough. Father hasn't been able to shake his illness, and so Walter is coming to stay with me for the Season."

"You and your cousins," Jeremy drawled. "You were always as thick as thieves. No one could pull one over on the Wilde boys at Eton."

Hugh gave a slow nod. It was true—he and his cousin Anthony had spent almost all their days together, running between their neighboring estates in their youth. Riding horses. Hunting. Failing at school. Well, when Hugh's marks started to fall, his father had threatened his inheritance. Hugh shaped up after that.

But Anthony never really seemed to take life seriously.

And then there was Walter, a few years younger. When he came to visit on holidays, he was like the runt of the group.

An annoying puppy always nipping at their heels. But manhood made all things equal, and now it seemed Hugh's father wanted Walter to spend the Season in London with Hugh.

"Well, perhaps you'll enjoy the company," Jeremy quipped.

"Very funny." Hugh didn't like company around the clock. He was his own man and kept to his own schedule. Jeremy was one of his few friends he kept in touch with. "I'll introduce Walter around at a few events, then let the invitations take over from there. He doesn't need my help. He's never had a problem making friends."

"Much like Anthony?"

The familiar pain of loss came sharp and swift, but it left almost as soon as it came. Months ago, it would have dwelled much longer. Even though Hugh and Anthony had been cousins, Hugh felt the loss of Anthony as if he'd lost a brother. They were even similar in appearance, though opposites in personality.

Anthony was always the center of any gathering and drew plenty of attention from the ladies. He had known everyone in London, and everyone knew him. It was both an advantage and his downfall. If Anthony had had fewer overeager friends and hadn't felt the need to please them all the time, perhaps he would be alive today. Perhaps he'd have a child on the way with his new wife, and Hugh wouldn't be facing a Season taking round their cousin Walter.

Once Hugh stepped into a ballroom, the matrons and their eligible daughters would see him as on the market. In his thirtieth year, and as the only son of the Marquess of Crawton, Hugh was considered a prime catch on the market for a wife.

"Anthony was one of a kind," Hugh said in a slow voice. "Not even our cousin Walter can measure up."

Jeremy chuckled. "I'll agree with you there, my friend. Anthony's wife must have been a diamond of the first water to snare the man. What's she like?"

"Anthony's widow?" Hugh said. "I have no idea. I've never met the woman."

Jeremy pulled his legs in and sat up. "What? How is that possible?"

Hugh shrugged and poured himself a brandy. "Anthony and I had become distant the last couple of years—he stayed in his rut, and I dug myself out. His widow had fled the estate by the time I returned home. Went to live with an aunt or someone. Wasn't interested in the Glenwood dower house, it seems. Anthony's mother was quite bitter about it all, and my mother took it upon herself to fill me in on the details."

"On the marriage or the runaway widow?"

"Both." It was no secret that Anthony and the lady in question had been caught in a compromising position at a social event. Hugh imagined that his cousin had let his lusts get the better of him, and well, the mistake was well paid for now. With Anthony's life. If Anthony hadn't offered for the woman, there wouldn't have been a wedding, and there wouldn't have been a wedding party, and Anthony wouldn't have drunkenly shot himself.

"I've never met her either," Jeremy said. "Sounds like one of those women who was after your family's money."

"Perhaps." Although if that were the case, why would Anthony's widow turn down the dower house at Glenwood? It was nicer than most homes of the *ton*, and she would continue being included in family events and hold an esteemed place in Society.

"Bridget was her name, right?" Jeremy persisted on the topic.

"I believe so, yes." Hugh very well knew her name to be Lady Bridget Reeve, or more accurately Lady Wilde. Because if Hugh were ever in the same room as her, he'd be sure to stay very far away. He didn't know if he'd be able to control the temper that had been simmering for over a year because of his cousin's tragic death. So what if Anthony had been a scoundrel and had dallied with the wrong woman? That didn't mean he should have married her and lost his life.

Not that it was exactly cause and effect, but it had happened, and there was no denying the facts. Because of Bridget Reeve, his cousin was dead. Because of Bridget Reeve, Hugh had a huge hole in his life. He'd never be able to reconcile with his cousin. They couldn't reminisce about their childhoods. They'd no longer share Christmases together.

It seemed there was a lot of unhappiness to blame on a woman he'd never met.

"You're coming with us, you know," Hugh told Jeremy.

"What?" Jeremy's eyes pulled wide.

"To the social events—I'm not going to be following Walter about—you and I can hit the card tables," Hugh said. "I need some sort of prize for playing the dutiful cousin."

Jeremy grinned. "You've had a letter from your mother, haven't you?"

Letters from his mother, letters from his father, letters from Walter himself. It seemed that the whole blasted family was looking for Hugh to save the family lineage. Anthony's death had put everyone on edge. If Hugh didn't produce an heir, then Walter was next in line, and no one wanted that. Least of all Hugh.

"You very well know my family's expectations," Hugh said. "It's the same in every family of the peerage."

Jeremy tapped his fingers against the armrest of his chair. "And? Is this where the woe-is-me begins?"

Hugh scoffed.

"Poor me, I'm going to be a marquess someday, and I'll be one of the richest men in the kingdom." Jeremy paused. "Should I go on?"

Hugh shook his head at his friend's idiocy.

"Poor me, I'll have to find a beautiful woman to be my wife who will want nothing more than to please me and bear my sons."

"That's enough," Hugh said, trying not to smile.

"Poor me, I'll have to go to a ball and dance with women who can't take their eyes off me. I might even have to kiss one or two of them just to see who is compatible."

Hugh threw his hands up. "It's getting late, don't you think? Shouldn't you be on your way home by now? Don't want to get caught in the rain."

Both he and Jeremy knew that the sky was bone dry.

Jeremy rose to his feet anyway. "Three is my maximum."

"Maximum for what?" Hugh asked.

"For social events," he said. "You forget, I'm two years younger than you are, which means I still have plenty of time before my mother starts writing me letters."

"I'm going to hold you to the three, then." Hugh shook his friend's hand. It was good to spend time with Jeremy. It almost brought him back to the old days—the days that included his cousin Anthony.

"And when does the first event take place?" Jeremy asked as Hugh walked him into the main hall.

"Tomorrow night," Hugh said. "Walter arrives in the afternoon, and we are to go to the Fords' ball."

"A ball? That's quite the introduction to your country cousin," Jeremy commented. "How long has he been traveling the continent?"

"About five years," Hugh said. "There was some scandal before he left, although I don't recall the details. I've conveniently forgotten them."

Jeremy chuckled. "Tomorrow night, then." He set off down the wide stairs in front of the town house that led to the street. There, he climbed in his carriage.

Hugh waved then gazed up at the sky, wishing it would rain. If it rained like mad, perhaps it would delay Walter's arrival. Or even better, perhaps Walter would stay at Glenwood.

Five

PHOEBE RUSHED INTO Bridget's room. "Can I borrow your blue ribbon?" she gushed.

Bridget turned from her own toilette to see her sister wearing a light-blue gown, her blonde hair hanging about her shoulders. "Your hair isn't even pinned up," Bridget said. "Harriet expects to leave within the hour."

"I know. Maren said she needs to weave in the ribbon right from the beginning," Phoebe said. "We tried the silver, but it's not wide enough."

Bridget rose from her vanity and walked to her wardrobe, where she kept her ribbons laid out in the top drawer. She selected the light-blue one and handed it over to Phoebe.

"Thank you," Phoebe said, then she paused. "And you look very pretty, sister."

Bridget smiled. "Go on with you. I'm not the one who will be getting the compliments tonight." Even so, after Phoebe left the bedchamber, Bridget stood before the full-length mirror to inspect her appearance. She was not on the shelf quite yet, but she was a widow. One who'd been caught up in a scandal before her marriage.

Many of the people she'd see tonight would remember the scandal and the subsequent marriage. A year wasn't nearly long enough to be forgotten, not at all. Bridget lifted her chin and turned her head to the right. Her hair was swept into a soft twist, with ringlets coming down on both sides. She no longer looked like a young miss but a woman who was older, wiser, and had seen her share of hardship.

She brought a hand to her décolletage. She was showing more skin than she had in a long time. Her black mourning dresses had been severe in their modesty. But this pale violet dress was a pretty and delicate garment, and she hoped she wouldn't be confused with the other young women in their first Season. For Bridget planned to keep a very close eye on her sister and wasn't at all interested in dancing any of the sets herself.

The last time she'd danced was at her wedding, in the arms of Anthony. She hadn't her father there to dance with, and Anthony's father, the Earl of Marsden, had no inclination to do her the honor.

It was just as well; his son was dead before the night was over, and Bridget had felt enough blame and incrimination from his parents to last her a lifetime. Bridget sat back down at her vanity table and clipped on her pearl earrings, then fastened her pearl necklace.

It was the wedding jewelry that Anthony had given her. They'd been the family pearls handed down from one of his great-grandmothers. Bridget hadn't been clear on the story, but she knew they were valuable, both in cost and sentiment. She hadn't worn the set since her wedding day, and it seemed only fitting that on her first night out in Society, she'd wear them again. They would be a sort of homage to her dead husband, no matter that she hadn't wanted to marry him, or that he wasn't in love with her. He'd still done her the honor of asking for her hand to avoid her ruination.

Wearing his family's jewels would give her the strength to hold her head up and take any barbs, verbal or silent, thrown her way. She was the widow of a known rake, and her marriage had lasted only hours, but she was still connected with the Earl of Marsden's family, and she would act accordingly.

By the time Bridget descended the stairs of her aunt's town house, her aunt was waiting at the bottom, tapping her foot. Her aunt was coming to this inaugural event to make her presence and recommendation known but would view the ball from a comfortable settee while holding a glass of lemonade. "Ah, there you are. Where is your sister?"

Bridget was not surprised that Phoebe wasn't quite ready, but it was yet five minutes before the hour, and Phoebe wasn't exactly late. "She is on her way," Bridget said, although she couldn't say for sure.

Her Aunt Harriet had dressed to the latest fashion, and although plenty of gray streaked through her hair, she still made an elegant presentation.

"You look well, Aunt," Bridget said.

Harriet's thin brows lifted. "Thank you. And you are a vision."

The words were automatic, spoken with little emotion, but Bridget didn't mind. In truth, she was used to this aunt of hers who had kept Bridget and her sister under her roof for ten years. When her parents were killed in a carriage accident, Harriet had been the first to step forward and offer to take the girls in. A widow herself, Harriet had no children from her marriage.

Bridget often wondered how different her life might be if her parents hadn't been killed. Would she have ever even met Anthony Wilde? No matter. The past couldn't be changed, and tragedies couldn't be erased. The only thing they could do was look toward the future.

And the future was descending the steps right now.

"Oh, lovely," Harriet exclaimed.

Bridget heard the pride in her aunt's voice and was glad for it. Phoebe truly looked lovely, like a beautiful oasis of color that would stand out in the ballroom. Bridget exhaled, and a tingle spread through her body. She touched the pearls at her neck. This was it. She was to face Society again after a full year, and she would be doing it with her younger sister.

"Do you like my hair?" Phoebe said in her sweet voice, giving a twirl so that her dress bloomed. She offered a view of her intricate hairdo intertwined with blue ribbon.

"You will be the talk of the *ton*," Harriet said in a breathless voice. "Come on, dear girl. Let's get you into the carriage."

Phoebe giggled, and Bridget followed after the pair.

"Mind the puddles," Aunt Harriet said.

The coachman handed her in after the other women were settled. It had rained a lot over the past two days, and the puddles of water could be disastrous to ballroom slippers.

As Harriet talked about all the people who should be at the Fords' ball and Phoebe listened wide-eyed, Bridget tried to tamp down the tightening of her stomach. Every movement of the carriage brought them closer to their destination, closer to members of the *ton* who had spread gossip about her.

By the time they reached the circular drive of the Fords' mansion, Bridget was gripping her hands so tightly together, she knew had she not been wearing her gloves, she'd be able to see the whites of her knuckles.

As the carriage waited its turn to pull before the wide steps leading to the front entrance, Phoebe leaned forward to get a better view of the elegant men and women exiting their carriages and ascending the steps.

"It's all like a dream," Phoebe said. "Do you think anyone will ask me to dance?"

Harriet gave a soft laugh. "You'll be invited to dance the moment you are spotted. The young men won't be able to keep their eyes off you."

Bridget's stomach only hardened, and she swallowed back her rising dread. Not only would she have to watch out for the men who would pay attention to Phoebe, she would have to deflect any negative comments sent in her direction.

Finally, it was their turn to alight from the carriage. The coachman opened the door for them, handing each of them down in turn. Harriet took Phoebe's arm as they started up the steps, and Bridget followed dutifully.

They were introduced to Mr. and Mrs. Ford, who were very polite in their greetings. Bridget felt no censure in their gazes, and she was warmly welcomed when she stepped forward. She began to relax a little; perhaps tonight would not be so difficult after all.

The music and the blazing candles inside the main ballroom cast warm golds about the room. Several couples were already dancing the cotillion, and Phoebe's gasp of delight echoed Bridget's sentiments exactly. If only Bridget hadn't suffered a scandal and a tragic wedding day, she might be dazzled just as her sister was at the beautiful gowns worn by the women and elegant suits worn by the men.

"Mrs. Thomas, Mr. Thomas," their aunt greeted a young gentleman who'd approached with an older woman who must have been his mother.

Thus, the introductions began. True to Harriet's prediction, Phoebe was asked to dance within minutes of their arrival. Bridget would be more than happy to play her aunt's companion, while observing Phoebe.

The women made their way to a group of settees, and Harriet claimed one for her own, immediately requesting that Bridget bring her a lemonade. Bridget obliged and fetched two glasses, one for Harriet and one for her sister, but when she reached Harriet again, Phoebe had already been collected for her first dance.

"Look, there," Harriet said, nodding her head toward the ballroom floor.

Moving in and out of the couples in the dance formation of the cotillion was Phoebe, practically floating, so light was she on her feet. Bridget stared at her sister, feeling the pride swell in her bosom. She was beautiful, and she was definitely getting noticed. Every man who passed by her turned his head, and every woman was paying attention.

The dance ended, and just as predicted, Phoebe was swept into the next dance. And another one. Bridget watched each man who led Phoebe out, and Harriet filled her in on each man's particular pedigree.

"Excuse me," a voice said to her left. "I hope I may be so bold as to approach you since we are related by your marriage."

Bridget looked up to see a young man, perhaps twenty-five in age. His dark-brown hair was tied back, as if he were from another time, but he was impeccably dressed in the latest fashion. He had polished manners, yet something about him seemed foreign, though Bridget couldn't quite place it since he had no accent.

Her aunt peered at the young gentleman too.

At what must have been a confused look on Bridget's face, the man took another step closer and explained. "Your husband, Anthony, is my cousin. I was traveling when the two of you married, and I regret I was not able to give you my regards before . . . he—"

"What is your name, young man?" Aunt Harriet cut in, using her most haughty voice.

At this point, Bridget was grateful for her aunt's brazenness. Was this Hugh? The cousin of Anthony's who'd been in Scotland?

"Walter," he said with a bow. When he straightened, his gaze met Bridget's. "Walter Stephens. At your service. My father is the younger brother of the Earl of Marsden."

He wasn't Hugh. She tried to place the name Walter and realized that it did sound familiar. Anthony's father had two brothers. One was a marquess, the other a baron. Walter must be the son of the baron.

Bridget swallowed against the dryness of her throat and wished she hadn't already finished her lemonade. She had never dreamed she would be faced with a family member of Anthony's . . . But it was inevitable that it would happen at some point. She tried to match her memory of Anthony with Walter's appearance. There was little resemblance. Anthony's hair had been dark, his eyes a deep green, his presence like a magnet. This man was more subtle in his appearance, but there was a worldliness about him that Bridget was unfamiliar with. As if he'd lived far and wide, and conventions in a London ballroom didn't stop him from seeking an introduction to a stranger, albeit their loose connection.

"Thank you for introducing yourself," Bridget said. "I am Lady Bridget Wilde, as you must know, and this is my Aunt Harriet. My sister is also here this evening."

"Ah," Mr. Walter Stephens said with a tentative smile. "Phoebe Reeve. She is the talk of the night already. What a debut!"

The breath left Bridget, and something akin to alarm rushed through her. She tried to shake the feeling, but it persisted. She had to think of how to get rid of this man. She had to ask her aunt what she knew of Walter Stephens.

But it was too late. "I'd be honored if you would dance the next set with me."

Bridget couldn't answer, couldn't think. He was asking *her* to dance? Because of their connection? Because she was the veritable wallflower? Because of Phoebe?

The silence had drawn out too long, and Mr. Stephens's expression fell. Guilt rushed through Bridget, and before she could think of any consequences, she said, "Thank you. I will stand up with you."

She thought she heard her aunt exhale, but Bridget didn't know if it was in relief or frustration. In any case, Mr. Stephens extended his hand, and Bridget was on her feet in one moment. In the very next moment, he was leading her to the dance floor.

It was then that she knew this had all been a monumental mistake. The next number was a waltz, which not only put her in close proximity with Mr. Stephens but required that she be in his arms the entire dance.

The last time she'd waltzed was with her husband . . .

"I—I am sorry," she said, backing away from Mr.

Stephens's outstretched hand. "I thought I could do this, but I cannot. I am only recently out of mourning."

Mr. Stephens's smile faltered, but then he quickly changed tactics. "Do not worry. I understand. Shall I escort you back to your aunt? Perhaps fetch you some lemonade?"

Bridget was trembling. "Yes," she managed to say.

Mr. Stephens said nothing as he escorted her back to Harriet. He merely bowed as he released her, then left to get the offered lemonade.

"Whatever is the matter?" Harriet asked when he was out of earshot.

Bridget pressed her lips together. She knew if she tried to explain, she would start crying. It was unfathomable really. She hadn't even been in love with Anthony. He had been a fool in more ways than one. Yet the waltz was what had set her off.

Harriet seemed to know not to press for information, this time, and patted her hand.

Mr. Stephens returned within minutes. His expression was unreadable as he handed over the lemonade. "Have an enjoyable evening, ladies. I hope to see more of you this Season." With that, he left.

Bridget brought the glass to her lips and took a long swallow. She closed her eyes as the sweet coolness soothed her throat. Perhaps it was too early to attend balls. Perhaps her year of mourning would turn into a lifetime of mourning. Not that she mourned her husband, but what might have been if she had never gone to that library.

Bridget opened her eyes. Another woman had come to sit on the other side of Harriet, and the two women struck up an immediate conversation.

Bridget scanned the waltzers for her sister, and after a moment, she saw Phoebe, who looked as if she were still enjoying herself.

Then Bridget caught sight of Mr. Walter Stephens weaving his way through the crowd. Guilt still plagued her, but he had been understanding enough. Perhaps Bridget would stay away from events that had dancing, except where would that leave Phoebe?

Bridget was still watching Mr. Stephens's progress when he stopped by a couple of other gentlemen who had by all appearances decided not to participate in the dancing either. Mr. Stephens certainly seemed animated as he spoke to the gentlemen, who had turned and were listening to him intently. One of the men was quite tall and lean, with brown, wavy hair. The second man was dark-haired, and when Mr. Stephens shifted to one side, Bridget got a clear view of him.

All warmth drained from her body, and she felt light-headed. It couldn't be. It was impossible. The man across the ballroom was Anthony.

Or a man who looked enough like him that there could be no doubt . . . he was the cousin never met. Anthony had said he and his cousin were similar in appearances, both of them taking after their fathers, who were brothers. The man staring at her now was the son of the Marquess of Crawton and the one whom Anthony had cursed more than once at the second wedding party. The cousin that Anthony had said would be a miserable marquess. And if anything happened to Hugh Wilde, Anthony was next in line to inherit and carry on the Wilde family name.

The man was staring straight at her, as Mr. Walter Stephens was surely filling this new cousin's mind with what had just transpired on the dance floor. Bridget grappled for her aunt's hand and squeezed tightly. She felt light-headed and sick at the same time. Much like she had when she'd fainted for the first time, which happened to be at her husband's death.

"What is it?" her aunt said, her voice sounding very far away.

Then Harriet gasped and squeezed Bridget's hand just as hard. "Oh my goodness. It's *him*."

Six

FROM THE MOMENT Walter said *Lady Bridget Wilde*, Hugh hadn't heard another word his cousin had spoken. Hugh looked past Walter and across the ballroom.

Several women sat on the settees which were usually reserved for the matrons or older chaperones. True to form, half a dozen such women were taking up space, most likely to remain there until their younger charges had danced the night through.

But there was a younger woman sitting next to a stern-looking matron.

Bridget. It had to be.

His dead cousin's wife. If Lady Bridget hadn't married Anthony, he would be alive today.

Hugh couldn't stop staring at her, and one thing stood out above all else that he might observe. Lady Bridget Wilde was lovely. Possibly enchanting. For a few brief moments, Hugh observed her as a man might look at a woman, as Anthony must have viewed her for the first time. The honey gold of her hair caught the light of the candle chandeliers, and her eyes were large, luminescent, really.

Her nose was a pert thing, but her mouth generous and nicely shaped, and he wondered what she might look like if she smiled. He quickly dismissed that thought, and instead perused the rest of her being.

Her dress was one of those flimsy layered things of a pale violet that made her look like she belonged in an illustrated book of children's fairy tales. Her shoulders were partly bare as the line of her dress followed the outline of her bosom and then proceeded to fall in soft folds along the rest of her body.

She was slender, that he could assess even though she was sitting down. She had a delicate frame, yet her gaze was full of enough assurance—or was it haughtiness?—that he had no doubt her delicacy was only a persona she was showing in the ballroom.

She held her chin up as she gazed directly back at him, and if he didn't know better, he'd have guessed that she was equally shocked to be faced with him as he was with her.

But then she broke her gaze from him and reached for the hand of the older woman who sat next to her. In the briefest of moments, something flittered across her face. From this distance, he couldn't be sure if it was disdain or grief or something else.

Her expression closed off again, and she tilted her head as the older woman seemed to be speaking rapidly. They had seen him, had recognized him as Anthony's cousin, and now . . . Hugh had to do the only thing that was left to be done. Introduce himself to his dead cousin's widow.

"She is crushed with grief, I tell you," Walter said as Hugh tuned into the conversation for the first time in several moments. "She accepted the dance, but once we stepped into waltz formation, she nearly started crying. From all accounts I've heard tonight, this is her first public appearance since Anthony's . . . death."

Hugh placed a hand on Walter's shoulder to stop his flow of words. The man was a veritable gossip—just like any of those matrons sitting along the wall. In the country, Walter might have spoken his thoughts quite openly, but here, in a London ballroom, eager listeners were only feet away. "We will discuss this all later," Hugh told his cousin, then caught

Jeremy's eye to get his meaning across. "I must give my regards to my, uh, cousin's widow. Please excuse me."

Walter made as if he was to follow, but Hugh stopped him with a shake of the head.

Thankfully, Walter understood and stayed back with Jeremy. Hugh would probably have to buy a drink or meal for Jeremy later to thank him for playing host to Walter. But as Hugh made his way around the dance floor, he was stopped more than once with greetings from acquaintances. He bore each brief delay with an outward calm that he didn't feel inside. If he'd known there was a chance for his cousin's widow to be in attendance tonight, he would have taken Walter to another event.

To have to meet Lady Bridget Wilde for the first time in a crush was not the ideal situation. Although, if Hugh truly considered any benefit, it would be that he'd be on his best behavior and not be tempted to hound her for explanation or plague her with accusations. This introduction would be all that was civil. And Hugh could only pray that he would never have to face her again.

"Lord Wilde," someone said, nearly bumping into him.

"Mr. Toliver." Hugh gave a short bow. The man was one of those inquisitive sorts who always seemed to ask a dozen questions.

"I didn't know you'd be here for the Season," Mr. Toliver continued.

"For only a short time." Hugh tried not to grit his teeth at the interruption. "I'm here with my cousin Walter. I'll introduce you to him later. I've got to speak with someone before they leave for the night."

"Very well," Mr. Toliver said, and opened his mouth to say more.

But Hugh slid past him. He moved around the refreshment table and finally arrived at the location where he'd last seen Lady Bridget Wilde.

But . . . she was not there.

Hugh narrowed his gaze and knew that the empty settee before him was where she'd been sitting just moments ago. He exhaled, his mind racing through the possibilities. Was she dancing? He scanned the nearby dancers. She couldn't have gone far. With no immediate sight of her violet gown, he turned to the refreshment tables. Perhaps he'd walked right past her, although he very much doubted it.

No. She was not at the refreshment table either.

He snapped his gaze to the empty settee. The woman's companion was gone too . . . Then he caught sight of a flash of violet just as a woman exited the terrace doors and disappeared into the dark beyond.

Hugh swallowed against the dryness of his throat. It wasn't an ideal situation to follow a woman into the gardens, but he'd do what he must. He deserved answers about his cousin.

Walking along the edge of the crush, heading toward the terrace, brought no more interruptions. Apparently the expression on his face warded off anyone who thought to give him a friendly greeting.

When he reached the exit, he waited as a foursome came through the terrace doors, chattering the night away and oblivious to Hugh's impatience. Then he stepped through the doors. The night was chilly, and he couldn't see how any lady wearing a ball gown wouldn't take the time to fetch her wrap first. Hugh's formal suit, in addition to the indignation boiling hot through him, kept him quite warm.

He crossed the terrace, passing a couple who stood quite close to each other. But Hugh wasn't looking for a man-and-woman pair. He was looking for two women. Descending the handful of steps, he scanned the garden area. Benches were situated among the hedges, and a winding path led toward what looked like a rose garden—half-frozen now, of course.

Hugh would follow that path. He started on his way, seeing that the path led toward a gazebo, then he slowed his step. Two women were walking toward him.

The moonlight made no secret that one of the women was indeed Lady Bridget. The women stood aside on the path before even looking at him as soon as they heard his footsteps, but Hugh had no intention of passing them by.

Then Lady Bridget lifted her eyes. Her lips parted in surprise, and her older companion gasped. Then both women paused and curtsied.

Hugh knew it wasn't out of respect for his title; no, it was merely a reflex of good manners. He could see in both women's eyes that they were none too happy to see him.

He offered his own brief bow, then found that his words had somehow stuck in his throat.

Lady Bridget and her companion hadn't donned their shawls, which gave Hugh plenty to see this close up to her. He'd been privy to the seductions of women aplenty, and he knew that the last thing he should be noticing about Lady Bridget was how well her gown fit her curves, especially when she was standing, and the raised hairs on her upper arms. He had a sudden urge to slip off his coat and drape it across her shoulders.

"Lord Wilde," the companion said, her voice reedy.

Hugh glanced at the older woman. "Whom may I have the pleasure of addressing?"

"I am Mrs. Harriet Reeve," the woman said. "And this is my niece, Lady Bridget Wilde. Who, of course, you must know."

"We have never met," Hugh said, his gaze cutting back to Lady Bridget.

Her eyes widened slightly as their gazes connected again, and she pressed her lips together.

Hugh continued. "And I very much would like to ask Lady Bridget a few questions." He looked to Mrs. Reeve. "If you don't mind giving us some privacy."

"Oh." Mrs. Reeve's brows drew together. "We were just about to return to the ball."

"I will return her directly to your company," Hugh said, keeping his voice calm, yet firm.

Mrs. Reeve's mouth opened, then closed. "I—I will wait near the terrace." She lifted her chin. "Propriety, and all—"

"Do as you wish, ma'am," Hugh cut in. "But I do not think that a man speaking to his cousin's widow would make the news in the gossip pages."

"Of—of course not," Mrs. Reeve said, her expression taking on a haughty edge. She turned to Lady Bridget. "You do not have to speak to this man if you do not want to."

Lady Bridget touched her aunt's arm. "Give us a moment, then I'll be inside shortly. Do not worry about me." Something in her eyes flashed. Determination? Anger?

Mrs. Reeve finally continued along the path, and Hugh glanced back to make sure the woman was out of hearing range before he turned back to Lady Bridget.

But when he turned back, she was moving in the opposite direction from him. At quite a rapid pace, which told him that she did *not* want to speak with him. It took a moment for Hugh's mind to catch up to what she was doing—she was running from him, giving him the cut direct.

Hugh exhaled and started after her. Even at her rapid pace, he had no trouble pursuing her and gaining ground. "Lady Bridget," he said in an urgent whisper, but she did not slow.

Perhaps she wanted to speak in the gazebo . . . but no, she continued past it, and then she was suddenly out of sight.

"Lady Bridget!" Hugh commanded a bit louder. How far would she go? And why did she think she could avoid him—her own relative?

Hugh hurried around the gazebo and saw her turning by a rather large hedge. In three strides, he caught up with her. He grasped her arm, bringing her to a stop, and he pivoted her to face him.

She was out of breath, as she should be, but she looked

up at him. The moonlight didn't let him decipher what he saw in the depths of her eyes—*Pain? Fear of him? Guilt?*

The skin of her arm was cold where he held her; in fact, she seemed to be trembling with cold. Despite the anger and questions tumbling through his mind, he couldn't watch this woman shiver. He released her and shrugged off his coat.

"I have questions," Hugh said, holding out the coat to her.

But the infernal woman folded her arms and stepped back.

Hugh's hand immediately shot out, and he grasped her arm. "Do not run from me," he said through gritted teeth. "You owe me answers."

She blinked a couple of times. She wasn't going to cry, was she?

Hugh moved closer, and he realized he could smell the faint scent of oranges. Oranges in winter? Lady Bridget must be wearing an orange blossom perfume. She shivered, and it brought him back to his senses.

He dropped his hand, then held out the coat again. "Take the coat. You'll freeze."

"I don't want anything from you, or your family," she said in a low voice, taking another step back. "I'd rather freeze to death than take your coat."

And the tiniest bit of guilt started to creep into Hugh's heart. He tamped it down right away. "Don't be foolish. You're shivering."

"I'm not shivering because it's cold out here," she said, but her trembling lips gave her away. "I'm shivering because I don't deserve your censure. I never wanted to marry your cousin. I would have been more happy living as a ruined woman in the country. I never wanted or needed Anthony. And I don't need or want anything from you or any of your family members. My marriage is over, and as far as I am concerned, I never want anything to do with the Wilde family again. Once my sister's future is secured this Season, I will gladly disappear from the Society that made my life a living hell."

Hugh stared at her. This he hadn't expected. He wasn't sure where all her accusations were coming from, but he supposed that the guilty were always the most defensive. He took a step closer, still holding his coat in his hand, and was gratified when she didn't shrink away.

She held his gaze, more confidently than he might have ever expected. Whatever her beliefs were, she was wholly convinced of them. Whatever mess she'd made of his cousin's short life, she certainly didn't take any blame for it.

Hugh wanted to know what had really happened between Anthony and this woman. And Hugh wanted the answers before the night was over. He shook out the coat and moved to set it about her shoulders. The orange blossom scent invaded his senses again, but before he could set the coat upon her shivering shoulders, she stepped forward.

Her body suddenly brushed against his on the narrow path, and at first he thought she might embrace him; but no, she merely pushed past, leaving him and his coat behind.

Hugh watched her go as she picked up her skirts and hurried toward the ballroom. He was suddenly weary. He wasn't going to pursue her. Not tonight, at least. But he would find those answers, one way or another.

Seven

"WHAT DID HE say?" Aunt Harriet asked Bridget as soon as she returned to the ball.

Bridget was still trembling from her encounter with her husband's cousin, Lord Hugh Wilde. She could not fathom the arrogance of a man who would hunt her down in the garden and practically accost her in front of her aunt.

She owed Lord Wilde nothing. Yes, she'd been married to his cousin, but Hugh Wilde hadn't bothered to return for their wedding, or her husband's funeral. Perhaps the closeness that Anthony claimed they had, "as close as brothers," was fictitious. Bridget had decided to put that entire portion of her life behind her. But now, it had caught up to her.

She took a deep breath and patted her aunt's hand. "He had questions about my courtship to Anthony. I told him that Anthony's parents had all of the information he should ever desire to know." This was a lie. But it was what she had to tell her aunt, or Harriet would continue with the questions, and Bridget didn't know how much longer she could hold off the tears.

This was Phoebe's night, and it would remain all about Phoebe. Not about Bridget and the feelings she'd thought she'd buried too deep to ever surface. Her betrothal to Anthony had been humiliating. She'd been seen as a fortune seeker by the *ton*, even though she had her own dowry. She had supposed that with the passage of time, the gossips would have turned their attention to other matters. But a quick marriage, and an even quicker widowhood, had once again brought all focus to Bridget.

She knew one thing. She could not be seen in Lord Hugh Wilde's company. Ever. If he was still in this ballroom, then she'd do whatever it took to avoid him. If only she could return home now and her aunt remain as chaperone. But no, then she'd have to explain more to Aunt Harriet.

"I thought he was very rude," Harriet said. "Not at all charming like his cousin was."

No, Bridget thought. Hugh's personality was not like Anthony's. They were similar in appearance, and there was no doubt they were related. Hugh was taller, broader, and he wore his hair shorter than Anthony had. The dark wave of their hair was close enough in color, but their eyes were different. Anthony's eyes had been an eternal source of amusement, whereas Hugh's eyes were hard. Serious. Bridget had noticed a scar along Hugh's jaw.

Perhaps he was a pugilist. Bridget couldn't imagine Anthony participating in fisticuffs because his frame was slight, and he seemed more interested in the pleasures of life, rather than demonstrating any sort of physical power. But Hugh . . . he was a Corinthian through and through.

Bridget tried to keep her demeanor calm as she glanced about the room to see if Lord Hugh Wilde was again staring at her. But there was no sign of him—no, not for another full hour. It was then that Bridget saw her sister dancing with Mr. Walter Stephens.

Phoebe was all smiles as they went through the movements of the dance together. Bridget narrowed her eyes, wondering how Mr. Stephens dared to ask her sister to dance, when their own dance had been rather disastrous.

"Oh, Phoebe is dancing with the other cousin," Harriet commented.

"Yes." Bridget pressed her mouth together.

"At least he isn't as dour as the older cousin," Harriet said. "Phoebe seems to be enjoying herself. We must find out more about him."

Bridget gritted her teeth. No matter Mr. Walter Stephens's character, she didn't want the two families interacting. The dance number ended, and Phoebe returned to them, bright-eyed and breathless.

"Do you know who that was?" Phoebe asked Bridget.

"Yes—" she started, but Phoebe cut her off.

"He told me that he's afraid you are upset with him because he asked you to dance the waltz," Phoebe said, settling on the settee between Bridget and their aunt.

"I'm not upset with him," Bridget said.

"Oh, I'm so glad," Phoebe said. "He is a sweet man." Her gaze scanned the room. "Everyone has been so complimentary and kind to me this evening. Are balls always like this?"

Harriet patted Phoebe's hand. "They are when you're the most beautiful girl in the room."

Phoebe giggled, and Bridget caught Harriet's eye.

"Oh, here comes . . ." Phoebe's voice trailed off as she studied the man. "Mr. Rowan."

Mr. Rowan turned out to be a tall, thin man with a trim mustache. He bowed elegantly over Phoebe's hand before leading her out to the floor.

Bridget watched her sister practically float off, and then she saw *him*. Lord Wilde was dancing with a red-haired woman who looked to be several years older than him. She was all smiles and made no secret with the cut of her dress that she'd been blessed with many feminine charms. Lord Wilde's face was mostly expressionless as he moved in time to the music.

Perhaps he was rude and abrupt with everyone. No matter how the redhead giggled and simpered, Lord Wilde didn't seem to appreciate what she was all about. This made Bridget sit up straighter and observe a little closer. Anthony would have never been cold to a flirtatious woman. Even at the handful of social events they'd attended together as an engaged couple. He was never too occupied with her to turn down a chance at flirting with any woman who looked his way.

Bridget felt the familiar anger and embarrassment start to rise within her over remembering the way Anthony had acted around her. She was like a playactor in his revenge plot against conventions. He had been determined to do everything that was opposite of his "perfect cousin—Hugh."

Once, on a curricle ride, he told her about the woman his parents had chosen for him to marry. She was the daughter of a marquess and had a significant dowry. "Hugh can have her for all I care," Anthony had touted. "She's like an ice queen and will never give him children. And with no heirs from Hugh, I'll be next in line." At that moment, he looked over at her, as if he were analyzing her child-bearing potential. "You'll never turn me out of your bed, will you, my dear?"

Bridget had flushed hot. She was about to marry and give herself to the one man in London who would never value her more than a broodmare. When she'd tried to complain to her aunt, Harriet had said, "Your children will become your world and solace. What's important is that you will be taken care of for life, and your sister will rise in Society."

Now, sitting in this ballroom and watching Lord Hugh Wilde turn up his nose at a flirtatious woman's conversation, she realized that nothing was ever what it seemed. The son of an earl envied his cousin's inheritance. Whereas the son of the marquess couldn't even enjoy his blessed life and relax at a social event. He had to follow after Bridget and interrogate her. Then he had to make another woman miserable by practically ignoring her on the dance floor.

"That poor woman," Harriet commented. "It seems that Lord Wilde is a veritable ogre with everyone."

"Yes, it does," Bridget murmured.

"His cousin is just the opposite," Harriet continued. "Everyone Mr. Walter Stephens dances with enjoys herself."

It took only a moment for Bridget to see where Mr. Stephens was dancing. Sure enough, he was smiling at his partner . . . Wait. He was smiling at someone else on his right side.

Phoebe. Bridget inhaled. Even though Phoebe and Mr. Stephens were dancing with other partners, they kept making eye contact and smiling.

Bridget's heart sank. This would not do. She would not let another Wilde infiltrate her family.

She looked about for Lord Hugh Wilde again and found him within a couple of moments. His expression hadn't changed, although the redhead seemed more demure than previously. Lord Wilde danced well, and it was obvious he'd been taught and trained, probably as early as the schoolroom. His form was elegant and exacting to the required steps of the dance. And it was quite obvious that the other women in the ballroom were keeping an eye on the most eligible bachelor in the room.

"How are you ladies doing this evening?" a woman's voice cut into Bridget's thoughts. She looked up to see one of her aunt's dearest friends, Mrs. Eliza Darby. The woman was about as round as she was tall, and she was also known for wearing more jewels than any royalty.

"Hello," Harriet said in a warm voice.

"You've brought Bridget with you," Mrs. Darby said. "How wonderful to see her in Society again."

Mrs. Darby always spoke as if Bridget wasn't in the same room. Bridget had stopped letting it bother her long ago.

"Yes, we've brought Phoebe for her first ball," her aunt said with obvious pride in her voice.

"Oh, have you?" Mrs. Darby clapped her puffy hands together. The multiple rings on her fingers clinked together. "Where is she? I must see her!"

Harriet pointed her out, and again Mrs. Darby clapped her hands.

"Sit with us," Harriet said, scooting quite close to Bridget so there was plenty of room for Mrs. Darby.

"I don't mind if I do." Mrs. Darby sighed as she sat by them. "My feet are absolutely aching."

"Mine too," said Harriet, although she'd hardly moved all night from her place.

The two women launched into detailed descriptions of their aches and pains. The current dance number ended, and Bridget watched Lord Wilde lead the redhead off the floor. Her expression was quite serious now, as if one dance with Lord Hugh Wilde had given her the blue devils.

"I couldn't believe it either when Mrs. Fransom told me he was in attendance tonight," Mrs. Darby was saying. "He's the most eligible man here tonight as an unmarried and handsome son of the Marquess of Crawton."

Bridget tuned into the conversation between the two women; it was clear Mrs. Darby was speaking of Lord Hugh Wilde.

"There is a family resemblance, as you can see, but Lord Wilde is nothing like his younger cousins." Mrs. Darby was speaking in a low voice, but it was loud enough for Bridget to hear every word. "They say that he just came out of mourning himself, which I think is odd because the cousins had a falling out."

"Oh? What happened?" her aunt prodded.

Bridget knew, at least from Anthony's viewpoint. She had never shared those details with her aunt, though.

"Some say there was a woman involved . . . one that divided their hearts."

Harriet released a small gasp. "You mean they were both in love with the same woman?"

Mrs. Darby gave a small giggle. "Apparently so. But it turns out that the lady didn't care for either Lord Anthony or Lord Hugh—she was in love with their *other* cousin."

"Mr. Walter Stephens?" Harriet shot out.

"You know him?" Mrs. Darby said. "Of course you know

him! He's . . ." She looked over at Bridget. "He's family to Lord Anthony."

"He's *here*, tonight," Harriet confided. "He introduced himself to us, and he danced with Phoebe."

Thankfully, Harriet didn't mention that he'd asked Bridget to dance as well. She didn't think she could fend off a dozen questions from Mrs. Darby right now.

As it was, Mrs. Darby's eyes had widened. "Oh my goodness. There must have been a significant reconciliation in the family."

"What happened with the woman the cousins had fought over? Did Mr. Stephens marry her?" Harriet's tone was both confused and curious. "I didn't know he was married."

"No, no. Mr. Stephens and the woman were caught—in a very compromising position, if you understand what I mean," Mrs. Darby said.

Harriet nodded gravely.

"Mr. Stephens was sent away, and I heard the woman was hastily married to some poor sop." Mrs. Darby tsked. "That was all years ago, and it seems that bygones are bygones with the Wilde family. Imagine, the two cousins at the same ball."

Bridget couldn't even look at Mrs. Darby. No wonder Lord Wilde was so angry with her. Seeing Bridget and being reminded of the compromising situation that had brought about her marriage to Anthony must have called to mind another dalliance—the one Walter had carried on with the woman Hugh loved."

"There he is now," Harriet said, tilting her head as Mr. Walter Stephens escorted another woman to the dance floor. "He is certainly making the rounds."

"Yes, it seems he is enjoying his return to Society," Mrs. Darby mused. "He's a nice-looking fellow, though. To be the cousin to the next Marquess of Crawton is indeed fortunate for him."

Bridget wondered if Lord Wilde was dancing again. She didn't see him, or the redhead, at the moment. Her aunt and

Mrs. Darby continued to chatter and gossip. Sometimes Bridget listened, other times she found herself quite lost in her own thoughts.

And then she almost gasped. Mr. Walter Stephens was leading out Phoebe. For a second dance.

Her aunt must have noticed the exact moment that Bridget did.

"Oh my goodness," Aunt Harriet said. "It's Mr. Stephens."

"He is practically announcing to the room that he intends to court Phoebe," Mrs. Darby exclaimed. "And at her first ball too!"

It seemed that Mrs. Darby saw nothing wrong or complicated in the fact that she'd just shared a scandalous story about Mr. Stephens, yet here he was, paying particular attention to her young and innocent sister.

Bridget gripped her aunt's hand, and Harriet squeezed back. At least her aunt agreed with her. This wasn't the place to make a scene; they'd both have to watch Phoebe complete the dance with Mr. Stephens.

And then, Bridget felt as if someone were watching her. It was an uncanny feeling. She looked about the room, only to see that in the original spot she'd first laid eyes upon Lord Hugh Wilde, he stood again, with the same gentleman friend as before. He was watching his cousin dance with Phoebe, and by the hard lines of his face, it was clear he didn't approve either. Good. It was probably the one thing they agreed on.

And then Lord Wilde looked at her, and Bridget knew he'd been watching her far longer than she'd been watching him.

This time, though, Lord Wilde didn't glower. A flash of understanding connected them. It seemed neither of them were pleased with the connection between the dancing couple on the ballroom floor. Then his expression softened and became contemplative, as if he were thinking about what she'd told him. About how she didn't want any association between their families.

She hoped that he didn't pity her, because if there was one thing she could not abide, it was pity.

Eight

HUGH PACED THE rug in the library of the family townhome. Walter would be down any moment and was intending to fetch Miss Phoebe Reeve and drive out to Hyde Park. When Hugh heard of his cousin's plans, he immediately balked.

Walter had just laughed. "You've turned into an old killjoy, Hugh! Maybe you should travel the continent like I did and see a bit more of the world. These London drawing rooms have turned you into a basket of nerves."

Hugh had gone silent at that. He'd traveled. And he stayed away from the London drawing rooms as much as possible. First, it was because the *ton* had thought he'd been jilted by Miss Sophia Benner. Then, it was to keep away from Anthony and his antics with the ladies and the growing friction between them as Hugh took on more and more responsibilities of his family's estates.

Antics as a young man were one thing, but once Hugh reached his mid-twenties, he'd lost his interest in drunken nights and gambling. Anthony continued, and Hugh had to pull him out of one episode after another. At one point, Anthony's father had threatened to cut Anthony off. That was right before Hugh went to Scotland and the whole marriage to Bridget had happened.

"I will see you later today, then?" Walter asked, stepping into the library.

Hugh stopped and looked toward his cousin. Walter was dressed as a veritable dandy, and Hugh wanted to send him back upstairs to change. But there was no time. Miss Phoebe was waiting, and it was never fashionable to keep a lady waiting.

The way that Walter gazed at him with something akin to a challenge irked Hugh. From what he could guess, Miss Phoebe had a modest dowry, and she was pleasant enough to look upon. But Hugh couldn't understand Walter's interest. Was this just a dalliance? Dalliance or not, Hugh couldn't allow it. Miss Phoebe's reputation must be protected because Hugh would not put up with another hasty wedding in the family. Especially to a Reeve woman.

"I'm coming with you," Hugh announced to Walter.

"What?" Hugh's brows drew together. "*I* don't need a chaperone. Certainly Miss Phoebe has an abigail for that."

"I've made up my mind," Hugh said, not giving any further explanation. "I believe the carriage is already out front, and I would like to pay my respects to the family." He moved past his cousin and snagged his coat from the front hall stand. Then he donned his hat.

Walter had no choice but to follow Hugh out to the carriage.

Hugh settled back on the seat and tapped the hood of the carriage to signal the driver to start. Walter just shook his head and stared out the window as he tapped his fingers along his knee.

Hugh hoped this act of his would dissuade Walter from pursuing the Reeve chit.

Moments later they pulled up to the townhome of Mrs. Harriet Reeve, only two streets away. Hugh hadn't realized their residences were so close together. Walter opened the door and climbed out of the carriage, and Hugh followed. He couldn't very well sit in the carriage while Walter fetched Miss Phoebe alone. It would be ill-mannered.

The front door to the town house swung open, and

Walter announced himself to the butler, not even naming Hugh. It didn't matter, Hugh decided. Miss Phoebe would find out soon enough.

The butler ushered the men into the front entryway, and Mrs. Harriet Reeve came out of what must have been the parlor. Her eyes widened at the sight of Hugh, but then she quickly covered it with a mollifying smile.

"Lord Wilde and Mr. Stephens, welcome," she said. "I didn't realize the both of you were to attend to Phoebe."

"I'm here to smooth over our less than ideal introductions from the other night," Hugh said.

"Oh, well then," Mrs. Reeve said, her face brightening. "Won't you come in to say hello to my nieces? Phoebe is looking forward to the drive."

Hugh should have expected this to be the result, no matter how much he might tell himself that he never intended to seek audience with Lady Bridget. He was about to give her the shock of her life, of that he was certain.

Mrs. Reeve led the way to the parlor, and Hugh and Walter followed.

Walter was still acting cold toward Hugh, but he didn't mind. Stepping into the room after Walter, Hugh felt like he'd entered a garden. Vases of flowers from the hothouse were perched on every flat surface in the room. Without doing an official count, he guessed there were over a dozen arrangements.

And sitting upon the settee were the two sisters. Miss Phoebe immediately rose, while Lady Bridget seemed absorbed in a book she was reading. Surely both women had heard the guests arrive at the door, so what did it mean that Lady Bridget was making her determination to continue reading known?

"Phoebe," Mrs. Reeve said. "Mr. Walter Stephens is here to take you riding." Stating the obvious had never been a favorite tactic of Hugh's. But what the woman did next was even less pleasant. "And Bridget, put that book away. You'll strain your eyes on this winter day."

"I can see fine," Bridget said in a murmured voice as if she didn't really want her aunt to hear her. Then she looked up, and her eyes connected with Hugh's.

First, Hugh noticed that the color of her eyes wasn't brown like he'd first thought. But he'd seen her up close only beneath the cold moonlight. Anyone's eyes would have looked dark. Her eyes were lighter, a blueish violet to be exact, like the mist on a spring morning.

Her hair was in a loose coif, and several dark-blonde curls brushed against her long, graceful neck. Her pale-green morning gown was edged in an ivory lace that made her look delicate and feminine, although Hugh knew firsthand that she had very decided opinions.

Lady Bridget snapped the book shut, still holding his gaze.

Miss Phoebe had risen from the settee and was donning her pelisse and gloves, but Lady Bridget remained sitting.

"Lady Wilde," he said with a nod of acknowledgment. There was no reason they couldn't be civil to each other. He wouldn't be seeing her after today, at least not if he had anything to do with it.

Bridget rose to her feet. Her voice wasn't much louder than her previous murmur to her aunt when she said, "Lord Wilde." She turned and took the few steps toward the hearth, where she paused, her back to him.

Hugh glanced at Walter and the other women. They'd gathered around one of the more extravagant flower displays. Walter appeared to be questioning Miss Phoebe on the gentlemen senders of the various vases of flowers, and Miss Phoebe chattered away about all her dance partners.

Hugh took the few steps toward Lady Bridget and stood next to her. She kept her gaze lowered, but this only gave him the advantage of scanning her face, her long lashes, the faint pink tinge upon her cheeks, the rose color of her lips. "Call me

Hugh," he said quickly. "We are related, are we not? Cousins by marriage, after all." Was he daft? Why was he further entrenching himself with this woman when all he wanted to do was forget she ever existed? If only he had returned for the wedding after all. He was certain Anthony wouldn't be dead if he'd been there. Perhaps he would have been able to talk his cousin into canceling the whole affair.

"I have broken all connection with your family, Lord Wilde," Bridget said in a stiff voice, keeping her gaze lowered. "I would like to keep it that way."

Hugh felt his face heat. This wasn't the conversation to be had when others were present, although they seemed to be still caught up in talking about the ball from the previous night. Miss Phoebe giggled, and Walter laughed. At least someone was enjoying himself.

"You made your repulsion clear last night," Hugh told Lady Bridget in a hushed voice. "At the time I was not aware of the attachment that your sister and my cousin have formed. It is for this purpose I have accompanied him today. I intend to put a stop to it."

This brought Bridget's gaze to his face. Her eyes were quite violet—there was no other word for it.

"You do?" she whispered. "I had hoped that you and I would be of one accord."

Her eyes were filled with such bright hope that he couldn't tamp down the satisfaction that filled his chest. She was looking at him like . . . like she was depending on him. "We are of one accord on this matter," he confirmed. Oh, how there was so much more he wished to question her about. Common sense told him that he'd never have the chance.

A sigh left her lips, and he could smell orange blossoms again. It took a measure of restraint to keep from leaning closer and inhaling. "I'm afraid my sister has paid particular attention to your cousin." Her eyes darted to the couple on the other side of the room. "And despite all the flowers delivered this morning, she has very much looked forward to riding with Mr. Stephens."

Hugh followed her gaze, but then he was drawn to looking at Lady Bridget again. "I will see what I can do. But you must not encourage her toward Walter."

"No," she said. "I have not, and I will not." Her tone changed as she spoke next, "Walter is a veritable scoundrel, and I will not have my sister bewitched by him."

"*Scoundrel?*" Hugh shot out, then bit his lip. He didn't want to draw attention to their conversation.

"Gossip has been resurrected with his appearance last night," Bridget said, the color of her cheeks becoming even more pink. "I had an earful, and I must say, the Wilde family and their relations seem hell-bent on their ruination of the fair sex."

Hugh just stared at her because he wasn't sure he'd heard right. The anger that had nearly simmered dry had now returned. "Do you really put stock in the gossips—?"

"What do you say, Hugh?" Walter cut in.

Hugh turned to see Walter crossing the room, coming toward them. "Say to what?" He felt suddenly on guard. What had been discussed without him?

"Let's make it a foursome," Walter continued, a bright gleam in his eye. "We will take both sisters out in the carriage to Hyde Park. Lady Bridget can replace any chaperone that might be needed."

Hugh opened his mouth, then shut it as Miss Phoebe rushed across the room and grasped her sister's hands. "Please come. It will be ever so much fun."

By the sudden paleness upon Lady Bridget's face, Hugh knew that *fun* was the last thing on her mind. Perhaps . . . perhaps they could use it to their advantage. Somehow, on this ride, they must convince both Walter and Phoebe they were a poor match.

He caught Lady Bridget's panicked gaze and said, "It would be an honor to have you accompany us." He kept his eyes on her, his gaze intense, hoping she'd understand what he was trying to say.

Her eyes widened, and she hesitated. "All right. I will fetch my things."

So it happened that Hugh found himself in a carriage with Lady Bridget, her sister, and Walter.

While Lady Bridget remained mostly silent in the beginning of their ride, Hugh asked the younger sister about those she'd danced with at the ball. As she listed names, he'd comment upon them, giving compliments and recommendations where they were due. He noticed Walter didn't seem too pleased. But Hugh wanted Miss Phoebe to know that she had many options.

Lady Bridget seemed to catch on, and soon she was adding her praises to certain gentlemen, although Hugh doubted she knew as much as half as she was claiming to know. From all accounts, she lived a very quiet life, almost reclusive. Or at least had done so since her widowhood.

Hugh found one thing interesting. Although he was certain Lady Bridget was bluffing through most of her side of the conversation, she was who he wanted to hear from the most.

Nine

THREE DAYS HAD passed since the ride in Hyde Park, and remarkably, Mr. Walter Stephens had not called upon Phoebe again.

Plenty of other gentlemen callers had come, of course, dazzling Phoebe with flowers and flattering words. She'd gone on another carriage ride through Hyde Park, which their abigail, Maren, had chaperoned this time around.

During all this time, Bridget couldn't get Lord Hugh Wilde out of her thoughts. He'd been surprisingly conciliatory toward her during the ride about the park. He and Bridget had practically teamed up in their praise of some of the gentlemen who'd danced with Phoebe, thus setting Mr. Stephens in his place. When the carriage had returned to her aunt's home, Hugh had also been the one to hand her down.

Yes, she was thinking of him as Hugh now. He was her cousin by marriage, no matter how determined she was to keep the family at a distance. It was impossible to entirely avoid him while he remained in London, especially while Bridget was escorting Phoebe to the social events. Tonight, they'd been invited to go to a small dinner party, then they'd accompany Mr. and Mrs. Darby to their opera box. She worried that Hugh and his cousin would be at the opera, though. She would have to avoid them if possible.

The offer from the Darbys was truly generous, although

Bridget couldn't help but wonder if Mrs. Darby just wanted to be on the cusp of any gossip about her sister. Phoebe had enjoyed so many visitors, specifically gentlemen callers, as well as inquisitive ladies claiming they wanted to form a better acquaintance. Bridget suspected that since Phoebe was a popular debutante, others wanted to be in their circle.

Their aunt certainly didn't mind. She eagerly greeted guests and continued ordering more tea and refreshments.

"Bridget," Phoebe said, opening the door to the bedchamber without knocking, per usual.

Bridget turned from her wardrobe where she'd lifted out her new gloves. They were soft, well made, and would do for tonight.

"Do you think the green is too matronly looking?" Phoebe asked as she did a slow twirl.

"The green makes your hair look like spun gold," Bridget said honestly. It seemed each day her sister grew more pretty. How was that possible? "You are the furthest thing from a matron."

Phoebe giggled. "Thank you. I knew I could count on you."

Bridget smiled. She was truly happy for her sister's success among the elite, but she always felt a bit on edge, waiting for something untoward to happen.

Phoebe flounced out of the room, all silk and ringlets, leaving behind the scent of jasmine. The perfume must have been a gift from one of her gentleman admirers. Bridget continued to smile as she pulled on her gloves and headed out of her room. She wanted to visit with Aunt Harriet before leaving for the dinner party. Her aunt had been feeling poorly all day and had kept to her room.

Bridget walked along the corridor until she reached Harriet's suite. She tapped on the door, then opened it when Harriet's voice bade her to enter. She found her aunt sitting up in bed, alert, although a bit pale.

A tea tray was on the other side of her and looked mostly untouched.

"How are you feeling?" Bridget asked.

"My head hurts, and I think I'm getting a cold," Harriet said with a sniffle. "Please give Mrs. Darby my most sincere apologies."

"Of course," Bridget said.

"And make sure Phoebe pays particular attention to Mr. Talbot," Harriet continued.

Mr. Talbot was a man whom Bridget could approve of. He was untouched by scandal and had an excellent reputation. She couldn't say the same for the beguiling Mr. Walter Stephens.

"If only we can get Phoebe a proposal before the season is half-over," Harriet said, pulling Bridget from her thoughts. "Then the happy couple could relax and enjoy the rest of the events together."

If only. There was nothing more Bridget wanted than to see her sister happily settled. Phoebe was young but of an age to marry. Bridget didn't mind being the widowed older sister. Four hours of marriage had been plenty for her.

By the time Bridget was ready, Phoebe was also ready. She seemed extra excited for tonight's event, and on the carriage ride over, she talked about all of those who would be in attendance at the dinner.

The evening at the Darbys' home went smoothly, and Mr. Talbot paid plenty of attention to Phoebe, which she seemed to soak up.

Time passed quickly, and soon the dinner party broke. Bridget followed after the Darbys to join them in their carriage, while Phoebe delayed a few moments to say goodbye to the guests who weren't going to the opera. Then Phoebe walked up to the carriage and poked her head in. "I've a bit of a headache. The Talbots have offered to take me home."

"Are you sure?" Mrs. Darby asked, leaning forward from her seat. "We can take you, dear."

"The Talbots are headed the same way as I am," Phoebe said.

"Of course you may go with them," Bridget said. It was more time in Mr. Talbot and his parents' company. "I hope you will get some rest."

After Phoebe left, Bridget settled back into the carriage. Time with the Darbys was pleasant enough, and she did enjoy the opera.

Thankfully, there was no sign of either Lord Hugh Wilde or his cousin at the opera, and Bridget found herself able to completely relax and enjoy the music.

Hours later, she returned home, exhilarated yet plenty exhausted. She was looking forward to climbing into bed and sleeping well into the morning hours. First, she'd check on Phoebe to make sure she was resting peacefully, then she'd turn in herself. Bridget only regretted having to wake Maren since her dress was impossible to get out of on her own.

Phoebe's room was dark; the only light came from the few glowing coals in the hearth. Bridget walked quietly to the bed and rested a hand on Phoebe's shoulder. But the lump Bridget assumed was her sister's shoulder was a cushion. Bridget scanned the length of the bed. A person wasn't lying in it, although the row of cushions might be mistaken for the form of a person at first glance.

Shock pulsed through Bridget. What kind of trick was Phoebe playing? When they were younger, these sorts of games were frequent . . . but the hard twisting in Bridget's stomach told her this was no game.

She drew back the coverlet to reveal the line of cushions, likely taken from the window seat on the other side of the room. "Phoebe?" Bridget hissed, looking about the room. Perhaps she fell asleep somewhere else? Or maybe she went to the kitchen to fetch something to eat or drink?

"Phoebe?" Bridget called again, opening the doors of the closet, even though she knew her sister wasn't there. Bridget hurried out of the room, and down the stairs she flew as much as her gown would allow.

She went into each room on the main floor, finding them dark and empty. Then she went to the kitchen. No Phoebe.

Heart hammering, Bridget went back up the stairs to her sister's room. She lit a lamp and drew back the covers of the bed even farther, searching for any sign of how long ago Phoebe had been in this room.

Then Bridget paused. Perhaps her sister had gone into Aunt Harriet's room and had fallen asleep in there? She could only hope. But as she turned to head out of the room again, she noticed an envelope on the small writing table. There was nothing unusual about an envelope being left on the tabletop, but a sinking feeling in her stomach drew Bridget closer.

Upon the outside of the envelope was written: *Bridget.*

It wasn't even sealed.

Bridget set the candle down and unfolded the letter with trembling fingers.

Dear Bridget,

Please do not worry about me. By the time you read this, I will be on my way to marry the love of my life. Walter and I will be man and wife soon. I know this is not what you imagined for your little sister, but Walter's cousin forbade us from seeing each other, so this was the only way. Now Hugh will be forced to accept our marriage. Vows made in Gretna Green are also recognized by England.

I will see you in a few weeks. Please let Aunt Harriet know that I love her and this was the best way for everyone.

Much love, Phoebe

The letter fell from Bridget's hand as tears built in her eyes. *No. No. No.* She looked wildly about the room. How long had her sister been gone? How had she left? Bridget dashed to the window and looked down upon the back garden. It was too high to jump, and there was no way to climb down safely.

Bridget turned and looked about the room. Nothing seemed disturbed except for the added cushions. She moved the wardrobe and opened drawer after drawer. Items were missing, but not many. Not enough to fill a trunk. She must have taken only a small traveling bag. Then Bridget opened the closet door again, and this time she searched for the green dress Phoebe had worn to dinner at the Darbys'.

It wasn't there, which meant that Phoebe hadn't come home at all after the dinner. Had she left that note before they'd even left that evening?

Bridget felt all energy drain from her. How long had Phoebe been planning her elopement? Anger shot through her, growing hotter and hotter. How could Phoebe do this to her, to their aunt? How could Mr. Walter Stephens swindle her sister this way? Hadn't the Wilde family ruined Bridget's family enough?

She scooped the letter from the floor, then remade the bed. She didn't want the abigail or Aunt Harriet to have the shock of their lives when they came in here. Maybe, just maybe, there was time to stop her sister from making this terrible mistake.

Bridget paused in the silent corridor. What if Mr. Stephens had threatened Phoebe? What if he had forced her to come with him? Bridget read through the letter again, analyzing the turns of phrase and whether or not the handwriting was shaky. It all looked smooth and eerily logical.

Still, Phoebe was no master schemer. She must have been seeing Mr. Stephens secretly. But how? Had they been writing letters? Meeting in private places? Sneaking out of their homes?

Maren. Bridget had to speak with Maren. Middle of the night or not. Bridget made her way down the stairs to the kitchen. Passing through the dark, silent room made her shiver. She opened the door that led to the bedchambers below.

She knew which room was Maren's, and Bridget didn't bother to knock. She opened the door and found Maren sound asleep in her bed. This didn't give Bridget much more hope.

Bridget called out to Maren in a quiet voice, and the woman stirred. Her eyes flew open when she saw Bridget standing in the middle of her room, holding a lit candle. When Bridget explained that Phoebe was missing and had possibly eloped, Maren gripped her blanket to her chest.

"Eloped? Gone?" she said in a terrified voice. "Are you sure? Maybe she is still out with someone."

Bridget waved the letter. "It's all here. Now, I want to know your part in all of this. What do you know?"

"I didn't know they planned to elope," Maren said. "I promise. I only delivered letters between Miss Reeve and Mr. Stephens."

Bridget saw the truth of it in the abigail's eyes. The maid had been only a conduit, and those letters likely had declarations of love and devotion mixed in with plans . . .

Maren climbed to her feet and pulled a robe about her shoulders.

"Wake James," Bridget said. "Tell him to ready the carriage. I am going to Lord Wilde's house. He needs to fix this." She took a deep breath. "First, unlace my dress. I need to change." She turned, and as Maren quickly worked the laces, Bridget hoped that these extra few moments wouldn't permanently put Phoebe in more danger.

The more she thought about the whole situation, the more she became angry with herself. She should have been more watchful, more aware, instead of having her mind on other matters. If she had been a better sister, this would have never happened.

Once her dress was loose enough to remove, Bridget clutched the front bodice, then hurried from the room and up the stairs to the kitchen. She moved as quietly as possible as she took the staircase from the foyer to the first floor. Inside her bedchamber, she stripped off her dress, tossed it over a chair, then pulled on the first dress she grabbed from her closet. Next, she gathered the same wrap she'd worn to the dinner, pocketed the letter, and hurried back downstairs.

Maren was waiting in the kitchen, dressed, and holding a cloak. "Best take this, ma'am," she said. "It's warmer than what you have, and the carriage will be cold."

Bridget swapped her wrap for the woolen cloak. "Thank you. Is the carriage ready?"

"Yes; do you want me to come with you?"

Bridget hesitated. "No, you stay here. Do not wake anyone and tell them. When my aunt wakes on the morrow, tell her we've gone out. I'm hoping to return with Phoebe before tomorrow afternoon. I just hope that Lord Wilde is a good horseman."

"Yes, ma'am," Maren said and dipped her head.

Moments later, Bridget was in the carriage, on her way to Lord Hugh Wilde's home in the middle of the night.

Ten

HUGH HAD JUST drifted off to sleep when he heard a banging. It took him a couple of moments to realize the sound was coming from his own front door. Hugh sat up in his bed and listened. All went quiet. Perhaps it was a drunkard mistaking his house.

Then the banging started up again, and this time he heard the voice of his butler, Mr. Peters, call out, "Coming!"

It took a lot to get beneath the stalwart Peters's skin, and Hugh might have smiled if it weren't the middle of the night and the knocking excessively discourteous.

"Walter, if that's you . . ." Hugh mumbled to himself. Even though Peters could very well escort a drunken Walter to bed, Hugh climbed out of his own bed and pulled on his trousers. He padded barefoot across his room and opened the door.

From his spot on the first-floor landing, he heard voices. And it wasn't the murmur of Peters's cracking voice mixed in with Walter's defensive murmurs . . . No, the voice was that of a woman.

Hugh was suddenly wide awake and alert. He hurried to the top of the stairs and nearly tripped down them when he saw who was standing at the front door, her face illuminated by the candle Peters held high as if trying to figure out if the woman was an apparition or a person of flesh and blood.

Lady Bridget. What was she doing here in the middle of the night?

"Wake your master if you have to," she said. "He'll want to hear what I have to say. This cannot wait until morning."

Hugh's previous irritation about the late-night intrusion was replaced by worry. Lady Bridget's voice sounded genuinely distressed, and they both knew that coming here in the middle of the night, apparently alone, would be fodder for the gossips. So Hugh surmised she must be on an urgent errand to risk whatever reputation she had left.

"I am awake, Peters," Hugh said, coming down the stairs.

As if she'd been doused with cold water, Bridget abruptly stopped speaking. Her eyes widened at the sight of him, and he realized he was in a state of undress, but that couldn't be helped. Plus, what did she expect in the middle of the night? Him to be trussed up as if he were attending a ball?

On the other hand, Bridget was dressed in a presentable manner, although he wasn't sure where she might have acquired such a plain woolen cloak.

He looked past the entryway. There was no sign of a carriage waiting for her. "Did you walk here?"

She glanced at Peters, then said, "I had my driver drop me off. I didn't want my carriage sitting in front of your home in the middle of the night."

Hugh puffed out a breath. He was more than curious to know what was so urgent that it couldn't wait until a decent hour. "That will be all, Peters. Thank you." Then, to Bridget, he said, "Come into library. I'll stoke the fire."

As Hugh led the way and Peters shut the front door, Hugh was tempted to send Bridget back where she came from right away—to insist on propriety—but he sensed she wasn't about to acquiesce. And he didn't want that sort of scene to play out in front of the household staff.

Inside the dark library, Hugh immediately lit the lamp, then crossed to the hearth and stoked the fire. He bent to retrieve a small log and set it up atop the embers. Soon, the log caught fire, and orange flames leaped and danced.

"My lord," Lady Bridget said. "I do not care about a warm room, and please do not offer me refreshment. Visiting homes in the middle of the night is not a habit of mine. I have come to see to the whereabouts of my sister."

Hugh straightened from the hearth and brushed his hands off. "Miss Phoebe?"

"Yes, Phoebe." Lady Bridget stepped forward and held out a letter that Hugh realized had been in her hand all this while. He had just now noticed it.

"What's this?" he asked, taking the letter, feeling a tightness in his stomach begin. What did he have to do with the sister?

"Read it." Lady Bridget's voice had grown quieter.

And why was he being asked to read a letter? Hugh unfolded the paper and scanned the words. The handwriting was decidedly feminine. To say that he was shocked at the content was an understatement. He'd forbidden Walter from continuing any sort of attachment with Miss Phoebe. There had been enough history and scandal between the two families, and in truth, Hugh didn't exactly trust his cousin's attentions toward the girl. There had been plenty of rumors about Walter's escapades across the continent.

He looked up to see Lady Bridget's eyes filled with fury.

"Is this true? Did they elope?" he asked.

"Phoebe is gone," Bridget's words came out like shards of ice. "She put cushions in her bed to make it look like she was there. Some of her clothing is missing but not a lot."

Hugh exhaled. "When did you last see your sister?"

Bridget explained how the evening had gone and how Phoebe had pleaded a headache. "She said she was leaving with the Talbots, although I am sure now that she never went with the Talbots at all. And that's why I'm at your home and not theirs."

"And what time was that?" he asked.

"About seven thirty," she said.

Hugh looked down at the letter in his hands and read the words a second time. "If they've truly eloped, they have almost five hours on us." He turned toward the clock that ticked on the mantel. "I haven't seen Walter since this afternoon. We planned to stay in this night, but then he decided to go to White's. I assumed he got involved in a card game, and so I didn't worry about him when I retired for the evening."

"Did you know of his plans to abduct my sister?" Lady Bridget asked, her voice rising in pitch.

"*Abduct*? Whatever you think of my cousin, he's not a kidnapper." How dare she accuse his cousin of such a thing? He wasn't happy with the situation either, but five hours on the road to Gretna Green might as well be twelve. "The letter makes that clear."

Lady Bridget scoffed and took a step closer. A far cry from any other reaction when they'd interacted. She always wanted to put more distance between them. "My sister is *seventeen*. Mr. Stephens is a *known* womanizer. Just like your other cousin Anthony, who ruined *my* life! I will *not* have my sister's life ruined too because your cousin can't keep his hands to himself!"

Hugh stared at her. There were so many things to address in her accusations. His temper was already pushing its way to the surface. "Your sister may be only seventeen, but if she is old enough to be presented to Society, she is old enough to take a husband. I understand being protective of her—but she clearly made her own choice."

Lady Bridget's face paled at his insinuation.

But Hugh wasn't finished. "To address your other accusation. You think Anthony ruined *your* life? What about *his*? He didn't have to offer for you—after you two were caught. *You* were the one who benefited, not him. Anthony's life was taken as a result of your sham marriage!"

"It was not a sham," she retorted, her eyes blazing. "Do you know what we were doing when we were supposedly caught? I walked into the library at the Arringtons', and Anthony was there, alone. Brooding, drinking, or contemplating his next conquest, I don't know. But I left as soon as I saw him. Before I could clear the doorway, Mr. and Mrs. Arrington were there—it was as if they'd followed me, had known Anthony was in the library. I was so startled I tripped, and Anthony was behind me. He caught me before I fell. That was our compromising position. If I'd had my way, I would have never spoken to your cousin again." She took a breath and plunged on, giving Hugh no edge to interrupt.

"Anthony was the worst of the scoundrels. Believe me, I had caught his attention weeks earlier, but his flirting was outrageous and even insulting. I vowed to stay away from him and to never accept an invitation to dance. It was as if the heavens were against me from the start. When we were forced upon each other, it was all I could do but keep up my end of the engagement. If it hadn't been for my sister and potential damage to her own reputation, I would have cried off and taken my losses to the country."

Hugh stared at her. This was a different scenario than he'd imagined. Lady Bridget turned away from him and paced the length of the room. She stopped by the shrouded window.

"What would you have had Anthony do?" Hugh finally asked. "Did he not do the honorable thing?"

Lady Bridget sniffled, and although she still wasn't looking at him, he guessed that she was crying.

"I will own that Anthony did act honorably in that instance," she said, in a trembling voice. "Although it was laden with a different agenda that I was soon to discover."

Hugh reached for his handkerchief, then realized he wasn't even wearing a waistcoat. There was nothing in the room he could offer her. "Many men change . . . after they marry. I am sure it will be the same for Walter. He has a good heart, and although I don't approve of his actions regarding your sister, it cannot be helped now."

Lady Bridget whirled. Her cheeks were streaked with

tears, but her voice held plenty of strength when she said, "Can it not be helped? Surely they will stop to eat and rest. Perhaps even seek a room for the night. Five hours, you said; five hours is not so much in a rented carriage with rented horses—which I presume they took."

He blinked. "You are suggesting that I hunt them down? Force them to return?"

She came toward him. "I am not suggesting it. I am demanding it. Your family owes me this."

He pressed his lips together. They could argue all night about what his family may or may not owe Bridget. She clearly felt that she'd been wronged in some extreme way. "Even if I had the fastest horse in London, I would not overtake them. And if I did, do you think I'd be able to talk your sister into returning with me? If she is in love with Walter as much as this letter indicates, do you think my sudden appearance will change her mind?"

"She does not know her mind," Lady Bridget ground out. "She's *seventeen.*"

"She's a woman who planned an elopement without a thought to how it might affect you or your aunt," Hugh said in a hard tone. "She had no consideration for you, so why are you willing to pursue her and drag her back home? For what purpose? So she can make your life a living hell with her moping and disobedience? She will only find the next opportunity to escape again and break your heart a second time. Not to mention the ensuing scandal. I can tell you that forcing her to do something against her will is not the answer. She will resent you and make your life even more miserable than you claim it already is. She will hate you, and you will have to live with the hatred." He cut himself off, breathing hard, as memories and pain and anger coursed through him.

Bridget was staring at him, and he knew, they *both* knew, he was no longer speaking of Phoebe.

What Bridget said next reached deep into his heart. "I have to try. What if she was coerced? What if she is trapped?

What if she realizes she made a mistake, and what if she wants to come home?"

He had no answer for that. Hugh turned back toward the infant fire. The room was suddenly too hot, the air too dry. His head hurt.

"We will take your carriage and ask along the way if anyone has seen them," Bridget said, coming to stand next to him.

Without looking at her, he could feel her desperation, her sincerity, her love for her wayward sister.

"We will make up for lost time because they will surely have to sleep at one point." She paused and placed a hand on his arm. Her touch was light, but the sensation of warmth was startling.

"Please, Hugh," she said. "We have to try. The journey on the road to Gretna Green is four days of travel, perhaps more. We can overtake them at some point."

Maybe it was the way she'd said his name in that soft voice of hers, or maybe it was the warmth spreading from her touch throughout his whole body, or perhaps it was how her pleading tone tugged at sympathies he'd thought he'd long since abandoned, but he turned to her. He looked into those violet eyes of hers and said, "I will leave immediately."

Her lips parted, and she exhaled. Then she leaned closer, her hand still on his arm, her touch still sending waves of warmth all the way to his toes. "I am coming with you."

Eleven

"No," Hugh said, his rejection short but firm. "A carriage will slow me down. And I can't be responsible for your reputation too. Responsibility for one woman from the Reeve family is plenty."

Bridget wasn't surprised that he was pushing back. But . . . he'd agreed to pursue Mr. Stephens and Phoebe. The first bridge had been crossed. Yet she wasn't ready to give up, despite the fact that every precious moment passing was another moment Phoebe drew closer to Gretna Green.

"I am a widow," she said, watching Hugh's eyes carefully. She had to convince him. She could not sit home with her aunt worrying and waiting to know if her life was going to come crashing down around her. "And I am your cousin by marriage. Traveling together might be questioned but not frowned upon. Besides, no one will know unless we tell them. We can overtake my sister and be back in London by tomorrow evening at the latest."

He blinked but said nothing, and Bridget moved closer. She could smell his spice, and it was a bit hard to concentrate on his face when the open collar of his nightshirt revealed a glimpse of a sturdy chest of golden skin.

Earlier, when she'd said *please* and spoken softly to him and touched his arm, something in him had seemed to shift. He'd let down his guard, and he'd really listened to her. If there was ever a time to use her womanly charms, it was now, no matter how distasteful she found acting a manipulative part to be. "Hugh," she said in a near whisper, lifting her hand and placing it higher on his arm. "Let me come with you. I need to see my sister. If I am forced to remain home, I fear I will go mad with not knowing what is happening. I must take action. I must *do* something." She felt the tears building but refused to let them fall again. "I am sure you understand how helpless I feel right now, and how much I need . . . your aid."

He was listening. He was looking at her with that intense gaze of his. When his gaze dipped to her mouth, then to her neck, as if he were considering something, Bridget's heart started to beat faster. For a moment, she thought he might—

"Did you pack a bag?" he asked.

The moment broke, but her heart soared. "I have this cloak, and I've brought some money. I don't need anything else. I'm not planning on sleeping or needing a change of clothing." She could feel his breath tickle the edges of her hair as he continued to study her. She wasn't sure if he was still truly looking at her or if his mind was elsewhere, thinking through all the schematics. "Should I meet you in the stable?"

"No." His eyes snapped back to focus. "Wait here. I'll be only a moment."

He stepped back, and her hand fell from his arm. The loss of the warmth between them was tangible. He moved past her, and she listened to him leave the room, cross the foyer, and then move to the first floor two steps at a time.

Bridget exhaled. He'd listened to her. They were going to rescue her sister.

She refolded the letter with trembling hands and slipped it into the cloak pocket. Then she smoothed back her hair, thinking of what Phoebe's reaction would be once they reached her. Was Hugh right? Would her sister hate her? No, Bridget couldn't think of that right now. Phoebe was barely more than a child. She was impulsive, innocent, and caught up in her first feelings of love. Walter Stephens was the predator here, and he shouldn't be allowed to get away with it. Not if Bridget had any say.

And whatever happened, at least she had Hugh on her side, for now.

By the time he returned to the library, Bridget had sunk into an armchair by the fire, giving in to the exhaustion the ordeal over the last hour had brought.

Hugh was fully dressed, Bridget noted, and she would not have to worry about accidentally ogling him.

"Are you all right?" he asked with concern.

She must look like death herself if Lord Hugh Wilde was concerned. She fought a yawn. "I am fine."

"If you are unwell, I will go on without you."

"No," Bridget hurried to say. "I am fine. We don't want to delay any longer." She gripped the edges of the armchair and began to rise.

Hugh stepped to her side and supported her elbow. Almost as quickly as he'd helped her, he released her. She followed him out of the library. The butler who Hugh had called Peters earlier was at the front door, holding it open. Outside was the Wilde family carriage, the driver already in position on his perch.

As Bridget started down the stairs, Hugh spoke briefly to the butler, then joined her at the carriage door. He opened the door and handed her up. When Hugh joined her inside and sat on the opposite side, he said, "There are blankets to keep warm."

Bridget looked at the end of her side of the bench. In addition to the blankets, she noticed a wicker basket on the floor.

"My housekeeper packed some food as well," Hugh said as the carriage pulled away from the house.

Every staff member in his household must have been awakened. "Thank you," Bridget breathed.

Hugh nodded, and there was very little conversation between them as the carriage rattled through the quiet streets of London. It wasn't until they left the city proper that Bridget started to let herself relax against the plush seat. The carriage was likely the most luxurious one she'd traveled in. Suddenly, she straightened again. "Did Mr. Stephens take one of your carriages?"

Hugh turned his head from where he was gazing out the window. "He must have hired one. He didn't want to incur my wrath on that account."

Bridget nodded. It made sense. She settled back into quiet, and for a short time she felt Hugh's gaze upon her. Who would have thought they would be traveling together in a carriage on a chase?

She closed her eyes, not to sleep, because she knew that wouldn't happen with her mind so keyed up, but to cut herself off from Hugh just a little. He was so different from Anthony. Yes, they were close cousins who'd grown up together, but she thought they'd have more in common. Whereas Anthony was the life of any party or event, Hugh was extremely reserved. He was every inch the type of man who she'd imagine would be a marquess. She could understand just a little how Anthony despised his cousin for having more wealth and privilege.

Anthony had grown up in the shadow of Hugh's estate. He had told Bridget that he planned to outlive Hugh and become the sole heir to the marquess. It was plain that Anthony had demons in his life, and he used his drinking, gambling, and seduction of women to combat those demons. Marrying Bridget had only been an act of willful stubbornness toward his parents and revenge against his older cousin.

Family relationships were so complicated, and it made Bridget even more tired trying to sort it all out. She let her breathing even out, and without meaning to, she drifted off to sleep.

When Bridget awoke, the carriage was traveling at a faster pace than it had been through London. She also had a blanket draped over her legs, which made her feel quite cozy. It took a moment for her eyes to adjust to the dimness inside the carriage, and when she did start to make out shapes and forms, she saw that Hugh was sound asleep.

He'd pulled a blanket over himself and used a second blanket as a pillow of sorts, pressing it between the side of the carriage and his head. His arms were folded across his chest as if he'd meant to close his eyes for a few moments. Bridget fought back a smile as she watched him. He looked much younger when he was asleep. The lines about his eyes and mouth had relaxed, and his dark eyelashes rested peacefully against his cheekbones.

She hadn't realized how dark his lashes were until now. His hair had fallen forward, across his forehead, and Bridget resisted the urge to smooth it back. Her touch would certainly wake him. Regardless, she leaned forward and pulled his blanket up higher, giving him more warmth. He didn't stir, and she moved back into place and adjusted her own blanket.

She'd never slept in the same room as a man before, let alone in the close confines of a carriage. But it was comforting somehow, and she felt safe and secure. They might be on a fool's errand, but this man had listened to her and was willing to track down her sister to make sure her foolish actions were not putting her into additional danger.

Bridget let her eyes slide shut again. Even though she'd told Hugh she wouldn't be sleeping, watching him sleep made her more tired.

The next time she awoke, she found that Hugh was awake too and was watching out the window. The glow from the outer lanterns on the carriage spilled inside enough so that she could see his face was etched with worry. He'd refolded both of his blankets, and they were stacked neatly on his bench. She moved to cover up her yawn, and he turned to look at her.

"I'm glad you slept," he said in a voice that sounded a little rough from sleep. But the worry on his face softened into a half smile.

This was the first time she remembered him smiling, even though it was only half a smile. Her cheeks warmed, and she was grateful for the dim interior of the carriage. "I didn't mean to."

"I know you didn't." He was almost teasing her.

"Have we made good time?" she asked, trying not to yawn again.

"We have." Hugh's somber tone was back. "It shouldn't be much longer to the next posting inn. We'll inquire within."

"All right," Bridget said. She hoped they'd find her sister at the next stop, or at least have word about her whereabouts and progress.

"Are you warm enough?" Hugh asked.

She was enjoying the deeper rasp of his voice, and she knew she shouldn't be thinking of things like that. This was the man whose cousin had manipulated Phoebe.

Hugh couldn't be very comfortable cooped up in such a small space. She scooted more to the right and said, "You can stretch out your legs; I don't mind."

He gave her the slightest nod and proceeded to do just that. Silence fell between them, but it was a comfortable silence.

After several moments, he said, "Do you think if Anthony had lived, you would have become fond of each other?"

Bridget felt as if she'd been dunked in icy water and couldn't help but shudder. "No." Her voice was a whisper, but she felt like screaming it. She didn't want to remember the foul things Anthony had said to her, but the memories were coming back whether she wanted them to or not.

"I didn't mean to make you upset." Hugh adjusted his legs and leaned toward her.

Bridget blinked a few times; she hadn't even realized tears had started. She was too numb to feel them.

Then, Hugh took her hands into his warm ones. His long fingers encased hers. "Perhaps with age, he would have mellowed and become a fine husband."

Bridget met Hugh's earnest gaze. Did he truly believe that

about his cousin? "Anthony told me he would give me one week as a faithful husband, but then he would return to his mistress. Yet he expected me to give him plenty of sons, regardless of his other relations."

Hugh drew in a breath, and his fingers tightened around hers. "The bastard."

Bridget couldn't agree more. She also knew that was how marriage was for many women. They paid a very high price to follow Society rules. A tear fell, and then another. Hugh released one of her hands and drew out a handkerchief from his coat pocket.

"I don't mean to be such a watering pot," she said.

Instead of handing over the handkerchief, he shifted over to her bench and sat right next to her. Then he dabbed at her cheeks. He was so close that Bridget imagined he could hear the rapid drumming of her heart.

"Anthony and I had quite a volatile relationship ourselves," Hugh said, lowering the handkerchief and keeping his gaze on her. "He was wild even as a child~~kid~~. I enjoyed some of the fun and games, but after Eton, even I couldn't keep up his pace. The more responsibilities I took on from my father, the less interested I was in Anthony's excessive indulgences."

Their shoulders and part of their arms kept touching as the carriage moved beneath them. Hugh didn't seem bothered by the contact, but Bridget was very much aware of every brush of their sleeves and every jostle.

"His father threatened to disinherit him more than once," Hugh continued. "My uncle pleaded for my help more than once. I could never understand . . . well, we were just different, that's all."

"What happened with the woman you were both in love with?"

Hugh chuckled and stretched his legs before him. He made no move to return to the other side of the carriage. "Every man in the county was in love with Miss Sophia

Benner. In fact, she had hair the same color as yours, but she was very short and reminded me of a cherub to tell the truth. I guess I noticed her like any red-blooded male, but I wouldn't say I was besotted." He shook his head. "It was more of a competition than anything. But Walter made a cake of himself, and they were caught kissing at one of our garden parties. Miss Sophia was sent away, and Walter left too."

Bridget exhaled. Hugh hadn't been in love with Sophia. Why did that make her so pleased to know he hadn't been jilted by the love of his life?

Twelve

HUGH COULDN'T HELP but think of his biggest question about Anthony and Lady Bridget. *Why* had Anthony offered to marry her? She was beautiful, yes, but she was an innocent . . . and Anthony had made it clear he preferred his mistress over his new wife. There were also plenty of women who fawned over Anthony who had much bigger dowries than the Reeve women.

Hugh knew his cousin enough to know that Anthony never did anything without a reason. Being a stand-up gentleman and proposing to Lady Bridget just wasn't in his character.

The carriage slowed; they were nearing the posting inn. Hugh quickly moved to the other bench to put the proper distance between him and Lady Bridget. She might be his cousin by marriage, but he didn't want any rumors started.

When the carriage stopped, Hugh opened the door and stepped out. He'd been cramped for so long that he wasn't surprised to feel the aches and pains as he unfolded his long body. He extended his hand to help Lady Bridget out of the carriage. Although they'd been traveling for hours, and she'd slept most of it, she didn't look any worse for the wear. Her hair had fallen out of its pins, but it only made her look more . . . Hugh snapped his attention away from the woman in front of him and released her hand. How long had he been holding it?

"I will go inquire straightaway," he said. "Do you want to order tea?"

Lady Bridget shook her head. "I don't want to delay. Besides, my body isn't sure if it's day or night."

Hugh understood how she felt. Dawn was still hours away, and he could only hope they'd get some information here. He walked into the inn while she waited by the carriage. The place was quiet, but a set of candles burned on a table near the door. A portly man shuffled toward the entryway from some other part of the inn. He looked as if he'd hastily pulled on a coat.

"Good evening, sir," the innkeeper said with a bow. "Do you need a room for the night?"

"Good evening," Hugh said. "I apologize for the lateness of the hour, but I'm in dire need of finding someone who I think has passed by here." He held out a few coins.

The innkeeper's eyes widened, and Hugh knew he'd selected the right amount to get this man to talk.

He described both Walter and Miss Phoebe, and the innkeeper nodded.

"You've seen them?" Hugh prodded.

"They stopped here and took their supper—although it was a bit late for supper," the innkeeper mused. "The gentleman wanted to book a room, but the young miss seemed very agitated. Had my wife take her aside to see if there was anything she needed, but the miss insisted she was fine. So they left, headed north I'd guess."

By the gleam in the innkeeper's eyes, Hugh guessed the man realized they were eloping.

"How long ago was that?" Hugh asked.

The innkeeper paused. "My wife was already abed, and I had to wake her up to heat the leftover stew. I would guess . . ." He tapped his bottom lip.

Hugh pulled out his pocket watch and showed the man the time.

"I'd say . . . three hours ago."

"Three?" Was that all? Had they made better time than Walter? Hugh wasn't entirely sure he was getting the most correct information, but at least he knew the couple had stopped here, and they were still traveling north. "Thank you." Hugh handed over another few coins.

"We've stew left, if you and your party would like to eat," the innkeeper said, all smiles. "It's a cold night out there. My wife thinks snow is on its way."

"We must keep to a schedule, but thank you again," Hugh said, then strode out of the inn.

Lady Bridget was leaning against the carriage, clutching her cloak about her, while the driver was back on his carriage perch, the horses already traded out.

He quickly informed Bridget of what the innkeeper had said, then he gave the directions to the driver.

Back inside the carriage, when they'd started on the road again, Hugh realized he was hungry. He picked up the basket. "Are you hungry?"

"My stomach is tied in knots," she said. "I couldn't possibly eat. Did the innkeeper really say three hours? Have we already closed that much in distance?"

"That's what he said," Hugh said. It was good news, but he didn't tell Bridget how the innkeeper had also said her sister seemed fretful. That could mean a few things, but most worrisome was that Phoebe might be regretting the elopement. If that was the case, and Walter forced her into a marriage or compromised her, there would be hell to pay.

The more time Hugh spent with Bridget, the more protective he felt toward her and her family.

"We'll be increasing our pace quite a bit when dawn arrives," Hugh said. "I don't dare go faster in the dark on unfamiliar roads."

Lady Bridget nodded.

Hugh didn't like the paleness of her face. "Are you sure you won't have anything to eat? There's a loaf of bread, cheese, some winter berries . . ."

"No thank you," she said in a faint voice.

Hugh persisted and held a handful of berries out to her.

She hesitated, then plucked one off his palm. Hugh watched her eat it, then swallow. He realized he was staring and that she was blushing.

"Thank you," she said again. "I'm fine."

Hugh ate the rest of the berries in his palm, then he put together a sort of sandwich with the bread and cheese. After he finished the food and had calmed the angry growl in his stomach, he unfolded a blanket and set it over Bridget.

She gave him a faint smile but said nothing.

"We're going to catch up with them," Hugh said. This melancholy Bridget was worrying him.

Her gaze flitted to his, and all he saw there was doubt, and maybe fear.

"What if you're right?" she asked. "What if Phoebe starts to hate me? What if this divides us forever? She's . . . she's my sister, but she's also my best friend, my only friend." She gave a soft laugh that wasn't really a laugh at all.

Hugh swallowed. "She'll know you care about her and that you chased her down because you love her. And you didn't want her to feel trapped."

"I hope so," Lady Bridget said in a voice that cracked. Then she turned her head toward the window, but Hugh knew she could see very little of the dark landscape beyond the yellow glow of the carriage lanterns.

"She'll also realize her decision affects more than herself, just like all our decisions do," he continued. Was he making her feel worse? "I don't know your sister well, but I believe she looks up to you. You've been like a mother to her." He could only assume this, but once the words were out, they felt like the truth.

Bridget sniffled and brought a hand to her mouth. She was trying to hold in her emotions.

Before he could think better of it, he moved to her bench and pulled her into his arms. She didn't resist, didn't stiffen. In fact, she seemed to melt against him, her head fitting neatly right below his chin and her cheek pressing against his neck.

Her shoulders started to shake as she cried, and Hugh held her tightly. After a few moments, she relaxed, the worst over, although she still clung to him. One of her arms was wrapped about his waist, anchoring them together, and her other hand clutched at the lapel of his coat. Her breathing evened out, and the comforting embrace started to turn into something else. Without either of them moving or changing position, the embrace became more intimate.

He could feel her soft breath at his neck and the silkiness of her hair against his chin. His heart rate increased, pumping hot blood through his veins. He should release her, put some distance between them. She'd stopped crying, and so he should return to his bench.

Instead, he ran a hand over her hair that had come unpinned, his fingers intertwining with the silky, blonde waves. She only nestled closer, and his mind shifted from relating to her pain and desperation to what it might be like to lift her chin and press a kiss on those rosy lips of hers. He imagined what it might be like to trail a line of kisses down her neck and breathe in the scent of her soft skin.

"You're not who I thought you were," she said in a half whisper.

"Is that good or bad?"

"It's good," she said.

He closed his eyes. "Then I'm glad." He paused. "You are definitely not the woman I imagined you to be."

"No, I should think not." She said it as a jest, but her words were like a caress against his skin. "Your cousin told me he wanted to marry me and get me with child so that his children would be older than any you might have," she continued. "We never . . . I mean, our marriage was never consummated. Once we married, he said he had a plan to get you disinherited, and once that happened, he'd already be established with a brood of children."

Hugh opened his eyes, not quite believing what he was hearing.

"Anthony painted you as some sort of cold, miserable man." She lifted her head, her gaze connecting with his. "He said he despised you, but I figured he was only envious of your greater title. I knew one day I'd meet you, but to be honest, I was worried. You had a lot of power over Anthony, which he hated, and when Anthony drank . . . well, I could see him capable of terrible things. Not only was my husband a rake and a gambler and a drunk, but he routinely made threats against his own cousin. I didn't even know you, but it terrified me to hear such venom from a man I was tied to."

Hugh was stunned. He literally had no words, and he could only stare into her violet eyes. He knew he'd made Anthony angry many times, especially when he was trying to help his uncle by doling out consequences for Anthony's debauched ways.

And this sweet, innocent woman had been drawn into Anthony's world, forced to hear and see him do things no woman should ever be exposed to. He'd been *using* her. If Anthony was still alive today, Hugh would call him out, even if they had to go to France to duel. He would aim his pistol right at his cousin's heart and shoot. *Blood be damned.*

Lady Bridget ran her fingers along Hugh's jaw; her touch was feather light, but it calmed the rising anger in him and instead sent a jolt of pleasure through him. A very dangerous jolt.

"But you're not cold, Hugh," Lady Bridget whispered, her voice low and intimate.

He liked how she'd called him by his Christian name, liked it very much indeed.

"I could never be cold around you, *Bridget.*"

A faint smile crossed her face. Then she sobered as she searched his gaze, and he finally understood the pain in her eyes he'd first seen that night he'd confronted her in the garden. He understood how she must have seen *him*, the cousin of a monster, and how much courage it had taken for her to stand up to him.

"You're nothing like Anthony told me you were," she continued. "You're the most honest man I've ever met. You're warm, and caring, and—"

Hugh stopped her words by pressing his mouth against hers.

This kiss had been inevitable, he supposed, from the moment he first saw her in the violet dress that showed off her cream-skinned shoulders. And anyone who thought he should stay away from this enchanting woman should go hang himself. Because Hugh had given up trying to stay away from her.

So he tangled his fingers into her hair and kissed her quite thoroughly.

And thankfully she didn't shy away. She didn't push him or slap him. In fact, she kissed him back.

Hugh was lost. In her touch. In her warmth. In her acceptance. In her desire for him. For he desired her more than anything or anyone he could ever remember. Lady Bridget Wilde had consumed him, possessed him, and even four horses couldn't drag him away.

And then one thought, and one thought only, forced him to pull away and release her. They were on their way to bring her sister home, and here he was, acting the part of a rake, in a carriage of all places.

"I'm sorry," he whispered. "I have taken advantage—"

He didn't finish because she kissed him again. He gave in and let himself become enveloped in everything that was Bridget. Her fingers caressed his neck, threading through his hair and pulling him even closer.

Hugh knew he should draw away from this intoxication.

She had no idea what she was doing to him, what passions she was awakening.

The carriage lurched and then slowed significantly, nearly sending both of them to the floor.

Hugh righted himself, holding on to Bridget. The landscape outside was gray and murky with the approaching dawn, but it was still some time before the sun would be up. The carriage had come to a full stop, and Hugh opened the door.

The driver met him at the door. "There's a carriage up ahead, sir," he said in a hushed voice. "Looks like it lost a wheel, but I fear it might be a trap."

Hugh exhaled. His mind was still foggy from all the kissing, and he needed a jug of cold water poured over his head. But the driver could be right—the broken carriage could be a trap. "Stay inside!" he commanded the startled Bridget. Then he grabbed his pistol and hopped out of the carriage.

"Let's check it out," he told the driver, after shutting the carriage door behind him.

The driver nodded and drew out his own pistol.

Hugh started to approach on one side of the road, while the driver walked the other side. The carriage up ahead had a broken wheel all right. There was nothing fancy or identifiable about the carriage itself, which told Hugh it was either hired or it belonged to a band of thieves that was now waiting in the trees to pounce.

He gripped the pistol tighter when he heard a sound in the trees. Swinging toward the sound, he saw the unmistakable dark form of a man.

"Watch out!" the driver screamed just as a gunshot split the air.

Hugh dove to the ground, and everything went silent.

Thirteen

BRIDGET SCREAMED WHEN she heard the gunshot. She scrambled for the door and tugged at the latch. An instant later, she'd tumbled out of the carriage, clutched at her skirts, and started to run for Hugh. He was on the ground, and she didn't care if an entire band of thieves was about to attack her, she wouldn't let them touch Hugh.

Just before she reached him, someone screamed, "Bridget!"

A woman's voice. Her *sister's* voice.

Bridget came to a stumbling halt and looked around, her heart nearly pounding out of her chest.

Then, from the copse of trees, her sister emerged, as if she were some apparition in the gray dawn of morning.

"Phoebe?" Bridget couldn't breathe, couldn't think.

Then Mr. Stephens appeared too. A pistol in his hand. His face was chalk white. "Did I shoot him?" he said in a choked voice. "Please tell me he's alive!"

Bridget turned toward Hugh where he was lying in the road, but he wasn't lying there anymore. He was sitting up, groaning, and clutching his shoulder.

"You're—you're alive." Bridget rushed toward him and knelt in the dirt next to a dazed Hugh. "Are you . . ." She froze when she saw the singed fabric of his coat sleeve.

"It missed," Hugh ground out, staring down at his shoulder in disbelief.

"Truly?"

He ran his hand over the burned fabric. "I'm not shot. The bullet missed."

The bottom dropped out of her stomach, and she threw her arms around Hugh. "You're alive!"

Hugh chuckled and squeezed her, then removed her arms from his neck. "We've quite the audience, dear."

Bridget sat back on her heels and gazed up at four pairs of eyes. Their driver, Mr. Stephens, Phoebe, and another man were all staring down at them.

"You're all right," Mr. Stephens said in an incredulous voice, tears of relief in his eyes. "Praise God. I thought I shot you. I didn't know it was you—until it was too late. I am so sorry. We broke down, and we thought we were going be attacked. I couldn't let anyone take advantage of Phoebe, so I—"

Hugh raised his hand to stop his cousin's spill of words. "Help me up, Walter, and then you have a lot of questions to answer."

Mr. Stephens extended his hand and pulled Hugh to his feet.

Bridget wanted to wrap her arms about Hugh and never let go, but he was right, they did have an audience. He was alive, and that's all Bridget cared about for now.

Hugh's gaze went to Phoebe, and Bridget studied her sister as well. All things considered, her sister looked tired but no worse for the wear.

"What are you doing here?" Phoebe asked, looking from Bridget to Hugh. "You—you came to stop us, didn't you?"

Bridget folded her arms. "Yes."

Phoebe's eyes filled with tears, and she took a step back, grabbing Mr. Stephens's hand. "No one can stop us. I am of age, and I love Walter."

Whatever Bridget had expected, it wasn't this.

Walter Stephens stood straight and tall, gripping Phoebe's hand as he lifted his chin. "What's all this about, cousin?" His gaze cut to Hugh.

"You've disobeyed me," Hugh said in a calm voice. "And you've brought an innocent woman into your deceit."

The man didn't blink. "I disobeyed *you*, yes," he said. "But I am making a new life with Phoebe. We refuse to live under anyone else's thumb. I know you don't believe I can make it in this world without you or our family, but I aim to provide well for her."

"How?" Hugh's words were blunt. No matter that the two drivers were hearing every word spoken—Hugh didn't seem to mind airing a private family matter.

"When I was in France, I befriended a man who owned a jewelry shop," Mr. Stephens said. "He told me if I'm ever in need of a trade, he'd take me on as a partner. He has no sons, you see."

"Trade? You want to go into a *trade*?" Hugh stared in disbelief. "You'll inherit property upon my father's death and be set for life."

"I'm finished with England," Mr. Stephens said.

Despite herself, Bridget was starting to like Walter Stephens.

"I don't want to live on handouts and play poppet to entitled relatives." Mr. Stephens glanced down at Phoebe. "Phoebe will become my wife, and then we'll settle in France. I'll be a jeweler, and Phoebe will be the most bejeweled woman in the county."

Phoebe smiled up at him.

Bridget's heart skipped.

Hugh was silent for a long time, and Bridget worried he'd demand that his cousin release Phoebe. Instead, Hugh looked at Phoebe. "Come here, Miss Reeve."

She swallowed and released Mr. Stephens's hand, obeying Hugh as she walked toward him.

He spoke in a soft tone when he asked her, "Do you want to marry Walter and live as a jeweler's wife?"

Phoebe nodded, her blonde curls bouncing. "Yes, I do."

Hugh clenched his jaw, then looked back toward his cousin. "You will marry her in a church, in the proper fashion. You owe the woman who will be your wife at least that decency. We will return to London immediately and keep this entire affair just between the few of us. No one will be the wiser. Your engagement will be announced in the papers and a wedding date set."

Bridget brought a hand to her mouth, fighting off tears.

"If you refuse, Miss Reeve will be coming back with us," Hugh continued. He waved at the broken carriage on the road. "You will remain here and clean up your mess."

Everyone was silent for several moments. The sun chose that exact time to lace orange and pink across the clouds in the eastern sky.

Mr. Stephens gazed at Phoebe from where he stood as the landscape brightened around him. "What do you think, love? Should we marry in a church?"

Phoebe laughed, then ran to him and threw her arms about his neck.

Bridget didn't know if she should be watching such an amorous display. Her heart swelled at the sight.

"I think that was a *yes*," Hugh said in a wry tone.

Bridget turned a full smile upon Hugh.

He gave her a wink, which sent a rush of warmth to her heart, then he headed toward the broken carriage. Mr. Stephens soon joined him with his amorous fiancée, and they transported their bags into Hugh's carriage.

Hugh handed over a coin purse to the driver of the hired carriage. "For your troubles and your repairs."

Once they were all loaded into Hugh's carriage, the women sitting on one bench with the men on the other bench, all propriety restored, Bridget felt as if a lifetime had passed since she found the letter written by Phoebe.

The ride back to London was nearly silent as everyone dozed on and off.

But Bridget couldn't sleep, couldn't relax. Yes, they'd saved her sister from a scandalous marriage, and now it appeared she'd be married properly and with adulations in a church. And hopefully Aunt Harriet would still be convalescing, and if Maren had done her job as promised, Harriet would be none the wiser.

Peace and happiness would be restored. Her sister would be a married woman, living in France of all places, but where did that leave Bridget? And Hugh?

She glanced over at him. He was staring out the window as the grays and blues of the sky rushed past them. It would be an unusually clear winter day. What had happened between them in the carriage . . . the way he'd comforted her . . . held her . . . *kissed her.*

She released a slow breath. This was the end. After today, she and Hugh would return to their formal relationship. There might be some reunion down the road, perhaps during Christmastide, if Phoebe and her husband visited England . . . But beyond that, Bridget and Hugh would return to being strangers.

Ironically, the closer they drew to London and restoring all that had gone wrong, the more Bridget's heart broke.

Hours later, when Bridget had nearly fallen asleep, they finally reached the outskirts of the city. Dread and anticipation reared within Bridget's breast. Had they been found out? What would her aunt do if she learned of this escapade?

But when the carriage pulled around to Aunt Harriet's home, everything seemed quiet. Hugh told the women to leave their bags in the carriage so as to not draw attention to them, and he'd find a way to deliver them later.

Bridget was only too happy to call an end to their journey

and said the briefest goodbye and thank you to Hugh. Phoebe came with Bridget quite cheerfully, and when they entered the house, Maren was the first to reach them. She told them Aunt Harriet had remained in her room all day and had been told the sisters had gone on calls for the afternoon.

"Thank you, thank you," Bridget said, gripping Maren's hands. "You have been a blessing to us. We will take tea in our rooms, and you can let our aunt know that both of us are staying in for the night. I'll visit her in a short time to check on her."

Maren nodded and went into the kitchen.

Bridget walked with Phoebe to her room. They hadn't spoken privately since they'd met on the road to Gretna Green, and now Bridget wondered how things would be between them.

"Bridget," Phoebe said, blocking the doorway of her room and not allowing Bridget to enter. "You may judge me, but I did the right thing, despite how it all turned out."

Bridget stared at her. "Why couldn't you and Mr. Stephens just come forward in the first place?"

"He did, with Hugh, but Walter was shut down," Phoebe said, blinking back tears. "We took the only course of action afforded to us. You cannot blame Walter for this."

Bridget's throat felt tight, and she had no time to reply before Phoebe quietly shut her door. Bridget walked back to her room and climbed into her bed without taking off her clothing. It was there that she fell into a deep, dreamless sleep.

"Ma'am?" someone was saying, touching her shoulder. "Ma'am?"

Bridget opened her eyes to see Maren standing over her. The room was filled with the dusky purple of the twilight hour.

"You have gentlemen callers," Maren said. "I didn't want to disturb you, but they said it was of utmost importance."

Bridget sat up, her mind catching up from the deep sleep.

Memories returned . . . *Phoebe's elopement . . . Hugh . . . the road to Gretna Green . . .*

"Who is it?" Bridget asked, blinking her dry eyes.

"Lord Wilde, and his father, the Marquess of Crawton."

Bridget went still. "Lord Wilde is here with his *father*?"

"Yes," Maren whispered, and then Bridget noticed that the poor woman was pale.

"Gracious. What could they want?" Panic jolted through her mind. Perhaps the marquess had forbidden Walter's marriage.

Bridget scrambled out of bed, then had to reach for a post to steady herself. Light-headedness swept over her for a moment. "Help me dress."

Maren rushed about, grabbing things.

Bridget caught one look at her reflection in the mirror and groaned. "My hair."

"We'll have you ready in a jiff," Maren reassured her, although the woman's rapid breathing told Bridget she was equally distressed.

By the time Bridget was dressed and coiffed, she wished Hugh had just sent a letter. That would have been less embarrassing for all of them. For a brief moment, she wished Aunt Harriet was well enough to attend to the gentlemen with her, but then there would be all kinds of questions to answer. It was better this way. Bridget would receive the news, then she would inform Phoebe.

Bridget left her bedchamber, feeling as if her heart was in her throat. When she walked into the front parlor to find Hugh and his father waiting, she marveled at the reaction she had upon seeing Hugh again. He'd changed his clothing and been shaved. The memory of their kisses skittered hot across her skin, and she had to will herself not to blush when their gazes connected.

Had it been only a few hours since she last saw Hugh? It felt as if it had been days.

She turned to his father, an older version of Hugh.

Bridget had never dreamed she'd have to face the marquess again. He had barely been cordial when she met him at her wedding to his nephew.

"Lady Wilde," Hugh said, drawing her attention as he stepped forward to greet her.

She offered him her hand, and he bent over it, pressing a kiss upon her bare skin. She was surprised because this show of conciliatory affection felt quite blatant in front of his father, and it also made the fluttering in her stomach increase tenfold.

Then, most extraordinarily, the marquess himself stepped forward and gave a slight bow. When he straightened, he said, "Lady Wilde, it's a pleasure to see you again."

Bridget had to make an effort not to let her mouth fall open.

The marquess didn't make any sort of move to step away either. "I arrived this morning at our town house only to find my son and nephew not in residence. When Hugh and Walter did return to the town house, imagine my surprise when I learned of the events that took place with Walter, and your, er, sister." The marquess paused.

Bridget felt cold all over. Here it came. The censure, the displeasure, the threat.

"As you may be aware, Walter has been the recipient of my hospitality, so I am somewhat involved in his business," the marquess continued. "Despite what happened on the road to Gretna Green, I find that I owe you an apology from our entire family, Lady Wilde. My nephew Anthony, God rest his soul, treated you in the most abominable manner. I learned the details only today when Hugh disclosed them to me. I hope you don't mind."

What could Bridget do but shake her head? The marquess didn't look upset—if anything he appeared remorseful.

He continued. "I entreated Hugh to see if he could think of a compensation from our family to yours to make up for the humiliation. You already turned down the dower~~ager~~ house on my brother's estate, which I doubt you are interested in considering again. But Hugh told me he had a different idea." At this point, the marquess looked toward his son.

Bridget followed his gaze and saw that Hugh was smiling. *Smiling at her!* It quite took her breath away.

"I will excuse myself and peruse your library for a few moments," the marquess said.

Bridget looked at the marquess in astonishment . . . He was *leaving* the room?

Hugh nodded at his father, then the marquess left the parlor, closing the door behind him.

Bridget exhaled. The marquess had come all this way to offer an apology on behalf of Anthony's father? And what did he mean that Hugh had an idea of how to compensate her? She'd made it more than clear that she didn't want any compensation or connection with the Wilde family.

She turned to find Hugh walking toward her. "What's this all about?" she asked.

"My father was at the house when Walter and I returned," he said, gazing down at her with—did she dare say—fondness? Hugh grasped her hands and pulled her toward him. "Did you think I'd let you get away that easily?"

She stared into those dark eyes of his. "What are you speaking of?"

"This," Hugh said, releasing her hands and reaching into his pocket. He pulled out a small jewelry case.

Bridget's pulse thudded in her ears.

Hugh took hold of one of her hands. "I'm pleased my father stepped out for a moment because I've come to ask you to marry me."

She stared at Hugh. She felt numb, like she was floating. "Is this a dream?"

His mouth quirked into a half smile, the expression that sent a thrill through her. "If it is, we're both in the same dream."

Her eyes started to fill with tears. How had this happened? How had this man become so dear to her?

Hugh kept hold of her hand while he knelt before her. "Bridget Reeve Wilde, will you be my wife?"

Even if this all turned out to be a dream, she would still say *yes* in her dream. The smile grew on her face. Leaning down, she placed one hand on his shoulder and whispered, "Yes."

Hugh slipped the ring on her finger, then drew her close while he was still kneeling and kissed her. A warm shiver traveled all the way to her toes. Then he stood and pulled her into his arms, kissing her over and over.

Bridget laughed as Hugh lifted her and spun her around. "Maybe we should have a double wedding," he said. "Do you think your sister would mind?"

Bridget kept her hands on his shoulders after he set her down. "You don't want to go to Gretna Green?"

Hugh smiled.

She loved his smile.

"Tempting," he said. "But you will be a marchioness, my dear. I think we'd better follow convention."

She tried not to think too deeply about that eventuality and whether she would fit the role. "You're right." She wrapped her arms about his waist, then laid her head against his chest. The drumming of his heart was just as fast as hers. "I love you."

He kissed the top of her head and ran his hand along her back in a caress. "And I love you, my dear Bridget. Always."

She closed her eyes and breathed him in. His words were the most endearing she'd heard in her entire life. And for a moment, she let them echo through her mind, before his father came back into the room, before she told Phoebe and Aunt Harriet of her engagement to Lord Hugh Wilde, and before her entire world changed.

Heather B. Moore is a four-time *USA Today* bestselling author. She writes historical thrillers under the pen name H.B. Moore; her latest thrillers include *The Killing Curse* and *Poetic Justice*. Under the name Heather B. Moore, she writes romance and women's fiction. Her newest releases include the historical romance *Love is Come* and *Ruth*. She's also one of the coauthors of the *USA Today* bestselling series: A Timeless Romance Anthology. Heather writes speculative fiction under the pen name Jane Redd; releases include the Solstice series and *Mistress Grim*. Heather is represented by Dystel, Goderich & Bourret.

For book updates, sign up for Heather's email list: hbmoore.com/contact

Website: HBMoore.com

Facebook: Fans of H. B. Moore

Blog: MyWritersLair.blogspot.com

Instagram: @authorhbmoore

Twitter: @HeatherBMoore

Made in United States
Orlando, FL
19 October 2025

70981704R00146